SEA BREEZE

PHANTOM QUEEN DIARIES BOOK 8

SHAYNE SILVERS

CAMERON O'CONNELL

ARGENTO
PUBLISHING

CONTENTS

SHAYNE AND CAMERON   vii

Remember when dead in the water was just an expression? Not anymore.   ix

Chapter 1   1
Chapter 2   3
Chapter 3   13
Chapter 4   21
Chapter 5   27
Chapter 6   32
Chapter 7   36
Chapter 8   42
Chapter 9   51
Chapter 10   57
Chapter 11   62
Chapter 12   66
Chapter 13   70
Chapter 14   75
Chapter 15   80
Chapter 16   83
Chapter 17   89
Chapter 18   93
Chapter 19   100
Chapter 20   105
Chapter 21   108
Chapter 22   112
Chapter 23   118
Chapter 24   122
Chapter 25   127
Chapter 26   133
Chapter 27   137
Chapter 28   141
Chapter 29   147
Chapter 30   152

Chapter 31   157
Chapter 32   162
Chapter 33   167
Chapter 34   172
Chapter 35   175
Chapter 36   186
Chapter 37   190
TRY: OBSIDIAN SON (NATE TEMPLE #1)   197
TRY: DEVIL'S DREAM (SHADE OF DEVIL #1)   202

MAKE A DIFFERENCE   207
BOOKS IN THE TEMPLE VERSE   209
ACKNOWLEDGMENTS   213
ABOUT SHAYNE SILVERS   215
ABOUT CAMERON O'CONNELL   217

Shayne Silvers & Cameron O'Connell

Sea Breeze

The Phantom Queen Diaries Book 8

A Temple Verse Series

ISBN 13: **978-1-947709-31-7**

© 2019, Shayne Silvers / Argento Publishing, LLC / Cameron O'Connell

info@shaynesilvers.com

SHAYNE AND CAMERON

Shayne Silvers, here.

Cameron O'Connell is one helluva writer, and he's worked tirelessly to merge a story into the Temple Verse that would provide a different and unique *voice*, but a complementary *tone* to my other novels. *SOME* people might say I'm hard to work with. But certainly, Cameron would never...

Hey! Pipe down over there, author monkey! Get back to your writing cave and finish the next Phantom Queen Novel!

Ahem. Now, where was I?

This is book 8 in the Phantom Queen Diaries, which is a series that ties into the existing Temple Verse with Nate Temple and Callie Penrose. This series could also be read independently if one so chose. Then again, you, the reader, will get SO much more out of my existing books (and this series) by reading them all in tandem.

But that's not up to us. It's up to you, the reader.

You tell us...

REMEMBER WHEN DEAD IN THE WATER WAS JUST AN EXPRESSION? NOT ANYMORE.

Fresh from her unplanned stay in the Otherworld, Quinn MacKenna is forced to wait in Fae's worst Air BnB—a grotesque gingerbread house in a forest full of breadcrumbs—for the captain who will guide her ship to the fabled Atlantis.

But just as idle hands are the Devil's workshop, idle minds are the Titans' torture chamber.

The last thing Quinn needs to do is climb down the rabbit hole of her own fears and self-doubts to confront her inner Beasts. She has enough on her mind as she struggles to rediscover her identity and frets over the whereabouts of an old friend bent on vengeance and mayhem. An old friend she may have to put in the grave, whether she wants to or not.

Before she can worry about any of that, Quinn will first have to heal old wounds, enlist the aid of allies old and new, and somehow survive the turbulent tides of fate. Unfortunately, in order to stay afloat, she'll have to sail into yet another unfamiliar world, a realm of monsters and men and gods so old they are known only as Titans.

It's all hands on deck—monsters, sea-dogs, and scallywags—as Quinn strives to save who can be saved and beat those who must be beaten. With new powers at her disposal and an ill-matched crew to manage, it will be up to her to navigate these troubled waters. Odysseus may as well have taken a leisure cruise back from Troy compared to Quinn's fatally fateful voyage.

Quinn will have to bring enough rum to get a Cyclops drunk. Or die trying. Because it's awfully hard to steer when gods are rocking the boat.

And the world desperately needs her to come back home.

~

DON'T FORGET! VIP's get early access to all sorts of Temple-Verse goodies, including signed copies, private giveaways, and advance notice of future projects. AND A FREE NOVELLA! Click the image or join here: www.shaynesilvers.com/l/38599

FOLLOW and LIKE:

Shayne's FACEBOOK PAGE

Cameron's FACEBOOK PAGE

We try our best to respond to all messages, so don't hesitate to drop us a line. Not interacting with readers is the biggest travesty that most authors can make. Let us fix that.

I straddled the line between darkness and light, lying on my back, body bisected—one half sun-kissed, the other bathed in starlight. The sensation was strange, but then so was my life; it hardly seemed fair to start throwing stones. The Twilight Valley, as I'd come to call this place, was one of many bizarre realms in Fae. Here the difference between day and night was a matter of distance, not time. I'd recently found I could walk from one side of the valley to the other and experience the passage of a day in a matter of minutes. Since finding the valley, I'd come here several times, fascinated by the strangeness of it, by the stark duality it represented. I supposed it had amused me, at first. Now, I felt like it embodied me, in a way. Caught between two extremes, trapped between two worlds, allegiances tugged in two directions.

You get the gist.

Fresh from a foray among the Otherworlders, I'd only recently come to terms with everything I'd gone through. Memories of my time there trickled in, often unbidden, like waking dreams...or nightmares. Some were pleasant things. Conversations. Embraces. Feelings of belonging. Some were less so, leaving bitterness and resentment in their wake. I recalled the face of a dead woman, the stickiness of dried blood between my fingers, the skin-blistering heat of a hateful atmosphere, the stench of rot. More often than not, these echoes led to thoughts of my mother. I dwelled on the legacy she'd passed on to me, wondering whether she'd known just how large a burden I'd be expected to carry.

I also tried to access her power. Not so long ago, I'd felt it roiling inside me—the mind-boggling capacity of a goddess. Enraged and vengeful, I'd stepped onto Fae soil with all that latent potential, prepared to smite to my heart's content, only to have it all stripped away from me in an instant—all my prodigious strength, my quickness, not to mention my newfound ability to bend shadows to my will. And yet, it was as though I could still sense the power lingering. As if it were merely hibernating within me; I held my hand up to the night sky and waved it into the light of day. It was like I could actually *feel* the darkness react, could feel it pressing against my flesh, clinging to me like cellophane.

That, or I was imagining things.

Of course, boredom can do that to you.

$\mathcal{I}$ think it's funny what some people consider a business trip and others consider a vacation. For instance, until recently I'd have thought sailing into uncharted waters a wonderful, life-altering experience, complete with fresh air and adventure, maybe even a romantic fling or two —a whirlwind affair featuring sun, sex, and hopefully sangria. So, why wasn't I more excited by the prospect? I could blame some of my reticence on homesickness; I'd been away for far too long. But the truth was I couldn't shake the feeling that I was going to get screwed on this trip, and not in the fun way, if you know what I mean.

Indeed, since receiving my mother's power, not to mention her final directive, I'd felt as though a cloud were following me. Something—a nondescript, and yet altogether foreboding apprehension—loomed on the peripheries, waiting in the wings to swoop down and ruin my Fae-cation. This nagging paranoia had stuck with me for several days now, getting progressively worse the longer I waited for the Goblin King to arrive with our guide in tow; Oberon had left us swearing he'd return as soon as he was able with someone qualified to lead us along Odysseus' Path. Though time moved differently in Fae, the ordinarily fixed law measured here in unfamiliar increments, it felt like several days, perhaps more, had passed since then.

Of course, it didn't help that my sole companions—an aggrieved sapling and a scathing, sarcastic mutt—had grown equally anxious; Eve, the budding Tree of Knowledge I'd been tasked with plant-sitting in perpetuity, stood firmly rooted on the far side of the room, limbs curled around her trunk as though she were hugging herself while Cathal, a faerie hound the size of a horse, gnawed on a long bone that might have belonged to a dinosaur. I'd spoken to neither in what felt like days, content to let Eve stew and Cathal be...well, Cathal. Unfortunately, aside from my trips to the Twilight Valley, proximity had become a bit of an issue; the safehouse Oberon had chosen for us—a cottage deep in the woods, surrounded by trees with glass leaves and stone trunks—was not exactly spacious.

I watched them both from the corner of my eyes as I rocked back and forth on a rickety chair, careful not to accidentally touch the rusty cages which hung from the rafters of the dilapidated gingerbread house we occupied; we'd found the clear sugar window panes shattered, the gumdrop shingles sunken with age, the brick oven fireplace coated with the ashes of a dead witch. Hansel and Gretel's handiwork, apparently. The two had even carved their names into the gingerbread walls. In German, of course.

Eve twitched, her roots writhing, restless. She did that a lot lately; ever since I'd pried her from her planter, it was like she had difficulty standing still. Ironic, given she had no legs. Unlike the Ents from Tolkien's imagination, Eve's root system refused to conveniently parse themselves into two functional limbs. If anything, she reminded me of an octopus in the way she slithered across the ground, roots coiling and uncoiling, cruising along with nary a bob or weave. Of course, the tic might also have been my fault: while it turned out only a few days had passed in the mortal realm since I'd traveled to the Otherworld, Eve still hadn't forgiven me for breaking my vow and stepping foot on Fae soil without her. My defense—that I'd had no say in any of it, not to mention the fact that I'd had plenty of other things to worry about at the time—had earned me nothing but a sullen silence.

Cathal, on the other side of the room, had given up on the bone and lay sprawled out on his side, snoring so loudly that you might have confused his breathing for the surf at high tide, his massive chest riddled with faint markings that flared to life whenever his dreams took a dark turn. The faerie hound had a bad habit of passing out whenever things got dull, which meant he'd gotten plenty of rest since we'd arrived.

Oddly enough, neither had questioned my motives when I relayed my plan to enlist the aid of pirates, sail across foreign seas, find the lost city of

Atlantis, and quite possibly confront the new Jack Frost—a murderous thief who happened to be one of my oldest friends. All of which, I might add, seemed less and less plausible with every passing day. Indeed, life in Fae had taken on such a surreal quality I wasn't entirely sure about anything; I found myself repeating my names and titles whenever I visited the valley, trying to determine which were masks and which were real. Was I Quinn MacKenna, heiress to the power of the Phantom Queen? Or was I Ceara Light-Bringer, cherished daughter of the Curaitl? Was I the woman who loathed bloodsuckers, who bought and sold magical goods, who practically bled silver, red, and nautical blue on football Sundays? Or was I the woman who'd survived the Blighted Lands, who'd sailed on the Jolly Roger, who'd reduced Balor One-Eye to dust? Only days before, I was certain I'd solved this particular riddle, that I'd found the solution to my identity crisis—the disparate voices in my head had merged, harmonizing like baying wolves. Now, I wasn't so sure. Had we really fused? And, if so, had they become me, or I become them? Lately, it was all I could do to wrestle with that question, to determine who—and what—I was supposed to be.

I stopped rocking abruptly, prepared to leave the gingerbread house and return to the Twilight Valley for more soul-searching. I wasn't sure I'd find any answers, but it beat the alternative; the gingerbread house smelled vaguely of pumpkin spice and white chocolate mixed with the odor of burnt meat and dog. Not a great combination. Before I could rise, however, Cathal's ears flicked up like antennae. A moment later, a knock sounded at the door. Cathal—who was apparently unable to deviate from the compulsions of his species—started barking his freaking head off.

"Would you tell that thing to shut up?" Eve hissed. That's what she'd taken to calling Cathal—that *thing*. Mostly, I think, because she had no idea what he was; despite our limited interactions, I'd discovered Eve's all-encompassing knowledge didn't extend to the Fae realm, nor its Other-worldly inhabitants. She'd nearly gone into hysterics yesterday when a flower she'd inadvertently stepped on had cursed her out and demanded an apology. I supposed that when you're the self-appointed Tree of Knowledge, ignorance isn't exactly blissful.

"Cathal!" I snapped, my Irish brogue cutting through the room like a butter knife for all the good it did; Cathal kept right on woofing until I finally reached up to cuff him on the ear, my hand comically small compared to his shaggy, blockish dome.

Cathal flinched, ear twitching, glaring at me side-eyed. "Don't do that."

I matched his fierce stare with one of my own. "Then at least pretend to be house trained, ye mongrel."

"Should have told him that before he set fire to the house," Eve muttered, one of her many branches angling awkwardly to gesture at a scorched stretch of gingerbread wall. A section of the crown molding, made entirely of frosting, had melted—the result of Cathal losing his temper and having what I liked to call a "flare up." Ever since then, Eve had avoided the hound out of self-preservation.

"Are any of you going to let me in?" the visitor called. I recognized Oberon's imperious rasp; the Goblin King had a distinct voice, even for one of the Fae. I sighed, marched to the door, and bent so close I could smell the sweet, mouth-watering aroma that wafted off the chocolate varnish.

"What's the password?" I called back.

"The...wait, what password?"

"Correct." I gripped the handle and eyed Cathal, trusting him to be prepared for anything. It wasn't so much that I didn't trust Oberon but that I'd learned to be cautious; one look around told me all I needed to know about Faeling hospitality. Besides, between pottymouth flowers and falling leaves that could impale you, the possibility of encountering an impostor hardly seemed much of a stretch. "What was the last t'ing ye said to me before ye left?"

"I told you to stay here and try to keep out of sight," Oberon replied.

Too general.

"Why?" I asked.

"Because there had been talk of Mordred's knights roaming the land. And we believed it possible that some of our people sided with him in opposition to Master Temple."

I nodded, though the mention of Master Temple—Nate Temple to be exact—twisted my gut. Nate was an integral player in the Fae realm's latest drama: a battle for the fate of the world. Both worlds, actually; according to Oberon, the scales that upheld the Fae and mortal realms would tip precariously depending on the outcome. Unfortunately, and as a result of what I could only imagine was some sort of karmic backlash, I'd inadvertently sided with the wizard by pitting myself against Mordred—King Arthur's son and would-be overlord.

"Welcome to Candy Castle," I said as I opened the door, shuffling to the right in a fighting stance, just in case it turned out I was wrong.

Oberon—in his diminutive, goblinoid form—eyed us all disdainfully, but raised both hands in a gesture of unconditional surrender. "I come in peace," he said, voice deadpan.

"Good thing, or you'd be leaving in pieces," Cathal growled.

Oberon grunted. "Is he always this grumpy?"

"Yes," Eve replied. "You should put him out of his misery," she suggested, her uppermost branches weaving in delight, her golden leaves shimmering. "Or perhaps remove his testicles. Did you know that aggression, roaming, and hard-headed behavior all tend to decrease in male dogs post-operation?"

Cathal's sides flared for a moment, the druidic markings that swirled along his body glowing orange before fading to a dull, ashen shade of grey. "I hate talking trees."

I cocked an eyebrow at the hound. "How many talkin' trees do ye know?"

"You'd be surprised."

"Been a long few days, I take it?" Oberon interjected, wryly.

"This isn't exactly the Ritz," I replied, waving my hand about. "And none of us are exactly designed to lay low." I'd already decided not to mention my trips to the Twilight Valley; I'd been careful to stay out of sight and had come across no one coming or going.

Oberon surveyed the three of us, noting the truth of that assertion. "My apologies. Hunting down your guides took more effort than I'd anticipated. The realms are somewhat...tumultuous, at the moment."

"Did ye say guides?" I asked, emphasizing the plural.

As if on cue, two cloaked figures stepped into the doorway behind Oberon. The first was about my height—a respectable six feet that I'd long ago embraced—while the second stood at a much shorter, much slimmer five-foot-nothing. The taller of the two removed his hood to reveal the startlingly attractive face of a young heartthrob, his skin tan and silky smooth, his eyes large and remarkably expressive, his bowed lips curving upward. He flashed me a megawatt smile which would have sent teenage girls everywhere squealing into their pillows. "Nice to see you again, Quinn MacKenna," Narcissus said, bowing slightly. "Not as nice as it must be to see me, of course, but there's nothing you can do about that."

"No, I suppose there isn't," I replied, immediately recognizing the world's most infamous egomaniac from my time aboard a cruise ship co-captained by the stunningly perverse Dorian Grey, though that had happened so long ago now that it felt like another lifetime. "You're our guide?"

"Oh no, dear. I'm mainly here for moral support. You know, because I'm so good at it." Narcissus reached out to squeeze the arm of his companion. "Ladies and gentle...well, whatever you all are," Narcissus said, waving his free hand in a flourish, "allow me to introduce you to the face that launched a thousand ships."

The cloaked figure hesitated before revealing herself, as if shy. But, when at last she did, I found I could only look at her in pieces. It was as if my eyes refused to take in the whole of her in one glance. I stared first at her flaxen hair, a mound of golden tresses piled upon her head, adorned with flowers and thin gold chains. Next, her downcast eyes, the irises a riveting shade of blue. She had double rows of dark lashes, almost impossibly thick. A mouth like a budding rose, petite and inviting. And yet, even in pieces, there was an allure to her, a magnetism to those prim lips and finely crafted features, that couldn't be denied; I found my hand reaching for her before I even realized what was happening, my fingers curled as if I might cup her chin.

"Best put that away, Helen," Narcissus whispered, coyly.

The woman did as Narcissus suggested, and I was finally able to look elsewhere. I glanced over my shoulder to find Cathal had been similarly entranced, a dopey, doe-eyed expression splashed across his muzzle. Eve, for her part, seemed unfazed; the expression on the face formed from a burl in the middle of her trunk displayed little more than curiosity. Meaning whatever pull this woman had, it wasn't enough to flog Eve's proverbial log.

I cleared my throat, feeling the tension in the room ease in perceptible increments until we could all stand easy. "I'm sorry, d'ye say Helen? As in, Helen of Troy?"

Oberon nodded as he showcased his two companions. "Indeed," he replied. "Very few remain who know of Odysseus' Path and where it leads, but even fewer who have been there before. I brought both."

I frowned, struggling to recall my hazy memory of Greek mythology. "And how would either of ye know how to get there? Ye weren't part of Odysseus' story," I insisted, pointing first at Narcissus, then at Helen, "and ye were taken back to Sparta by Menelaus after the fall of Troy."

Narcissus clapped delightedly. "Oh, she knows all about us!"

"I work in antiquities," I replied. "Or I did. Anyway, few cultures provided as many artifacts as the Greeks. It literally paid to know t'ings like that."

"It is true that I was taken back to Sparta by my husband," Helen interjected, the timbre of her voice surprisingly deep. She turned a bit, clearly staring at me from beneath the shadows of her cowl. "But Atlantis is known to all of the gods' children. It was not a city at all, but a sanctuary. An untainted place outside the influence of capricious deities where many heroes were laid to rest. My mother gave birth to me there before sending me to be raised by Leda."

"And I," Narcissus cut in, thrusting one hand dramatically over his heart, "was once given a map by a young sailor who sought to earn my affections. A very old map drawn up by Odysseus himself." The Greek patted his chest and winked. "I make it a habit to hold on to all my trophies, you see."

"And why are ye two offerin' to help us?" I asked, unsure why either of the Greeks would take the risk, though it was Narcissus—a man notorious for his self-serving nature—I turned to. "What's in it for ye?"

"They came because I asked," the Goblin King interjected, folding his arms across his bulky chest, suddenly standing a few inches taller. "Because I insisted they help you. Or don't you trust my judgment?"

I thought about that for a second. "It's not only your judgment I don't trust, but I wouldn't take that personally. I don't trust anyone these days."

Oberon's eye twitched. "Then what is it you have a problem with?"

"I guess I just prefer to know what drives people to do what they do. That way I can count on 'em to act in their own self-interest. I don't bother with nonsense like blind faith or misplaced optimism. Oaths can be broken, and hope is a double-edged sword."

Narcissus' sudden applause stole our attention, his booming laughter failing to echo despite the relatively high ceilings of the gingerbread house. "I could've said it better myself, of course," he declared, "but that was well put."

"So, does that mean ye two have a good reason for agreein' to join this little expedition of ours, after all?"

The two Greeks exchanged furtive glances that told me all I needed to know about their magnanimity; they clearly wanted something from this

9

voyage. Oberon, meanwhile, studied my face as if he'd never seen it before, his heavy-lidded eyes narrowed.

"Well?" I urged, pretending I hadn't noticed the Goblin King's interest.

"We wish to recover that which was lost," Helen replied, cryptically.

"Meanin' what, exactly?"

Helen hesitated before responding. "Atlantis was once a realm unto itself, beautiful and remote, a haven for those who wished to be free of the games played by the gods, the ceaseless infighting. Heroes and deities alike would find solace on its shores, leaving their cares and their material possessions behind. But when the Old Ones departed from the world of men, many of them to sleep and never awaken, Atlantis was no longer needed. Most believe it was swallowed by the sea, along with its many treasures."

"You're sayin' there are weapons in Atlantis?" I asked, hoping to confirm the story I'd been told by my mother when we last spoke.

"Weapons, books, jewels, metals so rare they haven't been seen by mankind since before Troy got sacked," Narcissus replied, eyes alight. Oberon coughed and nudged the rambunctious man-child, but Narcissus merely grunted—apparently oblivious to the social faux pas of referencing the sacking of Helen's adopted city. "What?" he asked.

"Alright, so which of those are ye lookin' for?" I asked, directing the question Helen's way; of the two would-be guides, she certainly seemed more reasonable.

The Greek turned from me to study the forest that lay beyond the gingerbread house, quiet for so long I thought she might not answer. "There is said to be a lyre," she replied, at last. "A musical instrument capable of swaying the gods. I wish to claim it for myself and use it to wake my mother from her eternal slumber."

"Your mother?"

"Nemesis," Helen replied. "As I said, Leda raised me, but Nemesis laid the egg I was hatched from."

Despite the peculiar nature of Helen's birth, I felt an eerie sense of kinship with the woman blossom as a result of her story; I, too, was the progeny of a goddess, raised by a mortal woman. Still, I got the feeling that there was more to her story—something she wasn't telling me. "Why d'ye want to wake her, exactly?"

"We have unfinished business," she replied, cagily. "Family business."

"Right. And what about ye, then? What's in it for Narcissus?" I asked, turning to the other Greek.

"Who, me?" Narcissus asked, sliding his hand in slow circles over his chest. "Why, I'm simply tagging along because I want to ask Helen's dear mother a favor. She cursed me once, you know. Thankfully, my dearest Helen offered to put a word in." Narcissus slid his arm over his companion's shoulders and squeezed. "We're besties, you see."

"Oh? And what happened to Dorian?" I asked.

Narcissus rolled his eyes. "I'm more than enough for anyone, but Dorian is all about quantity over quality, if you know what I mean."

I cringed inwardly at the implication, afraid I knew all too well what he was referring to; Dorian Grey had a habit of throwing lavish, decadent parties when he wasn't putting together underground fights for Freaks— essentially anyone who wasn't human or Fae—everywhere. I'd slept in his orgy-sized bed once and immediately felt the need to shower with bleach.

"Narcissus is the only person I can rely on," Helen added. "He has to come with me."

"Narcissus?" I asked, unable to keep the disbelief off my face. "He's a lot of t'ings, but reliable doesn't come to mind."

"You wound me," Narcissus insisted. "I'm the most reliable man alive. No one can be depended on more than I can."

Helen patted her companion's arm. "Narcissus' self-love is so strong it renders him completely immune to me, which means he's the only person I can let my guard down around."

"Immune to what, exactly?" I asked.

Narcissus burst out a laugh. "To *what*, she says. To this face!"

The Greek man reached into Helen's cowl and squeezed her barely visible cheeks. The slightest glimpse of her rosy flesh made me want to do the same, to slide my fingers along her skin. I shivered and looked away, unable to overcome my sudden desire, aware of her in a way I hadn't been a moment before. "I see what ye mean."

"You'll all have plenty of time to get to know each other better on the ship," Oberon interjected, his face turned away as if looking for enemies lurking among the stone trees. "Time is against you."

"Speaking of that, where is this ship of yours, dear?" Narcissus asked, peering over my shoulder as if the sea were somehow behind me.

"It's waitin' for us in Neverland," I replied. The whole truth—that I had no idea whether Hook would help us, or whether I'd be able to enlist the aid of Peter Pan and the Lost People—I kept to myself; there was no point filling them in just yet. Besides, I still wasn't certain whether I trusted our guides. Best to compartmentalize until I knew for sure where their allegiances lay, one way or the other.

Oberon coughed into his hand. "About that...we may have a problem."

I grimaced, sensing that dark cloud hovering over me once again, my chest tight with the knowledge that something was wrong. Was this what I'd been dreading, or was it simply another hurdle to be overcome? I sighed and gestured for Oberon to fill me in, aware that—the way my life had been going lately—this turbulent mess was the closest thing to a pleasure cruise I was likely to go on for quite some time.

So much for that romantic getaway.

3

*N*everland was dead.

I knew it the instant the six of us landed on the beach; where once there had been a glittering sea of white gold sand, green grass, and rolling hills there was now a coarse grey clay, withered grass, and a shelf of cragged, sun-bleached rocks. In a way, Neverland's decayed remains reminded me of the Blighted Lands—a hellish landscape I hoped never to see again. Except that whereas the Blighted Lands had seemed sick, even diseased, Neverland felt like a long dead corpse, its bones picked clean of flesh, the stench of rot long faded.

"How long?" I asked.

"Hard to say," Oberon replied, understanding my question immediately. "Time never did hold much sway over this island. Even the Fae knew to avoid it. Most blamed the Manling children, but eventually our people embraced the legend of the land that would not age, telling horrific tales of those who inhabited it, of the island's growing bloodthirst. That's how I heard of Captain Hook and his flying ship, and why I thought to recruit him," the Goblin King explained, referring to the time he'd enlisted Hook and his men to join his armada against the Fomorians—a battle we'd fought together in what felt like simpler times. "But it seems something must have changed," he added, gesturing to the desolate landscape.

"Must have," I agreed halfheartedly, though I knew what that something was; I'd seen the hole left in the Hangman's Tree where a single grain of sand had once halted the flow of time. I knew that Nate Temple's parents—a power couple responsible for a great many plots and more than a few catastrophes—had removed the grain, though I had no idea why. I knew all this because Peter Pan had confided in me once, asking nothing in return except that I come back someday. He'd been a man in his mid-thirties then, living out his life as a husband and father; time had already reasserted itself upon my arrival, though what had happened here could only be measured in centuries, not mere years. Which meant I was very, very late. "What about Peter Pan?" I asked. "The Lost People. Where are they? Where did they go?"

Oberon turned away, staring at the sea. At first I thought he was refusing to meet my eyes, that perhaps he knew the answers to my questions but did not want to voice them. But then I saw what had caught his eye: black sails materializing on the horizon. The *Jolly Roger*, its sleek black sides gleaming in the light of day, sailed towards us.

"When I sent my goblins here to check on the Neverlanders," Oberon said, "all they found was Hook's ship. The rest of the island was deserted. They tried to board the ship, but it fled whenever they got close."

I frowned, wondering why Hook would run from Oberon's goblins. Sure, they were an ugly bunch, not to mention dumb as rocks, but that hardly made them a threat. I began walking the beach, waving my arms about. I didn't bother yelling; as far out as the ship was, there was no way the pirates could hear me. But hopefully the sight of a woman on this barren beach would draw the pirates in. Maybe then I'd get some answers.

Unfortunately, as the ship drew closer, I realized how unlikely that was; no shapes flitted across the deck, no one manned the rudder, and the crow's nest appeared empty. I stopped at the edge of the shoreline, the tide brushing up against my boots, and watched the seemingly abandoned vessel drift towards us. My companions followed, massing at my back, and I wondered what they were thinking; none had been to Neverland before, which meant they likely had no idea what was going on. No clue what had been lost here.

"What's that?" Narcissus asked, jabbing a finger towards the top sail. A moment later, I saw it, too; a pink ball of light spinning around the mast, dust trailing behind it like the tail of a comet. The ball darted faster, dipping and ducking along the sails and rigging, leaving a trail of light that seemed to stain the ship with the faintest blush, a rosy glow that spread and spread until the whole vessel shone pink. In seconds, the vessel began to rise out of the water, liquid spilling off the hull to join the waves below, leaving a frothing surface behind as it climbed into the sky, stopping to hover perhaps ten feet above the waves. As we watched, the pirate ship resumed its approach.

"Is no one going to answer me?" Narcissus asked, sounding remarkably put out.

"Looks like a flying ship to me," Cathal ventured, his grumbling voice seething with the scathing brand of sarcasm I'd long grown accustomed to —though it was admittedly refreshing to have it directed at someone else.

"Obviously," Eve added.

Narcissus looked back and forth between the talking tree and talking pooch, then let out an exasperated huff. "Your pets are being rude," he said, glaring at me.

"Not at all," Eve interjected, testily. "Rude would be the mutt confusing you for a snack."

Cathal licked his chops. "I do like snacks."

Narcissus gulped but was saved having to respond by the lowering of a rope ladder from the ship as it approached. Soon, all I could make out was the ship's keel; the *Jolly Roger* settled in above us, casting a massive shadow. Above the rope ladder, a young man's face appeared, peeking out over the edge—one I thought I recognized.

"James?" I asked, unable to mask my disbelief.

"Come on up," the young man said before disappearing back the way he'd come.

Unable to believe my eyes, I took hold of the ladder after it collided with the ground and quickly worked my way up, pausing only for a moment to glance down at Cathal and Eve—neither of whom could reasonably be expected to follow.

"Go," Cathal insisted, "I'll make sure no one sets fire to the tree."

Eve said nothing, though I could tell she was upset to be left behind; she was hugging herself again, her bright leaves turned down like the ears of a kicked dog. Still, seeing as how there wasn't much I could do to mend her hurt feelings, I flashed Cathal a thumbs up and continued up the ladder. At the top, I found myself pulled to the deck by a man in his early twenties. James Pan—Peter Pan's adopted son—held me at arm's length for a long moment before stepping away, resting one hand on a familiar sword—the cutlass that had once belonged to his biological father, the notorious Captain James Hook.

"Who are you? And what are you doing here?" he asked as my companions joined me on the deck, searching my face as if he might find the answers written there.

"Ye don't remember me, then?" I asked. As if they'd been waiting for my response before showing themselves, two figures emerged from the Captain's cabin. Both I recognized, though I had fond memories of neither. The first was Tiger Lily, now a woman at least my age. Covered in animal skins, her face painted to mimic a human skull, and having razor sharp teeth, the brave may as well have been an advertisement for all things barbaric. The other was Tinkerbell, a pixie the size of my middle finger who'd tried very hard to stab me, once upon a time. She floated in midair, her wings bustling, body emitting more of that pink light we'd seen earlier.

"It's you!" Tinkerbell hissed as she closed the distance between us, her expression irate.

"You know her, Tink?" James asked.

"She is the one who fought alongside Hook during our final battle," Tiger Lily acknowledged, answering the young man's question. "Our people sang songs of her and her guardian for many moons. The children soon lived in fear of the creature wreathed in flame."

It took me a moment to remember what Tiger Lily was referring to, and by then all three of the ship's inhabitants had crowded closer. I held up a hand, hoping to deescalate the situation, only too aware of the irony that the task should fall to me. "That was a long time ago. And it wasn't personal," I explained. "I wasn't in control of meself." And neither was Alucard, I thought, but didn't say—better if we bypassed the Louisiana born daywalker and his pyrotechnic display altogether; from what I could recall, he'd immolated a ridiculous number of pixies and braves that day.

"Wait," James said, holding out one arm to stay his companions. "I do remember her."

"Yes, she was the one I told you about. The one who—" Tinkerbell began.

"No, not from your stories," James interrupted, shaking his head. "I met her once. I did, didn't I? When I was younger, in my father's...in Peter's house." The instant James said the name, it was as if sadness had reached out and slapped each of their faces. Grief-stricken—that's what they were. Which told me all I needed to know about poor Peter Pan.

"What happened?" I asked, brushing aside the implications of Peter's death for the time being; he and I hadn't known each other long, but in our brief time together he'd patched up my wounds, offered me sage advice as well as sanctuary, and had put both himself and his people at risk for my sake. No matter who I'd become since then, no matter how many lives I lived, I would forever mourn the loss of a man like that.

"Time happened here," Tiger Lily replied, her response gruff and concise.

"How long was I gone?" I asked. "Do any of ye know?"

James cocked his head. "How old was I when we last met?"

"Eleven or twelve years old, maybe," I shrugged, unsure. In my mind's eye, I pictured the bookish child who'd helped his mother set the table, who'd disdained his adoptive father's attempts at humor. He'd been young, yes, but I remembered how those blue eyes tracked me, how thoughtful his questions had been.

"And how old am I, now?"

I grinned but quickly realized the lad wasn't joking. "Don't ye know?"

James looked away and said nothing.

Strangely enough, it was Oberon who answered my question, his voice shattering the sudden silence. "It seems the boy has been living among our kind," the Goblin King explained, gesturing at Tinkerbell and Tiger Lily with one long, crooked finger. "We don't age the way Manlings do. He probably has no idea how old he is."

I studied Hook's son, taking Oberon's point; in a realm outside of time, a realm without birthdays or anniversaries, it would be hard to keep track of something as arbitrary as one's age. "I'd say you're in your early twenties, if I had to guess," I said to James. "Perhaps ten years older than when we met, give or take."

"Ten years...is it a long time for us?" James asked in response—a question so odd it took me a moment to realize what Oberon had actually meant; thanks to his upbringing, not only was James incapable of determining his own age, but his grasp of time as a concept had been compromised.

"Not so very long," Oberon replied, his voice soft and surprisingly gentle. "A tenth of a Manling's lifespan, if he's fortunate."

James nodded, his scowl so deep I couldn't help but see the resemblance between him and his birth father—a man whose grizzled aspect had haunted the dreams of many a child. Indeed, standing as he was, his feet wide, his arms crossed, with his face turned towards the island, I found a great deal of his father in him. He had the old man's dark, wavy hair, his lean musculature, the pointed tilt of his nose and chin. How had Peter fared, I wondered, raising a child who so resembled his greatest adversary? Or had he even been around to see it?

"The island died," James explained, answering my question at last. "The Hangman's Tree was the first to go. Then the forests. The rivers and lakes of Tiger Lily's people dried up next, but by then most of the Lost People were already gone." He flicked his eyes to me. "Time had finally caught up to them. That's what Peter said before he passed. It happened fast, I think. One day he was simply old, the next, gone." James cleared his throat, but no tears stained his cheeks, nothing to show how much it had hurt to see his father fade and die. "Mother lasted longer. Long enough to find Hook and bargain for the rest of us."

I frowned. "And where's Hook now?"

"He's gone, too. He made the mistake of stepping on the island, along with the rest of his men. Looking back, I think they knew what would happen. Anyway, they survived long enough to escort my sister and the other children to a safe place, but that was it."

"And what about ye?" I asked after a moment of silence, fighting against a second wave of grief as I realized that the man I'd fought alongside— disreputable scalawag though he'd been—had also passed away. In some ways, this news hit me harder. It was difficult to imagine a world without Captain James Hook; I'd assumed he at least would find a way to survive—a trait I'd admired, even then.

"What about me?"

"Why are ye here? Why d'ye leave your sister?"

"He refused to leave us behind," Tiger Lily answered, staring at the young man with an expression that went beyond gratitude. "He knew my people had nowhere to go and no way to get there, and so he returned with Tinkerbell in Hook's ship."

"Tink found me after Peter died," James explained, perhaps sensing my next question as he glanced back at the pixie, on whose face sorrow and guilt warred.

"I should have been with him," Tinkerbell said, though I could tell it was a line she'd repeated so often to herself that it had lost all meaning. "I always thought we would have our time together again. That he'd come find me, and we'd play like we used to."

"James escorted my braves to new lands," Tiger Lily continued as though Tinkerbell hadn't spoken. "And now I stay with him, to honor the boon he gave us. Perhaps even repay him, one day."

"Alright, but why not return to your sister, now? What's keepin' ye here?" I asked. Oberon coughed and nudged me with his shoulder, clearly suggesting I enlist the services of the young man and his motley crew of Neverland castaways. It wasn't the worst idea; with Hook and Peter gone, my options were increasingly limited. But I wouldn't. The three of them had been through enough already. I'd find another way. Somehow.

"I was told to wait here," James replied.

"By whom?"

"He was a man. Like me, but older. He told me to sail the coast and wait for a tall woman with hair the color of flame to arrive. He even described your companions, though I'm not sure who is whom." James began counting off on his fingers, apparently recalling a list. "The grieving god. The flower. The seducer. The guardian. And the savior."

I cocked an eyebrow at the titles, unable to place them all, myself. "And what made ye t'ink he was tellin' the truth?"

Tiger Lily pursed her painted lips. "I will admit I was suspicious, but what he promised us was too great a thing to ignore."

"And what did he promise?"

"He said you would save Neverland," James replied, eagerly.

I froze, startled. "He said what?"

James repeated himself, which only confused me further. I hated to think it, but I was fairly certain someone had blatantly lied to the poor kid —albeit someone with enough foresight to predict my arrival. I turned to study the barren landscape that had once teemed with life. For some reason, it seemed fitting to me that it should have died with Pan and Hook; with them gone, Neverland would never be whole again, anyway.

"Listen, James, I'm not sure who told ye I could—" I began.

"He was a Manling," Tiger Lily interjected, as if she were afraid I'd leave

Neverland to its fate without more information—and rightfully so, considering there was little else I could do. "A Manling who called himself a wizard. A Manling who could move through time. He had a Manling name. An odd one."

"Merlin," James chimed in. "He called himself Merlin."

4

*O*beron and I exchanged shocked glances, taken aback by the alleged name of the man who'd insisted I could resuscitate a freaking island. Merlin, arguably the greatest wizard of all time, if not the most notorious, was a figure known around the world for his role in King Arthur's ascension, though accounts of his exploits varied to an almost comical degree. He was also my father, though that seemed to have been left off his list of achievements. Until now, I hadn't even known whether or not he was still alive. In fact, the only person I'd spoken with who'd even crossed paths with my father—the enchantress, Morgan le Fay—had felt strongly that he'd moved on, content to let the world spin without his influence. Before leaving Ipswich, I'd learned the two had once been lovers, though I'd never pressed for more details; seemed a tad unkind, asking her to relive a centuries-old breakup. Not to mention inappropriate, given our respective roles.

Morgan le Fay had also been the one to identify Merlin as my father, citing my inheritance of time-bending magic and Merlin's impressive height as evidence. Unfortunately, that bit of trivia accounted for everything I knew about the man physically; I'd heard his voice before, but never seen his face, which meant asking what the time traveler had looked like wouldn't be much help.

"Well, what'd he look like?" Narcissus asked, plainly curious.

I sighed.

"What?" Narcissus shrugged. "I thought it was a great question."

The Neverlanders looked at each other in turn as if trying to come to a consensus, as if Merlin were inexplicably hard to describe. Tiger Lily spoke first. "He was a very tall Manling, dressed in the hides of strange creatures. Like yours," she insisted, gesturing vaguely at my black scoop neck shirt and dark denim jeans.

"He wore a hat. Like Hook's, but shaped like this," Tinkerbell added, gesticulating. "He used it to hide his face."

"Anythin' else?" I asked, unable to help myself; if they really were talking about my father, then this would be the first time he'd ever been described to me. As a young girl, I'd obsessed about such things. I'd drawn him, clumsily, the way a child would. Tall, like me. Dark, curly hair, like my Aunt Dez's. I drew him in suits, like the men on the news, like the principal at my school. Later, I'd imagined him in a black leather jacket and sunglasses, behind the wheel a fast car or on the back of a throaty motorcycle. Eventually, I met a young man who resembled that—gorgeous and suave, he talked fast and lived on the edge. Only it turned out he wasn't a man at all, but a vampire. A bloodsucker. It wasn't until after he realized he couldn't drain me dry—thanks to my immunity to all things supernatural—that he'd shown his true colors; starved for affection, I'd let the bastard treat me like shit for months before I abandoned him in a burning building.

Oddly enough, now that I thought about it, I realized I had no emotional attachment to that story, to that horrific period of my life. Not so long ago, looking back on those moments had felt like prying shards of glass from my palms. Now, it was as if I held a river-worn stone. Had enough time passed, or had I simply become numb to the traumas of my own life? For some reason, I didn't think either of those were the case. Instead, it seemed as though those things had happened to someone else, someone I could only pity—a young woman so immersed in her own pain that she began lashing out at anyone who got too close, afraid to open her heart again, especially after discovering she could love with such abandon that she'd forgive her partner anything.

"He knew things," James replied at last, startling me. "But most of what he said made no sense. He knew about Hook and my mother, but he called me someone else. It was odd. Sometimes it felt like he was looking right past me, like I wasn't even there."

"What did he call you?" Narcissus asked.

"What?"

"You said he called you someone else. Who was it?"

James shook his head. "It wasn't even a name. He called me Shake Spear. And he called me Captain."

"He called ye Captain Shakespeare?" I asked, dumbfounded.

"Strange, right? Tiger Lily and I almost ran him off, after that. But then he began talking about the Lost People, about Neverland. He told us about you. Said you would save the island, that you would make it even better than it was before if I swore to aid you and your companions." James seemed to be looking inward, now, wringing his hands together over and over again. "We'd lost hope, you see. Neverland was our home. Leaving it behind, watching it fade and die…"

I could tell James had more to say, but that it would be difficult for him to go on, so I reached out and squeezed his shoulder in reassurance. I'd felt as he did, once; after my battle with Balor, I'd returned to the charred remains of my aunt's house, the memories of a caring home ruined forever by the sight of it in ruin. "I understand, but—" I began.

Oberon coughed delicately into his fist.

"What?" I asked, eyes narrowed.

"If it was him, then maybe it's possible…"

I shook my head, finding the circumstances incredibly hard to swallow. Because, if it were true—if the great and powerful Merlin had indeed dropped by on a portentous errand—it meant my father had spent decades avoiding me, only to show up long after I'd given up hope, and then only to set me up for failure. Why couldn't he have appeared the instant we arrived —or hell, years ago, when I'd actually needed him? "Did the time traveler happen to say how I was goin' to restore your island?" I asked the Neverlanders, my infamous temper boiling to the surface at last.

The blank stares I received told me all I needed to know about the quality of Merlin's divinations—not that I'd had high expectations. That was the problem with prophetic mumbo jumbo: it rarely offered practical advantages. More often than not, it wasn't until *after* the portentous events unfolded that it all made sense, that you could sit back and feel properly stupid for not having puzzled it out sooner. Which meant the time traveler's promises were worth about as much as the lifeless island he'd insisted I could revive.

"Listen, James..." I began, preparing to let the young man down as gently as I could. Afterwards, I'd talk to Oberon, see if I could use one of the ships from the armada he'd amassed to fight Balor. If not, maybe I'd try and call in a few favors in the mortal realm. See what turned up. With the new Jack Frost at least a week ahead of us, I couldn't afford to sit on my hands, but this was clearly a dead end.

"Quinn!" Eve yelled before I could say more. Surprised, I glanced over the side of the ship only to find my uprooted houseplant waving at me with several of her limbs. Cathal lay beside her, ears cocked. Had they heard everything we'd said?

"What is it?" I called down.

"I need you to come with me, but leave the others. They'll just be liabilities."

Taken aback by her tone, it was all I could do not to ask a dozen questions. But, unlike Oberon and his chosen guides, I trusted Eve; if she had something to say to me, I knew it would be important. Still, judging by the expressions of those around me, I could tell the others weren't happy being called liabilities. Or maybe it was the bit about being left behind. Either way, the situation called for a little comedy. Something to lighten the mood.

"Oh? D'ye say ye want me to leaf 'em behind?" I asked, grinning, one hand pressed comically to my ear.

"Is she always like this? Or does it get better?" Cathal asked, plenty loud enough for everyone to overhear.

"She used to be worse. I've been working on it," Eve replied.

I glared down at them both, then let out a long, ragged sigh as though I were being put upon. Then, shoulders slumped, I turned to the others. "She can be a real pain. Anyway, let me go see what she has to say, alright? Maybe she has an idea."

The Neverlanders brightened at that, but I could tell Oberon wasn't buying it. Narcissus simply pouted. If Helen thought anything out of the ordinary, I couldn't tell; safe behind her cowl, it seemed the face that launched a thousand ships had nothing to say regarding this one. Funnily enough, I wasn't sure why I'd felt the need to put on an act in front of the others, only that I did. Confusion to my enemies might have been a little extreme under the circumstances, but I wasn't certain I had any friends on board, either. Never hurt to play with my cards close to my chest.

"And am I supposed to just wait here?" Oberon asked as I approached the ladder, clearly ticked off. "I have..." the Goblin King drifted off and glanced at his audience, apparently disinclined to reveal his true identity to James and his friends—though why that was, I had no idea. "I have a job to do, as you well know," he concluded.

I nodded, acknowledging Oberon's gripe; I'd kept him from his duties as a ruler for several days amidst the potential outbreak of a war that could see his subjects caught in the crossfire, and he had brought the guides he'd promised. It would be unfair to ask him to linger on my account, even if our goals paralleled each other's. Maybe that was why I didn't trust him, plain and simple; the Goblin King had his own agenda, and I wasn't yet sure whether that agenda aligned with my own. Stop the new Jack Frost? Steal back the devourer I'd recovered from Balor's ashes? Find the first Jewel of the Tuatha de Dannan? It all sounded reasonable, if a bit implausible, and yet—even if I somehow succeeded—what would I do, then? Would I take on Mordred, or confront Nate Temple? What if, by the time I returned, there was no war to be fought? Or worse, what if someone had already won?

"I promise not to be gone long," I said.

"See that you aren't. We each have a great deal to do, and very little time to do it in."

"And what happens if I fail?" I asked, studying Oberon's face, searching for the faintest sign of doubt. "Let's say I save the island. We sail away from here, follow the path, and find Atlantis. What if Ryan got there first? What if we fight, and he wins? What then?"

The Goblin King favored me with a humorless smile. "Then we're doomed. Or maybe something else happens, something we can't predict." He shrugged, a raw pain flashing behind his eyes, his expression unnaturally tortured, like a cracked mask put on display. Power, a great suffocating wave of it, rode my skin for an instant before dissipating. "Whatever happens," Oberon continued, as though nothing out of the ordinary had happened, "I'll stand with my subjects and lead them on a Hunt they'll never forget."

The last was said with such animalistic ferocity that everyone but Tiger Lily and I took a step back, caught off balance by the sudden burst of power and subsequent vow. Indeed, the only reason I stayed put was because I knew—deep down—that Oberon was no threat to me. Not as things stood now, at any rate. The Goblin King simply had too much to lose.

While the others recovered, Tiger Lily took a step forward, touching the back of her clawed hand to her forehead and bowing slightly at the waist. "Lord of the Wild Host," she said, "forgive me for not honoring you sooner."

Oberon quickly returned the gesture and waved her off, almost as if he were embarrassed to have been discovered. "Nevermind all that, Tiger Lily," he replied. After a moment's scrutiny, I realized it wasn't embarrassment affecting the Goblin King, but nervousness. Why?

"Quinn!" Eve called again, sounding impatient.

"Comin'!" I replied, pausing at the top of the ladder to look back at Oberon, who studied me with an inscrutable expression. I found myself sympathizing with the Faeling and his role in what was to come; something about his agonized expression earlier had triggered memories of my own identity crisis, my own suffering. "Don't let Temple's war become your war," I warned, though I wasn't sure where the sudden concern stemmed from. "Keep your subjects safe."

Oberon scoffed. "Wars aren't kind to cowards, Quinn MacKenna. But don't worry, we'll all have our parts to play in this. Even you." His eyes narrowed. "Perhaps especially you."

"All the world's a stage, eh?" I teased, gaze shifting inexorably to James— the earnest Captain Shakespeare, or so the time traveler would have it—as I bastardized one of the Bard's most famous lines in an attempt to leave things between Oberon and me on a lighter, perhaps even friendlier, note.

"Let us hope not," Helen interjected, speaking for the first time since we'd stepped onto the ship, her voice a dramatic contralto. "Stages can burn."

Well, so much for improving the mood.

$\mathcal{C}$athal padded alongside me, his almost impossibly large, lanky frame making it easy for him to clamber up and over the array of jagged boulders that lined the shore. Up ahead, Eve seemed to be having even less trouble; she moved between the rocks like a spider, her roots diving between the crevices, keeping her level. In fact, she churned forward with such ease that I could barely keep up. I called after her to slow down, but she either didn't hear or chose to ignore me. Despite her recent chattiness, I had a gut feeling that it was the latter; few wounds close with the passing of time alone, and emotional scars bleed more than most.

Unable to keep pace and unwilling to die trying, I stopped to catch my breath, hazarding a look over one shoulder. The *Jolly Roger* continued to hover in the sky, though the pink blush had faded considerably. The Neverlanders stood apart from the Greeks and the Goblin King, though all were watching our progress from the railing. I couldn't quite make out their faces but suspected they were filled with hope, perhaps even expectation. Rage surged through me for a brief instant—how dare my father, if it really had been him, promise those poor people such a thing? What if I failed? The cruelty of losing your home twice—once to circumstance, and again to a broken vow—was staggering. Cathal nudged me with his muzzle, nearly sending me flying off my temporary perch in the process.

"Easy," I cautioned as I reset my feet. "Not all of us have four legs."

"Yes, well, we can't all be perfect."

I rolled my eyes but resumed the march, working my way between the stones, using my hands as often as my feet, beads of sweat pricking my brow. Cathal fell in behind me, loping from stone to stone the way a child might play hopscotch.

"Your tree," he said, a moment later, "what is she?"

"What?"

Cathal quickly overtook me and set atop a particularly tall stone, eyes locked on Eve as she glided among the rocks, ears cocked. He didn't speak until I joined him, my breath coming in short bursts, sweat now running down into my eyes; after spending months training to master the spear in the Otherworld, I'd developed impressive reserves of stamina, but seemingly had very little tolerance for the heat.

"She is learning," Cathal replied as I sidled between two stones, mindful of the deeper crevices lest I slip and break something. His tone suggested he wasn't entirely sure that was a good thing.

"Aye, she does that," I replied, patting his flank. "Ye might even say it's her sole occupation."

"No, not like that. Humans learn by seeing, by doing. The Coin Sithe learn the way of the world by drinking the milk of our mothers. What she is doing is more like that." Cathal raised his haunting, amber-colored eyes to the sky, muzzle twitching as he scented the air. "Something strange is happening here. I can smell it."

Caught off guard by Cathal's sudden loquaciousness, it was all I could do to process what he'd told me. The faerie hound rarely spoke of his kin or his upbringing, and I knew it pained him to do so. Which meant he'd thought it important I comprehend the distinction. But, before I could respond, the hound took off after Eve, leaving me to fumble onward, cursing my body's current limitations; having endurance was all well and good, but without the mind-numbing speed and prodigious strength I'd been granted my first time here, I was irrevocably, irritatingly human.

Surprisingly, I didn't consider this a humbling experience; I'd been a relatively frail creature for most of my life and had made the most of it, routinely surviving experiences which might have broken stronger, more capable people. In fact, until recently, I'd prided myself on that achievement. Looking back, it was clear I'd built a life around it—that so much of my self-worth had hinged upon surviving the worst of the worst, my psyche caught somewhere between an adrenaline rush and a death wish. Honestly, that's all my chosen profession had boiled down to: as an arms dealer, I had an excuse to play in the monster's sandbox, to steal their toys and kick down their castles.

It was only now, upon reflection, that I realized how delusional I'd been. That it hadn't been my gift for navigating the precarious black market or my talent for tough negotiation which had driven me to pit myself against the worst possible odds. No, it was the chase, the thrill, which had appealed to me. Still appealed to me, if I was being honest. And yet, something had changed along the way.

I'd grown up.

Perhaps it was the obscene advantage I'd been given when I'd first arrived in Fae—a competitive edge so vast it mocked all my years of training, all my hard work. Of course, it wasn't like I'd suddenly begun playing with a stacked deck; back then just about everyone I associated with had a trump card to play—be it the ability to shift into a ravenous animal, to weave illusions, to wield magic, or what have you, it had felt for a while there like truly gimmickless, powerless individuals had ceased to exist. And yet, with every new power I discovered, the stakes had seemed to diminish. I was no longer the little girl playing in the monster's sandbox. I'd become the schoolyard bully.

Except that wasn't entirely true. Deep down, I continued to thrive on chaos, eager to test my mettle. So what if I was no longer the underdog? A fight was a fight. That aspect of my personality hadn't changed at all. The only difference now was that I no longer held any illusions about my chances. This tumultuous, often bloody life I led—little more than setting myself against one impossible task after another—was not going to end quietly in the wee hours of the night years and years from now. In fact, if Oberon was right and there *was* some cosmic hand of destiny guiding this mess, then I had a sneaking suspicion I was being prepared for a tragedy—a final act forged in fire and bathed in blood. And yet, I realized that didn't really bother me; I had and always would live in the moment, partially convinced my next breath could be my last. To do anything else would be to invite the sort of self-doubt that so often plagued those listless, ambitionless people I could never entirely relate to. In this, all three of my selves had agreed.

Fuck being weak.

"Quinn," Eve said, her voice surprisingly close.

I halted and found myself standing on the final outcropping of rocks, overlooking a vast valley utterly devoid of life—a flat, nearly empty surface of solid dirt, cracked and broken. The remains of a small lake, perhaps, judging by the shape. As I watched, Eve plunged her roots into that lifeless soil and began to march further out, ploughing as she went, trailed by a furrow at least as wide and deep as a man. Together, Cathal and I followed on either side, covering ground much quicker now that I wasn't forced to labor after them. Still, we had to hang back a bit; dirt clods soared high into the air, threatening to crash down on our heads if we weren't careful.

"What's she doin'?" I called to my canine companion.

"What's it look like?"

I frowned. "Ye don't know either, do ye?"

"Nope."

I fetched a loose mound of dirt and tried to chuck it at the faerie hound, but Cathal dodged it with alarming ease, not so much as sparing me a glance. I sighed but resolved to keep walking and let the mystery unfold on Eve's terms; I owed her that much, at least.

While I walked, I began to poke at the other mystery I'd uncovered—Merlin's alleged involvement. Putting my emotions aside for the moment, I had to admit the circumstances surrounding his fortuitous arrival were suspicious, at best. Assuming he was alive, why urge James to help me? Was it because we sought Lugh's Spear? According to my mother, it had been his responsibility to keep it safe. Or was it something else, something to do with the destiny my parents had bestowed upon me?

I wasn't sure, and not knowing irritated me. When I'd first agreed to sail to Atlantis, I'd considered it a sort of favor, a way to repay the debt I owed to my mother's spirit for looking after me in the only way she'd been able. Coupled with the fact that Ryan planned to use what he'd stolen from me to power an incredibly dangerous artifact—presumably so he could wage war on potentially innocent Faelings—and the whole affair felt more and more like fate, as opposed to mere providence.

But now...now it seemed like the possibility of meeting my father—once perhaps my most ardent wish in the whole world, in all the worlds—was no longer a fantasy. What if he was waiting for me at the end of this insane voyage? What would I have to say to him, and him to me? Would he apologize for abandoning me, or claim it was all part of the "divine" plan? Could I forgive him, either way? Such questions provoked a roil of emotions: anger, frustration, hope, longing.

Would it be a ceasefire, or a siege?

"We're here," Eve said, drawing me back to the present so quickly I nearly tumbled into the massive ditch she'd created. I halted and squinted skyward, surprised by what she'd found, by where she'd led us. The Hangman's Tree, its branches skeletal, its trunk sunken and grey, loomed over us all. I did a slow turn, realizing we stood not far from the settlement I'd once visited; I could see remnants of the wall in the distance, the logs toppled to form misshapen lumps against the horizon. I stared for a moment, surprised by the lump in my throat. There had been people living there. Most of them had looked my age, maybe a bit older. The sheer waste sickened me so much I had to look away.

Peter Pan was dead. Hook was dead. Neverland was no more.

Somehow, I'd let those truths sink in, but not the others. Not the fact that the Lost People, that Hook's crew, had also perished. How easy it is to forget the nameless, faceless folk who sit in the backgrounds of our bedtime stories—to weigh the passing of a legend against the deaths of hundreds. "Why here?" I asked, throat tight.

Cathal leapt to my side of the ditch and sat back on his hind legs, his tongue pulsing, teeth bared as he drew great, laboring breaths. I frowned and glanced back the way we'd come, surprised to find the distant rocks little more than a smudge. It seemed we'd walked a couple miles while I'd been lost in thought.

"I'll get to that," Eve replied. "But first, I want to talk to you about Eden."

6

"*A*nd then there was light."

"Shut up, it's my story to tell," Eve replied peevishly, obviously displeased with my offhand comment. "Besides, it should have gone: and then there was *consciousness*. Light and darkness are merely realities imposed by the natural world. It was you humans who decided to use them to represent wisdom and ignorance, and only then because you idiots can't see in the dark."

"Heh, good one," Cathal chimed in.

I held both hands up in mock surrender, though admittedly I was glad to see Eve back in her natural state; giving me shit was how Eve showed affection—or at least I hoped that was the case. "I wasn't tryin' to be flippant," I said. "Just sayin' the first t'ing that came to mind, is all."

"Another regrettable human trait," she replied.

"Hah hah. I won't interrupt again, I swear. Go on."

Eve seemed to gather herself for a moment. "If I'm being honest, I have a very muddled understanding of what you might call Creation. What was passed on to me from that time is fragmented, mainly sensations, not actual memories." Eve pressed one limb to her trunk in a remarkably human gesture, as if struggling to think. "I've made sense of some of it by analyzing the allegories, by testing the myths against my own feelings in order to determine what really happened."

Cathal, whose heavy breathing had finally subsided, dropped to the ground and laid his shaggy head on his paws, staring up at the tree like a child waiting for a delightful bedtime story full of romance and adventure. But it wasn't that sort of story.

"The Garden of Eden," Eve began, "once defied everything mankind has come to despise or fear. Disease, rot, sorrow, death. These realities did not yet exist, not even as abstract concepts. Back then, the known world was touched by divine light. Unchanging, unyielding. But then something changed." Eve's limbs twitched. "There was a war. A battle for the fate of Heaven, unlike anything your kind would ever know because it was unlike any war you've ever seen. It was waged in different dimensions, scaled from the atomic level all the way to the cosmic, occurring outside time and space as you understand it."

I cocked my head as Eve fell silent, trying to reconcile her story with the Biblical events I'd learned about during my Catholic school years. She was talking, presumably, about the angelic rebellion. Lucifer's rebellion. For some reason, Eve's story conjured up an image: a stained-glass window depicting Michael the Archangel with his spear pressed against the throat of a conquered dragon, his foot pinning the wing of his fallen foe. "And Eden?" I asked. "What about Adam and Eve and the apple? Isn't that what ye wanted to tell us about?"

"I was getting to that," Eve replied, waving one limb dismissively. "First of all, you mustn't think of the Garden as a fixed place. It can be, but like so many of the realms that brush against your own, it's only partially touching the mortal world. As the other realms exist, stretching out like peninsulas, so, too, does Eden. Even when it was first fashioned, it was as much a concept as a location—as much a dream as a reality. Indeed, it can grow anywhere and thrive under any name. Places like Avalon, like Nysa, Annwn, Lintukoto, and so many others long forgotten."

I shook my head not in disbelief, exactly, but in confusion. I grasped the underlying principle well enough; if Heaven and Hell could exist across multiple pantheons, why not the Garden of Eden? A mythical paradise non-angelic beings could inhabit, so long as their deeds were worthy, their hearts pure. Having seen so many fictions come to life before my very eyes, I certainly wasn't going to discount the possibility. But what did all this— Eve's perspective on the angelic war, the long-winded explanation—have to do with Neverland?

"Why are ye tellin' us this?" I asked, perhaps a tad impatiently.

Shockingly, Eve laughed; it was the first time I'd ever heard the sound—a rustling outburst that made me think of an animal surging through forest brush. "Here I am, trying to fill you in on a period of history that some theologians might actually kill for, and you want me to get to the 'good' part," she said, branches curling to form air quotes. "Sometimes I find it inexplicable that fate brought us together, Quinn. I've not met many of your kind, admittedly, but I doubt there are many who care so little for knowledge."

I cocked an eyebrow at that. It wasn't that she was entirely wrong, of course; most people were innately curious, unable to help themselves. Had Eve been given to an academic of any sort, they'd likely still be pumping her for information. "It isn't that I don't care," I said, in my defense. "It's that me priorities are different. Some people aren't happy unless they know every-thin' there is to know. I'm not happy unless I know everythin' I *need* to know. There's a big gap between the two, that's all."

"Yes, I'm aware," Eve countered, lightly. "I can't say it's an admirable trait, but I am glad it was you who found me. You have used me for your own gain, but far less often than you might have if you were someone else." She sounded sad, then. "Very well, we'll leave this story for the appropriate time. Ask the question you so clearly wish to ask."

Struck by the notion that Eve's tale had merit, I almost asked her to go on. But with the others waiting on the *Jolly Roger*, I simply couldn't wait; there was no guarantee that Oberon would hang around if we dallied. Which meant, if we failed to save the island, we'd be more or less stranded here. I coughed into one fist, clearing my throat. "D'ye know how to revive Neverland?"

"In a manner of speaking."

"I'm listenin'."

"That's a first," Eve quipped, caressing the trunk of the Hangman's Tree with one limb. "Alright. Well, first of all, you should know that the island is not dead."

"Come again?" That was news to me. The island sure *looked* dead; I had no idea what the standard of living was for a landmass, but I knew from personal experience what a wasteland looked like.

"She lives, still. We've been communicating, she and I." Eve plunged her roots deep into the earth beneath our feet, and I realized she'd firmly entrenched herself while we'd been talking. "The island has told me about herself, shown me the memories of this place. Wonderful, horrible memories. She shows me images, visions of the blood that has been shed on her soil, of the battles that have been waged, of the children she once sheltered." Eve's voice drifted as she spoke, becoming almost monotone, as if she were reading from a script. It reminded me of when I'd first spoken to her, of how artificial she'd once sounded.

"Does that mean ye can bring her back?" I asked. "Return the land to what it once was, somehow?"

"No, Quinn, I cannot. What Neverland once was can never be again. Her consciousness, awakened by the blood of Manling and Fae alike, is fading. As I am, now, it is all I can do to share her memories. To keep her company."

"As ye are, now? Eve, please, I don't understand."

Eve shook herself, limbs rattling in the process, clearly agitated. "I see now that it had to happen this way. I see so many things, now. All these seemingly unconnected incidents, all designed to draw you here, one way or another. This island, this tree, in the land of Fae..." Eve drifted off. "I cannot believe he planned it, but the sheer coincidence is staggering."

"He?" I echoed, feeling remarkably out of my depth. "He, who?"

"Merlin," Eve replied. "The wizard who created this place."

7

I stood in silence for a full minute, wheels turning as I played back Eve's words in my head. The implications were, of course, mind-numbing—literally; I couldn't begin to grasp the full extent of the revelation. I opened my mouth, closed it, then opened it again. But every question seemed less important than the next, each "how" followed by a "why" followed by another "how." Eventually, I settled on the simplest, most direct inquiry I could think of.

"He did what?"

"Well, perhaps 'created' is the wrong word," Eve allowed. "The island itself existed long before Merlin arrived, merely another landmass among many throughout the Fae realm, occupied by pixies and a tribe of wild Faelings who would one day be called 'braves' by the mortals who encountered them."

I frowned, realizing Eve was describing Neverland as it must have existed before the coming of Peter Pan and his Lost Boys, before Wendy Darling and her brothers, before Hook and his pirates. An island untouched by mankind. Since she'd essentially hacked the island's brain, she must have accessed those memories—though how she was engaging with them, I had no idea.

"Alright, let's say I believe any of this. And that's a big ask, mind ye. What could have possibly brought Merlin here?"

"It seems Merlin had a unique interest in islands at the time," Eve replied, tilting a bit as if to shrug. "Something to do with Arthur Pendragon and Easter Island. A derivative of Avalon, perhaps? Or maybe he was searching for something? I'm afraid he never shared his plans. Whatever his reasons, it was on this island that Merlin planted the seed which would create what you call Neverland. The undying island. An island outside of time. Perhaps Merlin thought to create his own paradise, here? Or perhaps he foresaw what this place would become? All I know is he came alone." Eve tapped the side of the Hangman's Tree. "It was he who brought her here to house the seed."

"Hold on, just hold on." I began waving my hands about, unable to process the wealth of information being thrown at me. I mean, Merlin wandering Neverland? Merlin creating a paradise in Fae? It seemed impossible. Not because it couldn't be true, but because it felt like a storybook mash-up. Like one tale had bled over into another—as improbable as a "so-and-so walked into a bar" joke. And yet, was it so unlikely? *Someone* had altered this island—why not my father?

"Do you remember what Peter showed you when you were here last?" Eve asked.

"What he..." I drifted off as I tried to remember what all Peter had shown me during my previous trip to Neverland. Together we'd toured his settlement, stayed in his house, even met with his family. But that wasn't what she meant, and I knew it; Eve had led us here for a reason. I found myself staring up at the pathetic remains of the Hangman's Tree. Back then, it had stood tall and proud, almost impossibly large. Peter had escorted me inside —knowing it would be easier to show me than to explain. And it was there I'd discovered the truth, that I'd learned why time had returned to Neverland. "The missin' grain of sand," I muttered.

"Yes," Eve replied. "The very grain Merlin placed here—back then merely one piece of a much larger, much more powerful whole. The grain he grafted to this very tree. The same grain the Temples later retrieved." Eve fell silent for a moment, then spoke so softly it seemed she was talking entirely to herself. "They saw what he'd built here and were horrified by it. A paradise fueled by the blood of children. They must have thought themselves noble for removing it. And perhaps, in a way, they were."

"Eve, wait," I said, holding up a placating hand as I tried to process everything she was telling me. I mean, I knew they'd visited Neverland themselves when Nate was a child. Peter had told me as much. But Eve was insinuating *they* were the ones who'd stolen the grain of sand. And why? What was it Eve had said? "What d'ye mean, 'fueled by the blood of children'?" I asked.

"That was the price. The cost of keeping the island and its inhabitants young forever. Blood. The fact that lost children were among the victims still haunts her. But it was for this task she was made, you see." Eve's tone sounded so distant, so impartial, that it might as well have been a robot with her voice. "Paradise is an expensive commodity."

Struck by Eve's take on the island's alarming origin story, I glanced down at Cathal, wondering if he were as bothered as I was. But the hound hardly seemed interested; he'd closed his eyes, content to listen but not speak. Taking a cue from the faerie hound, I took a calming breath and turned back to my ward. "Even assumin' it's all true, what does this have to do with us? With me?"

"Don't you see? It's all tied to you. Always has been. You came once before, subconsciously responding to her call. But the grain was already gone, and the power inside you dormant. Indeed, it's possible you were never supposed to use it, to awaken it on your own. Regardless, here you are again, against all odds. And she's been waiting for you."

"She? Ye can't mean the island?"

"In a manner of speaking. This tree was left unattended, and her roots have grown. In this respect, she is both the tree and the island—a brain and a body."

"And she's been waitin' for me, why?" I asked.

"Because she believes you hold the key to the island's salvation. You are of the same bloodline, after all. Merlin's blood, his power, his ability to bend time to his will—all of these you possess. It seems this undying island was designed for him, only he never returned to claim it as his own. But then you came along, and she hoped that you might find a way to halt the flow of time, as he did. Or at least set her free. Only it seemed you couldn't hear her."

I shook my head, trying to recall my time on this island, to think whether or not I'd heard or felt anything out of the ordinary. "I couldn't, not that I'd have known what to do, anyway. I don't know what I can do for her, now. But wait," I interjected, nagged by a growing sense of confusion. "If the Temples took the grain, how is she still alive?"

"The grain held back the tide of time, but it didn't sustain her, or this place. Neverland—the name she chose for herself so long ago—is a sentient creature, one of a few such beings living throughout the realms. It was her task to shelter the grain and pass along the power she drew from her victims, to facilitate the island's perpetuity. But, with the grain removed, the sudden influx of time sought to ravage this place. And so Neverland used her own life force to delay, to slow the inevitable march of time. But the Manlings stopped coming. The children grew up. The pirates grew old. The battles ended, and she was no longer able to sustain herself with their blood. Eventually, she was forced to draw on the island's very essence. In the end, though she'd held back the tide as long as she could, it overpowered her. The island lives on beneath the surface, but barely."

I had to step away with a hand pressed to my head, overwhelmed by the sheer scope of what Eve was suggesting. The notion that this timeless island —with its lust for blood—had somehow been created for a purpose, albeit an unfulfilled one, struck me as profoundly upsetting. And yet, who was I to gainsay the Tree of Knowledge? It was, as I'd mentioned to Cathal earlier, Eve's thing. If she was certain of what had happened here, if she really did have that level of insight, then how could I argue?

"Assumin' this isn't a delirious fever dream you're sufferin' from after putting your roots in some strange island," I said, choosing my next words carefully, "what now? How are we supposed to save the island? And, more importantly—knowing what we know now—should we? What if more children show up, and she starts feeding again out of habit?"

"Do you think her evil, Quinn MacKenna, for being what she was meant to be? For doing what she was tasked to do?"

The question caught me off guard. Did I blame the island itself for being a staging ground for decades worth of brutality? No, I blamed my father. Knowingly or unknowingly, if what Eve said was true, then he was the one responsible for what had happened here. "That isn't it," I replied. "I just want to be sure we're doin' the right t'ing. Even if ye know how, we can't revive the island if she means to harm people. It's not fair, I know, but I won't have blood on me hands."

"Then would you free her, instead?"

I scowled, wondering what freedom might mean for a creature who'd fed on blood for centuries, if not longer. "Depends. What would she do if she were free?" I asked, warily.

Eve shuddered, a fraction of emotion spilling into her voice. "She's become a being whose sole understanding of the world is pain and pleasure in equal parts. For so long, all she's known is violence. Violence and joy. She sees war as a game and associates it with the laughter of children. Setting one of her kind free would be dangerous enough, but, given her predispositions, the consequences could be catastrophic."

"Well, then I'd have to say no, obviously," I said, simultaneously horrified and exasperated. Frankly, I wanted to know where all this was going; Eve had to have known I'd have reservations when it came to reviving the island, not to mention how unlikely it was I'd free Neverland under those circumstances, and yet she'd insisted we come all the way out here. What was she playing at?

"And what if you could bring her back from the brink under your rule?" Eve asked. "What if you could bind her, as your father once did?"

"Think carefully before you answer," Cathal interjected, opening one eye. He raised his head a bit to stare up at Eve, his expression impossible to read. "You should tell her what it means to say yes."

"It is in your power," Eve explained, drawing my attention back to her, "to not only save Neverland, but to redress her wrongs. To show her a different way. But first, you will have to subjugate her. If you do not, if she in turn defeats you, then Neverland will drain you of everything you are. After that, she could use her newfound strength to break her own shackles."

"Define 'drain me of everythin' I am,'" I said, discernibly concerned by the metaphor.

"She will devour you. Your mind, your spirit, and your power. You will become a catatonic shell of yourself, assuming your body survives."

I gulped. "And if I win?"

"If you win, she will be yours to command."

"And the island? Would I be able to return it to what it once was?"

"If you wish it, the island will flourish once more," Eve replied, cryptically. "Of course, that would be but a small thing compared to what all you might achieve. A bond with one of her kind is like attaching yourself to a massive battery. It would bolster you in ways you could not begin to imagine."

I cringed, shaking my head reflexively at the notion of amassing more power than I already had; before breaking my vow, I'd been endowed with an unprecedented degree of potential, so much so that I'd only begun to scratch the surface of what I was capable of. "I don't care about that, Eve. I just want to give the Neverlanders their home back. Preferably one that won't feed on 'em."

Eve seemed to shrug, her limbs rising and falling almost imperceptibly, as if to say it was my decision. "As I said, it would be in your power."

I frowned, realizing it felt as though I had no choice; if I wanted to keep my promise to James and his friends, to honor the commitment the time traveler had signed me up for, to chase after a Jewel of the Tuatha de Danann, and confront Ryan, I had to do this. And yet, part of me railed against the notion that I *had* to do anything. Hadn't I earned the right to say no, by now? Especially if it meant I wouldn't have to risk my life? I ran a hand through my hair, fighting the urge to curse, to cut and run. But I knew I wouldn't. That I couldn't, not and live with myself. "Fine," I said, at last. "How do we do this?"

"I've already prepared the way," Eve replied, gesturing at the furrow she'd gouged into the earth. "Though there are a few additional things I must prepare. Your role, however, will be to provide Neverland with what she craves, with the only form of energy she understands."

"Blood," I muttered, feeling silly for not seeing it sooner. "Ye mean blood."

"Yes."

"How much blood?"

"Depends which of you wins," Eve replied, matter-of-factly.

8

I sat with my back pressed against the dead trunk of a storybook tree my father had allegedly created to house a magical artifact which had absorbed the blood of children and pirates for decades, all to create some sort of timeless oasis—a design he'd clearly abandoned. If I looked at it that way, I felt for Neverland and her burden; we'd both been discarded, in our own ways, forced to make do with what we had. Eve had gone on to clarify a few concepts I hadn't entirely grasped, though she'd made it clear most of it was conjecture. Like the notion that Neverland and I were somehow linked through my father, that she and I had been drawn together for a reason. Maybe it was the residual time magic echoing my own innate abilities, or maybe it was Merlin's deteriorating bond with Neverland calling to me. Whatever the cause, she doubted circumstance alone had led me here of all places, and even I had to admit it was unlikely. Hell, if I hadn't been so damn busy lately, I'd have come back to honor my promise to Peter months ago. Maybe then none of this would have happened.

"That might not have been for the best," Eve had admitted. "Neverland was dying, but not yet as weak as she is, now. She might have sought you out proactively, forcing herself on you the way a drowning man grabs at anything he can."

"So, what, you're sayin' she's vulnerable, now? That I wouldn't have stood a chance before?"

"That depends. If she'd tried when you first arrived, she would likely have won. But you're different, now. You've awakened your birthright since then. And what your mother bequeathed to you before you returned to Fae was far more than power. In many ways, it as though you have ascended."

"Ascended?"

"Best to think of it like the tiers of a pyramid. On the bottom, occupying the most space, you have mortals. Above them, what you call Freaks, all of whom are internally ranked, depending on their skills and reservoirs of power. The Fae run parallel in this analogy, though in their element many can seem more powerful than gods. Next, you have godlings—beings with immense power, on par with gods, but who are able to exercise them freely in the sense that there are no natural impositions. The man you call Temple is one of these, though the more I hear about him, the more I suspect he belongs in the tier above." Eve hesitated for a moment, as if she wanted to say something else, but quickly moved on. "Anyway, those above godlings are what you might call gods, at least in terms of their influence, their power. Some belong to pantheons, some do not. Some are immortal, some aren't. There are those who demanded blood sacrifice, and those who never had a single worshipper. They range from the omniscient and all-knowing to the petty and spiteful. All any of them really have in common is that they belong on this top tier, forming the pinnacle in which resides a catastrophic degree of power. So much so, in fact, that a cosmic balance has been enforced upon them, either internally or externally."

I held up a hand at that point. "Wait a second. I get the bit about the tiers. Humans, here. Freaks, here." I'd put my hand low, then higher, then higher still. "But that third level? Ye mean, what, demigods? Angels? Demons?"

"No, not really. There are a few powerful enough to be considered godlings among them. Michael and Gabriel, the Fallen princes, perhaps a few others. Similarly, there are some minor deities I would put in the third tier. Gods who are often so overlooked they can get away with influencing the realms." Eve had rattled her limbs, swaying them back and forth. "That's not important. What matters is that you see the distinction between checked and unchecked power."

I felt a suspicion tickle the back of my mind, snagged on something Eve had said a moment ago. "What makes ye t'ink Temple is a god, and not a godling?" I asked, stressing the difference between the two terms.

"The same thing that makes me wonder where you fall," she confessed.

"Go on..."

"Imagine a balanced scale. Or the symbol for yin and yang. Whatever image comes to mind, the reality is the same. For every action, there is an equal and opposite reaction. It is a law of the universe that some might argue gods are exempt from, and yet they bow to the necessity of it more than any other group. For every God, there must be a Devil. For every savior, a destroyer. Without those poles, the cosmos cannot turn. And turning—the inevitability of change—is what makes consciousness worthwhile."

"Alright," I replied as I struggled to wrap my head around the abstract concept. What she said made sense; I'd encountered similar notions in Catholic school, though of course they'd been skewed towards the Biblical. What made less sense, however, was where I fit in. "And what about me, then? Which tier do I belong to?"

"Well, that depends."

"On?"

"On whether you have an opposite, or not. You have to keep in mind that, in the height of their power, your mother and her two sisters combined to become a supremely powerful force. The Morrigan once drove the Fomorians from the island of her chosen people with the strength of her voice alone. She was a deity tied to death and sovereignty, to fate and prophecy. Among her own kind, she was opposed in ability only by the Dagda, the greatest of the Tuatha de Dannan. To contain even a third of her capacity is astounding. And yet, you also carry the blood of a sorcerer whose legacy continues to shape the world, and whose own lineage is riddled with controversy. And let's not forget you possess the ability to manipulate time, making you even more volatile than you might have otherwise been."

"It's not like I go around stoppin' clocks whenever it suits me," I countered, indignantly. Frankly, I didn't like the way the conversation was going; I'd always considered myself dangerous, true, but in an applied way. Eve made it sound like I was a bomb just waiting to explode at the slightest impact.

"Exactly my point. So much of what you're capable of is unknown.

Untested. Are you a goddess bound by the laws of the universe, or a mortal with the capacity to reshape the world? Quinn, have you ever asked yourself what the former might mean? Not in the grand scheme of things, but simply for yourself? You could be immortal. It's possible you may never age from this point forward. You may never die, though everyone around you might. If you ever plan to have children, you could be passing on a legacy you don't fully understand. And that's not even accounting for what might happen if your opposite—"

"That's enough, Eve," I snapped.

I'd cut the conversation off there and had retreated behind the tree where I now sat, leaving Eve to finish her preparations on her own. The thing is, I hadn't exactly been horrified by what Eve proposed; I'd had such thoughts in the past, though I'd quickly dismissed them. I wasn't worried about living forever, not with the shit I put myself through day in and day out. As for the rest, well, remaining relatively young until my time came didn't sound so bad, I'd already had plenty of people die on me from a lot worse than old age, and the notion of childbirth had always physically repulsed me. Basically, I'd made peace with all that.

No, in hindsight, what bothered me most was the fact that I'd had no say in any of it. That no one had ever asked me what I wanted. Not my mother. Definitely not my father. Not the scheming Temples. Sitting there, alone, I had to wonder if Nate Temple was out there somewhere, feeling the same way. Feeling wronged, like a tool created with only one purpose in mind. I'd always figured him for an entitled prick because he'd been born rich. Envied him for having loving parents. Resented his charm, his easy way with people, his relationships with Othello and Callie Penrose—two women I'd desperately wanted to like me. Granted, the self-proclaimed King of St. Louis hadn't made things easier by hijacking my Uber and breaking into my apartment, but I could at least admit to myself now that I'd been biased, my animosity fueled by jealousy and spite. That I'd seen in Nate a reflection of my own upbringing, my own coping mechanisms, my own faults, and had been compelled to look away.

A reflection...now that was a troubling thought.

I took a deep breath and let it out as slowly as I could manage, forcing myself to think about the task at hand. To decide whether or not I was up to the challenge. I held my hand up, staring at the lines criss-crossing my palm, the callouses I'd developed from training with the spear, the silvered scars representing decades' worth of pain. Pain, I knew, was coming; blood wasn't the only thing needed to reinvigorate the island. According to Eve, the bonding process was unique to each individual who experienced it, which meant she couldn't predict exactly what would happen to me once I offered Neverland my father's legacy. Only that it would be difficult. Oh, and that it would hurt.

"Nothing can occupy the space of another thing without friction," she'd said, moments after confirming that my blood was the key. "That's why the bonding processes responsible for creating life are often pleasurable, and those for causing death so painful. What you are doing here requires both. In order to fashion a new bond, you must first kill the old. You must take the reins and give her a new purpose. Create something better than what came before."

"So we'd be, what, making a new Eden?"

"No!" Eve insisted, vehemently. "Not Eden. Not ever. You have to create something better. Not some timeless paradise."

"If not Eden, then what?"

"I can't tell you. If you can control her, it'll be your decision—it'll be your will which shapes this place. But please, be mindful of what you want from her. A fortress cut off from the rest of the world, accessible only to a chosen few, may keep you and your loved ones safe, but no fortress stands forever. Eden's walls kept far more out than it kept safe, and as such became more of a punishment than a reward. To see such a glorious place, only to be cast out, to watch it fade, is the worst sort of cruelty."

She looked impossibly sad, then. I thought about asking her if she regretted this life of hers, if she resented me for my role in her existence. I wouldn't have blamed her; she hadn't asked for any of this shit, either. But I didn't. I was too afraid of what she'd say. Instead, I resolved to do what I could for her, to bond with Neverland and give Eve a home she could be proud of. Of course, we hadn't discussed what her role would be—whether she'd want to remain here, or not. But I sensed she felt a connection with this place, with Neverland; they had a great deal in common.

I sighed, realizing that I was merely delaying the inevitable—moping behind the tree like a child who didn't get the present she wanted for Christmas this year. And so I lowered my hand and pressed it to the cracked, barren dirt, preparing to rise, when Cathal lumbered into sight. The faerie hound plopped down beside me, seemingly oblivious to my sudden resolve. I settled back, curious what he had to say, even if it meant another delay. At this point, I wasn't worried about the others. If the Goblin King ran off, I'd manage, and the Neverlanders would definitely wait. As for the Greeks, well, I considered it an opportunity to see how committed they were to our journey; for some reason, I couldn't work my head around Narcissus tagging along with us, even if his logic seemed perfectly sound. Helen just bugged me. Maybe it was that she always hid her face. Or maybe it was the fact that, when she didn't, I swore I could hear "Heartache Tonight" by the *Eagles* playing in the background.

"It's funny," Cathal said, his silhouette blocking out what little light the gloomy sky offered, "we travelled together for a while, but we never talked much about ourselves. Turns out there was a lot I didn't know about you."

"Been talkin' to the tree, have ye?"

"She's not what I expected. Neither of you are."

I shrugged, thought about making a joke about books and covers, but went with, "Everyone judges. If they get it mostly right, we call 'em perceptive. If they get it wrong, they're judgmental. T'ing is, most end up believin' what they want to believe, no matter what their eyes and ears tell 'em. Takes guts to admit ye were wrong, but to yourself most of all."

Cathal made a sound low in his throat, as though he agreed.

"Anyway, I wouldn't worry about it," I said. "Neither of us are big on sharin'."

"No point looking backwards if all you see is pain."

I turned to study the hound, trying to analyze his expression beneath all that hair. Dogs, in my experience, had oddly expressive faces; aside from the exceedingly dopey ones, you could tell a lot from how they stared up at you, from the way their brows knit or their lips curled. And yet, I doubted I'd ever seen regret flash across a dog's face. I'd seen pain, the kind animals lashed out against, and even contrition. But never sorrow, never true anguish. Eventually, I turned away, fighting the urge to reflect on everything that had been taken from me, everything I'd lost—as I was certain Cathal was doing. Perhaps that's why neither of us shared our stories; we'd seen enough of each other's scars to know what it meant to pick at old wounds. "Aye," I replied, at last, thinking of my supposed destiny and the ridiculous journey ahead, "though I'm not sure if the future is that much brighter."

"Your tree disagrees."

I raised an eyebrow at that. "Gone all optimistic, has she?"

"Did you know your mother killed my master?" Cathal asked, changing the subject abruptly. His tone was surprisingly casual, given the accusation; the faerie hound continued to look to the horizon, his muzzle in profile.

I, meanwhile, could only gape at the question. I certainly hadn't known, though perhaps I should have. The trouble was that my mother played both prominent and supporting roles in a great many Celtic myths, many of which I'd been hesitant to read; it had felt a little weird, getting to know her that way. It didn't help that a great deal of the literature contradicted itself; one tale claimed she'd seduced the Dagda while straddling a river, another that she was a vicious, vindictive hag who routinely led people to their doom.

"It was a long time ago," Cathal continued. "My master refused to love her despite her beauty, and so she brought about his ruin. It's an old story. A long one." He huffed, chest vibrating from the force of his own breath. "I hate long stories. But you should know that when I was told to guide you, and where, I wasn't happy about it."

"Ye don't say," I said, recalling how short the hound had been with me during those first few hours, not to mention how caustic our relationship had become before we'd had to rely on one another to survive. I still wasn't sure where he and I stood now that we'd left the Otherworld behind. He'd saved my life, and I'd saved his. Once, I might have been naive enough to think that meant we'd formed a bond, even a friendship. But now I knew that wasn't enough. If it were, I wouldn't be chasing after Ryan, trying to save him from himself.

"No matter how you look at it," Cathal said, swiveling his head to look down at my arm, "it seems we were destined to meet. Destined to become linked."

I followed the hound's gaze, eyes drawn to the faint impression of teeth on my pale white skin—evidence of Cathal's bite, a mark that seemingly shackled the two of us together, though neither of us seemed to know which role to play. Was I his master? Was he some sort of familiar, forced to answer my call whenever I needed him? Either way, I wished there was some way to remove it. Cathal was his own person, not a creature to be leashed. Unfortunately, the irony that I was about to try and collar Neverland before the day was through was not lost on me. Still, Cathal and I had yet to hash any of that out, and I secretly hoped that wasn't where this conversation was going; I had a feeling it would be a long, potentially fruit-less chat.

"Destiny can go screw itself," I muttered.

Cathal grunted. "Pretty sure it's busy screwing you."

"Hah hah. Say what ye came to say, already, ye mongrel."

"You reminded me of him, you know, when we first met. Of my master. He, too, chased after life, noseblind to what was happening around him, always believing he'd relax when he finally caught it," Cathal said, shifting his weight so his shoulder rested gently against mine. Which was good, considering the hound could have crushed me to death with just one of his paws if he felt the urge. "But lately, not so much."

I thought about that, then nodded. "I've been doin' some self-assessment, that's all. Seemed like the t'ing to do, after what happened in the Other-world. After what we went through in the Blighted Lands."

"Yeah, well, the tree has noticed, too. I think that's why she's so opti-mistic about the future. Why she wants you to do this." Cathal rose to all fours, towering over me so that all I could see was his faintly pink belly poking out beneath wisps of grey-white hairs. Mercifully, the rest of him hid behind the dense muscles of his hind legs; I'd caught glimpses of what lay between, but never in such close proximity. "This thing you plan to do," he said, sounding oddly thoughtful, "I have heard tales of others who have attempted it. I know it seems the only way forward, but you should not take this lightly. Beasts like this one are not so easy to tame."

I rose, joining the hound, my head in line with his shoulder. Dirt clung to my hands where I'd pressed them to the earth. As I rubbed them clean, I considered Eve's request, wondering what I'd make of this place when the time came. As an amateur interior designer, I had to admit I had a certain flair; anyone who'd been invited to my apartment said as much. But land-scaping was a unicorn of a different color; I couldn't begin to imagine what a tropical paradise would look like, or even something more architectural in nature. No, what I wanted had to be simple. It had to be able to sustain the Neverlanders, of course, but it wouldn't be Neverland. Not anymore. Peter Pan no longer played his games here. Hook no longer sailed. The heart and soul of this place had vanished. Which meant, if I had to risk my heart and soul in exchange, I was going to get something worthwhile in the bargain.

"I can't say I know what I'm doin'," I said. "Or what I'm about to put meself through. But, in a weird way, it feels like this island and I are related.

Like we're already bound." I tapped a finger to my head. "Maybe it's all in me head, but I can't help feelin' responsible for this, somehow. If I'd done this sooner, come back earlier, maybe Peter and Hook would still be alive."

"Don't be an idiot." Cathal had to walk a circle to face me, giving me more eye contact in the process than most men do on a first date. "You know, you could just leave it all behind. Not only this island, but all of it. Return to the mortal realm, let the others settle into their new home, and leave this realm to its fate. Your problem is you keep assuming it wouldn't survive without you. That, and you seem to have this issue with saving everyone and everything, even if it costs you your life."

I could tell the faerie hound was baiting me, perhaps trying to get me to defend my decisions, but his take was simply too much; I had to laugh, wondering what my nearest and dearest would think hearing me described as a martyr of any sort. Guess I really had changed. Still, he was right; I wasn't at the center of this conflict, so why was I rushing towards the enemy's front lines? Why dig myself in deeper? The truth wasn't as cut and dried as I'd have liked, so I gave him what I could. "Maybe I'm just craving a little absolution," I said. "I have someone I called a friend out there, prepared to wreak havoc so long as he gets what he wants. A friend whose pain I was blind to, someone I might have helped if I'd been less self-involved. I'm not sure if there's anythin' left to save, but I owe it to him to try. That's why I'm goin'. I'll let everyone else worry about the fate of the realms."

"Sounds like you have a hero complex, to me," Eve chimed in from the other side of the tree, having apparently overheard at least a portion of our conversation.

"Come on," I said with a sigh, nudging Cathal, "let's go see if the Eves-dropper's ready." I nudged him harder. "Get it? Evesdropper?"

Cathal winced, baring his fangs on the one side. "Humans are the worst."

he three of us gathered in front of the decrepit remains of the Hangman's Tree, Eve facing Cathal and I as though she were about to announce us woman and dog. Indeed, with her limbs spread wide, she rather looked like an officiant, moments away from giving us her blessing. Except it wasn't a benediction we were receiving—it was a lecture, complete with redundancies.

"Whatever happens, whatever you experience, don't let your guard down," she insisted for the third time since I'd returned. "Neverland is weaker than she once was, but that might make her more desperate. Like an animal lashing out when it feels cornered."

"I thought ye two were connected," I said, struck by the simplicity of what that meant. "Can't ye just tell her to roll over and let me win? Avoid the bloodsheddin' bit altogether?"

"She's not a creature of reason, Quinn. Once perhaps, but she has been severely diminished since she was first deposited here. Without me translating, without me filtering her memories and emotions, you'd never have been able to communicate with her at all. Besides, it's not in their nature to simply roll over, any more than it is in yours. Imagine how you'd react if I asked you to lay down and show me your belly."

I wrinkled my nose, studying the ground. "Bit dirty, but if ye insist—"

"Hold out your hand," Eve snapped.

I did as she asked, though with more reticence than I would have displayed if she'd had me lay down; there was something intimate about offering someone your hand. Something primal in us resists that urge, recognizing perhaps how valuable the hand is as a tool, how easily mangled it could become. But Eve didn't reach out and crush it, nor did she cut it open—which is what I'd really feared would happen. Instead, she deposited a pip the size of a walnut. It was light and dry, the outer skin bright as the gold of Eve's leaves, as though it had been dipped in metallic paint. Unsure what to do with it, I simply stared.

"Aren't you going to ask what it's for?" Eve asked, snarkily.

"Wasn't plannin' on it. Figured you'd tell me if ye wanted me to know."

"You know, sometimes I wonder why I bother."

"I wonder why ye do, too. And not only sometimes." I grinned a bit and drew my hand back, the seed cupped in the palm of my hand. "Anyway, what's it for?"

Eve sighed. "Just keep it with you. Don't let go of it for any reason, alright?"

I nodded, feeling a bit silly for teasing her under the circumstances. Morosely, I wondered if this wasn't some sort of memento, something for me to take with me to the afterlife. A parting gift for the soon-to-be-departed. If so, at least it was pretty; a girl's gotta have some standards. "So, what's next?" I asked, raising my gaze from the pip to Eve.

Except Eve wasn't there.

In her place was a young girl sitting on the lip of a fountain, seemingly captivated by the pages of the book which lay cradled in her lap. She wore a gray cardigan beneath a blue jacket, her hair tied back with a blue ribbon, though that didn't stop her frizzy locks from poking out in all directions. Perhaps that's why she wore a straw hat; it, too, had a ribbon, and partially shaded her face. Crossed at the ankles, her legs were covered by a pair of long white socks which disappeared beneath the curve of her skirt, her shoes so scuffed I couldn't tell if they'd once been a color other than black.

I spun round, expecting to see the shelf of rocks behind me, but found myself in a different place entirely; the courtyard was a quaint little place, surrounded on all sides by paths leading off into what must have been a park of some sort. Trees, their leaves burnished in shades of autumn, were visible in the distance. The fountain itself was a drab thing, meant more for pigeons to enjoy than people. And yet, the girl didn't seem to mind; she thumbed another page, biting her lip. I considered waving to her, if only to confirm that I wasn't dreaming, but she was far too engrossed to notice some strange woman hailing her from a dozen feet away. Better if I approached her, I thought. Maybe she could tell me where I was.

Except I couldn't. I could turn, even wave, but I was firmly rooted to the spot upon which I stood—as though I were meant to observe, not interfere. I tried to speak, but nothing came out. Indeed, now that I thought about it, I realized there was no sound at all; the fountain should have gurgled, the birds chirped, the faint breeze whispered past my ears. I began to panic. What the hell was going on? Where had Eve gone? Was this part of the test? Had it already begun?

I felt a sudden weight in my palm. I found Eve's seed there and squeezed, reassured that I held it, still. If this was a dream, perhaps that meant it was one in which I had at least some control of. Focus, that's what I needed to do. I glanced back up, expecting to find the girl sitting alone, still immersed in her book. But she wasn't alone. A boy, perhaps only a bit younger than the girl, watched her from the other side of the fountain, dressed in what appeared to be rags. The child had that unique color of hair that couldn't decide if it wanted to be blond or not—streaks of shimmering gold ran between large swathes of auburn. But it was his face I couldn't look away from. He had a faintly pointed chin and sallow cheeks, his eyes large and round and breathtakingly blue. Overall, there was an impish cast to him that could only belong to a child; as a man, his beard would obscure much of his elfen features. Only the eyes would remain—the eyes of the man who'd patched me up after I fell from the sky.

As I watched, the boy crept across the courtyard, slinking comically towards the girl, whose back was turned to him. Indeed, his steps were so elaborate, so artfully placed, that it seemed alien, somehow. Like a dancer defying the laws of physics for one spectacular leap—except over and over again. It was then I realized why; the boy's feet weren't touching the ground. Unable to keep up the game for long, the boy rushed the last few feet, throwing his arms wide, mouth opening in what seemed a silent scream. The girl leapt to her feet and danced backwards, though I could only imagine the sound of her feet skittering across the ground. Her shout of surprise. She began waving the book about manically, jabbing it in the boy's direction. But he was too busy laughing to notice. He'd doubled over in mid-air, floating on his back like a spider hanging from a web.

Peter Pan, the Boy Who Wouldn't Grow Up.

The instant I thought his name, it was as if someone hit the mute button a second time; a crescendo of sounds descended, so loud I flinched, taking a step backwards. So, I could move, as well. Good to know, I thought, as I tuned into the situation at hand.

"You can't keep doing that to me, Peter," the girl was saying in accented English, her voice deeper than I would have expected for a girl her age, more mature. It made me tick her up a couple years. A teenager, at least. "It's a dreadful thing to do, sneaking up on a young lady."

Peter, lounging in mid-air, propped his head up with one hand and yawned. "You're always telling me what I can't do, when you know I can do anything I want." He rolled over, turning his back to the girl.

"Except grow up," the girl muttered, stuffing her book into a satchel I hadn't noticed her carrying. She glanced up at the sky and sighed. "Oh well, looks like I'd have been late if you hadn't distracted me from my book. So I guess I should thank you, really."

Peter flipped back around, grinning wildly. "Does that mean you'll come play?"

The girl shook her head. "Not today, Peter."

"Oh, come on. I'd have you back in no time."

"Last time you said that, you brought me back so late I had to beg John not to tell our parents. Do you remember what you said to me, then?"

Peter pinched his lips together as though he were trying not to laugh. "I said," he began, voice breaking with humor, "I said—"

"You said no time means whenever you want it to mean. That if I wanted a *specific* time, I should have said so," she declared, sounding cross. "You should know better than to try and pull the same trick on me twice, Peter Pan. You're not that clever."

The humor on Peter's face drained away so quickly it was as if it had never been there at all. In fact, his expression went cold. Inhumanly cold, like those of centuries old vampires or long-lived Fae. Only the really old ones could pull off that level of disdain—as if everyone and everything were beneath their notice. Frankly, to see that look on the face of a boy Peter's age was more than a bit disturbing. And yet, the girl didn't seem the least bit fazed; she took one look at him, turned on her heel, and marched off. Straight towards me.

I shuffled out of the way as she passed, though she barely seemed to register I was there. She offered a muffled "excuse me" as she went, pressing one hand to the hat on her head as if afraid it might fly off. A moment later, I saw why: Peter had flown above us and now hovered over her, hands splayed like claws, hoping to snatch it away and lead her on a chase. From where I stood, the girl looked a bit beleaguered, if not worn down completely. It wasn't hard to understand why, what with Peter Pan playing poltergeist above her head.

After perhaps a dozen feet, she stopped to glare up at the boy. "Peter, go home. I mean it, I'm not in the mood."

Peter let his hands drop, arms dangling towards her, but without malice. He, too, seemed upset. He wilted a bit, drifting towards the ground. Just before he landed, however, he perked up. "I know! I'll ask Michael. He'll come with me."

"Peter, no!" the girl cried. But the boy was already twenty feet in the air, bathing in a sudden beam of sunlight, radiating joy. The rags, I realized, were formed of leaves and twigs, pasted together with thick slabs of sap, lending Peter a less homely, but infinitely more wild aspect. The girl began running after him, but it was no use; he wasn't listening. I hurried after her, afraid I'd miss something if I didn't. Whatever was happening here, something told me these two were the key.

"You can't keep taking him, Peter," the girl mumbled to herself, too wrapped up in her own emotions to even notice me. "It's not safe." She yanked off her hat, clenching it tight with one fist. "Do you hear me, Peter?! If something happens to him, I'll never forgive you!"

"It's all just fun and games, Wendy!" Peter yelled back, fists planted on his hips. I noticed the hilt of a short sword poking out from his left side just as he slid his fingers over the pommel, as if he were subconsciously aware of the contradiction. "I'll have him back in no time!"

And, with that, Peter Pan launched himself forward. He performed a half-dozen barrel rolls, whooping as he went, clearly showing off. Soon, nothing remained of him but a speck in the distance. And yet, there was something of his spirit left behind. I could feel it riding the air—a manic delight that made me want to do something reckless. The only reason I noticed it at all, I think, was because—until recently—I'd always felt that way. Impulse-driven, I'd lacked the inhibitions that governed most people. Over time, of course, I'd learned how to slow down, to think before I acted. I'd never have survived adolescence, otherwise. But it hadn't come easily, not the way it had for everyone else I knew—those people who thought of self-preservation as part of the human condition.

"I hate you, Peter Pan," Wendy Darling—for who else could she be—whispered as she donned her hat once more, oblivious to the crease she'd created. "And I wish you'd just leave us alone."

I almost reached out in that moment. I even tried to speak, though no sound emerged. But I knew it would make no difference; what had happened here—if it had happened at all—had taken place long before I was born. Long before I ever met the man Peter Pan would become. My role here, assuming I had one, was strictly to observe. Which is perhaps why I wasn't surprised to find that, between one blink and the next, Wendy and the park were gone.

And I'd returned to Neverland.

$\mathcal{T}$his was not the Neverland I'd left behind, however, but the Neverland of ages past. Looking around, I realized this was how it must have appeared before my time, before the Lost People carved out a space for themselves; I was surrounded by the splayed trunks of banyan trees, their many limbs thrust high overhead, their canopies blocking out all but the faintest golden light. There were no signs of deforestation, no indication that anyone had ever stepped foot here. Not, that is, until I heard the distinct snap of a twig to my right.

I whirled, tracking the sound, and spotted a young man approaching a familiar landmark. Although, among its fellows and bearing none of the trademark elements I'd seen upon my visit, I almost didn't recognize the Hangman's Tree. But there was no mistaking it; even now it exuded the slightest air of authority, a humming sort of power I could sense in the air. Now that I knew what I was looking at, my eyes were drawn to the tree as though it had been staged, like a famous painting mounted on an otherwise empty wall. The young man, meanwhile, seemed equally fascinated. He trudged through the undergrowth with a steady determination, and I realized he was humming. It was a shanty—a pirate's song.

Sensing what I was about to see unfold, I hurried to catch up, glad to find I'd retained my mobility. Soon, I was close enough to observe details, to note the ragged appearance of his brocaded blue jacket, to discern he'd been washed ashore; the stench of salt water and brine lingered wherever he walked, he wore no shoes, and he clearly suffered from an awful sunburn which had blistered his hands and face. Still, despite his youth and sorry condition, I knew who I was looking at the instant I saw his face in profile —if only because he and his son looked so alike.

Captain James Hook, though perhaps not yet a Captain at all, cursed as an errant vine tripped him, sending him sprawling on all fours. A giggle emerged from the eaves, chiming as clearly as a doorbell. Hook rose quickly, producing a small dagger and brandishing it with his right hand. "It's bad form to laugh at a man when he's down," Hook called, scouring the canopy above for the offender. "Come down or be labeled a coward!"

"You talk funny."

Peter Pan, looking much as I'd last seen him, sat in the crook formed by branching limbs, his head resting against the trunk of the Hangman's Tree. I'd never seen him look so at home, so at peace, so...comfortable. It took me a moment to realize why; unlike before, Peter seemed to have forsaken his childlike affectations. Or perhaps he'd yet to learn them. Either way, while a manic gleam continued to twinkle behind his eyes, the Boy Who Wouldn't Grow Up studied Hook with a cool, calculating gaze.

The dagger vanished as quickly as it had appeared. The sailor, clearly realizing he was addressing a mere child, bowed. He rose a moment later and ran his hand along his bristled jawline, clearly chagrined. "Sorry about that, my boy. Caught me by surprise, that's all. Can you tell me where I am, and who I have the pleasure of addressing?"

"I'm Peter. Peter Pan."

"Pleasure to make your acquaintance, Peter Pan." Hook bowed a second time. "Midshipman Killian Jones, at your service."

"This is Neverland," Peter said, jerking a thumb at the Hangman's Tree. "She's mine."

Hook—going by his original name, I gathered—nodded, slowly, the way you might when talking to a crazy person. He spun in a small circle, studying the landscape, then squinted up at the sky. "Any chance Neverland has another name? India, maybe? Africa?" He flicked his gaze to Peter. "Where are your parents, anyway?"

"Parents?"

"Yes. Your mother and father..." Hook drifted off, perhaps noticing for the first time what the boy was wearing. I could practically see the wheels

58

turning in his head—no respectable, God-fearing parents would allow their child to run around on his own, and dressed like a native, no less.

"Neverland wants to know what you mean. What is a mother?" Peter asked, pressing his cheek against the bark of the Hangman's Tree, which seemed somehow to curve into him, cradling the tilt of his head like a pillow. Had that lip always been there, or had the Hangman's Tree really just molded itself to the boy?

"I am sorry, my boy, but I need to know if there are any adults around here. Anyone I can speak to who might know where I am."

"Any what?"

"Adults," Hook said, patience wearing thin. "Someone older, perhaps taller. Like me."

Peter laughed. "There's no one like you around here. Neverland, do you know any adults?" Peter asked, putting an odd stress on the last word, the way you might try to pronounce something obviously foreign. A moment later, Peter laughed. "She says no."

"Who on earth are you talking to, boy?"

Peter rolled his eyes. "I already told you." A pause, then another laugh. "Neverland says you could always talk to the mermaids. They live in the lagoon."

"The what?"

"If not them, maybe the skin-wearers," Peter continued, pointing off into the distance. "They're on the ridge."

"And who are they?" Hook asked.

Peter shrugged.

"Is there anything you do know?"

A grin split the boy's features. "I know you aren't what you say you are."

"Listen, I don't know what you're playing at, but—"

"You're a pirate," Peter said, with relish. "That's what Neverland said. She told me you stole that coat from a man with his own ship, that you cut him from gut to gizzard. Only now you're lost, same as the rest." The boy hopped up so quickly it seemed to happen in the blink of an eye. He stood with his hands on his hips, perched on the lip of a single bough in a defiance of gravity. "I think we're going to have fun together, Jones."

The Hangman's Tree seemed to shudder beneath the boy's feet. He reached out, patting the bark, and whispered something I couldn't make out. Hook, meanwhile, seemed preoccupied. At first, I thought him simply incredulous; a child he'd never met had just poked holes in his cover story and was currently thwarting physics, to boot. But I quickly disabused that notion as a slow, lazy smile spread across the pirate's face. "I am not one for games, Peter Pan."

At that moment, everything—myself included—froze.

Suddenly, voices began thundering overhead—as though there were speakers in the sky, the volume cranked way up. The first was Cathal's. He sounded anxious, a thin whine trickling through his words. "What's happening to her?"

"Neverland happened," Eve replied, brusquely. "She's latched on to Quinn, somehow. She's taken her mind, though I have no idea where."

"Can you snap her out of it?"

"I don't know. This wasn't supposed to happen. Quinn was supposed to initiate the bond. Offer up her blood, lure her in, and establish control. It's possible Neverland let me think she was weaker than she was. All I know is that if Quinn stays under too long, Neverland won't let her go. The island will have won."

"We have to do something."

"If only Quinn could..."

Eve's voice drifted away.

I craned my ears, unable to do anything else, wishing I'd caught the tail end of what Eve had said. Maybe then I'd know what to do—how to stop Neverland from playing show-and-tell until I literally lost my mind. What was the point of all this, anyway? Why show me Peter and Hook's first interaction? Why show me the scene with Wendy?

An emotion flared, so strong it registered in my head as a thought. But it wasn't my emotion. This was external, coming from everywhere all at once, like a strobe of blinding light. Suddenly able to move, I cringed, recognizing the heady weight of regret—so thick, so cloying it made me want to curl up in a ball and cry. Indeed, I could feel tears slipping down my cheeks. Mine, and yet not mine. Hers.

I found myself spun around as though someone had grabbed me by the shoulders, forcing me to look directly at the Boy Who Wouldn't Grow Up. That feeling of regret intensified, but—with it—I sensed something else. Something profound and deep, an emotion so lacking in subtlety it hurt: love. So much love. More than I could ever have imagined possible, and not just from this sentient creature, but from anything. Hers was a selfless, inexhaustible fount. In that moment, it was as if I could read her mind, as if I could recall her memories. I could see Peter, again and again, flying off with his friends. I watched him fight. I watched him crow. I watched him play. I mourned with him when things failed to turn out how he wished they would. I leapt for joy when he succeeded. I envied those he chose to spend his time with but never begrudged him their company. When he asked for things from his imagination, I provided them, like the sword he used to sever the hand of the man he called Hook. I changed my shape for him, transforming to become the shelter he needed. I gave him everything he asked for, until one day I could not. I'd become too distracted. I had forgotten my purpose. Peter began to change. To age.

This time, when the regret hit, I fell to my knees, sobbing.

"Mother," I said, hardly able to form the word through my choked throat. That's what she was, what she'd been to Peter, even if he'd forgotten. Once, they'd been each other's only companions. He, an abandoned child. She, an abandoned guardian. They'd formed a different sort of bond. Not that of a master and servant, but of a mother and son. Except now, he was gone, and she had no one to give all this love to, no one to take away all this grief. Suddenly, I could sense it—her desire. The reason she'd brought me here. The reason she'd offered me snapshots of Peter's life. She wanted me to understand, to feel her suffering, so when the time came, I wouldn't hesitate.

Neverland wished to die.

And she wanted me to kill her.

11

I came to, sitting upright, back pressed against something warm, bulky, and breathing. I lay still for a moment, content to rise and fall in slight increments. The murky sky above was unchanged from when I'd last seen it, so I doubted I'd been out long. I shifted my gaze to find I'd been propped up against Cathal; the faerie hound had his head on his paws, eyes shut. Eve, meanwhile, stood with her limbs pressed against the Hangman's Tree, her roots withdrawn from the soil. I felt something itch above my left eye but winced the moment I touched it—my fingers came away wet and sticky with blood. Cathal must have felt the movement, because he immediately perked up, ears spiked. He swiveled his head around at an awkward angle, his tail thumping against the ground.

"You're back," he said, sounding relieved.

Back. It was a curious word. Not awake, as if I'd been unconscious or sleeping, but back. I held out my hand, curling my fingers one by one, aware of the sensations I'd been missing only moments before, back in the landscape of memories I'd shared with Neverland. It was odd, I thought, how dreams could feel so real, despite the fact that in them you had so little control of your senses; I hadn't once concerned myself with the state of my own body beyond being able to move it. Now that I was back—as Cathal had put it—everything seemed to have a higher resolution, a more severe degree. I could feel the dull ache of my muscles from having climbed and walked all the way out here, the burning itch above my eye, the pounding of my head from the fall I must have taken when I'd been snatched away. Other minor discomforts, too, ranging from the slight dryness of my skin to the press of hard surface against my tailbone.

"Aye," I replied, moving my neck back and forth to relieve the stiffness. "T'anks for lettin' me lay on ye."

Eve came rustling over, branches rattling together in her hurry to stand by my side. She bowed slightly, one limb curling beneath my chin, forcing me to look into her eyes—such as they were. "How did you escape?"

"I didn't. Pretty sure she let me go." I reached up, gave Eve's limb a brief squeeze to let her know I was alright, then made to stand. I needed to stand, to get the blood pumping, if only to think clearly. Cathal helped, as did Eve, propping me up between themselves until they were sure I wouldn't topple over.

"I don't understand," Eve said, sounding uncharacteristically distraught. "When we linked consciousness, I was certain she was too weak to do what she did to you, or I'd have warned you. But she had you, so why let you go?"

"She's craftier than she made herself out to be, Eve. Don't beat yourself up." I grimaced as the wound above my left eye reopened. I could feel the trickle of blood inch down my face but couldn't be bothered to mess with it, just yet. "She probably fed ye what she thought ye wanted to see. She's suspicious by nature, and you're about as foreign as they come, even here."

I realized upon saying it that I knew it all to be true, that somehow I'd linked with Neverland's consciousness long enough to get a feel for the type of being she was. Sentient, yes, but with animalistic instincts. She'd lash out when in pain, would protect herself if she felt threatened. In a way, I suspected that had contributed to her suffering; animals experience loss differently, occasionally more severely, than we do. Having experienced hers in real time, I understood her compulsion, her desire to end it all, even if I hated the idea.

"I underestimated her, then," Eve said.

"No, that's not it. Ye just t'ink differently, is all. She'd only have shared everythin' with ye if she felt like she had the upper hand. If she were dominant, in control." I shook my head. "Anyway, it's not worth dwellin' on."

"What happened when your spirit left?" Cathal interjected.

I sighed. "Neverland showed me bits and pieces of her life. Memories of Peter Pan filtered through her perspective. It was all a tad cinematic.

Surreal, even. I could hear ye two talkin' at one point..." I drifted off, realizing my memories of what had transpired were getting hazier, that I was left only with impressions, the way you'd recall a vivid dream. Damn it. "There was a meetin' with Wendy. She was older than he was, on her way to becomin' a woman. Lots of regret, there. Then Hook, the first time he met Peter Pan."

"Why those memories?" Eve asked, sounding puzzled.

I scowled, wishing I had an answer; I'd wondered the same thing, at the time. Had Neverland shown me those two scenes specifically, or simply chosen two at random? Was there a connection in there, somewhere? "I'm not sure," I replied, at last. "She seemed scattered, when we finally interacted. The first wasn't even on the island. Which means she could watch Peter even when he wasn't here."

"That's...odd. Is it possible Peter Pan became her master?" Eve mused aloud.

"Not her master. He was her companion. Her first friend. In time, she grew to love him and thought of him as hers. It wasn't Merlin's directive that she sacrificed herself and the island for, it was Peter. She didn't want him to grow up, to grow old." An idea struck. "Maybe that's why she showed me Wendy. The girl who left Neverland to grow up, who grew to resent Peter and his childishness. It's possible she wanted me to see what she feared would happen."

"And Hook?" Cathal asked.

"Maybe who she feared he would become?" I shook my head. "Either way, Peter is gone, and she's devastated. She released me so I could find a way to kill her." Even saying it aloud sounded horrific. Funny how, not so long ago, I'd considered letting Neverland waste away for the good of everyone involved. Now that I'd communicated with her, now that I knew she was a thinking, feeling creature, I found myself compelled to do the opposite.

"If you do that, then you'll have to find another way to go after your friend," Eve cautioned.

"But ye know how I can, don't ye?" I asked, studying my companion.

Eve looked away.

"We talked about it while you were gone," Cathal said, clearly speaking for her. "It would be difficult, but not impossible. The Beast may be stronger than the tree thought, but she is still wounded. Still vulnerable."

I cocked an eyebrow. "You've called Neverland that before. Why?"

"That is what the Otherworlders call her kind. It is an old name, from another time."

"I think it would be a mistake to kill her," Eve cut in. Not for the first time, I wondered whether Eve saw something of herself in Neverland—if she felt a kinship with this unique, isolated creature. Would she resent me if I did as Neverland wished? Probably. But then, she wouldn't be the only one.

"If we can find another way, I'll try it," I agreed. "But she's in more pain than I'd have thought possible, and I won't leave her to suffer."

"If you bond with her, it's possible you could strip away those memories," Eve suggested. "I'm sure you'd be able to influence her emotions. Perhaps communicate directly."

I was already shaking my head. "I won't lobotomize her. She's entitled to feel, even if that means she wants to die. Just because I think it's short-sighted, doesn't mean I have the right to override her wishes."

"There might be another way," Cathal said, breaking up what might have become an awkward silence. "Neither of you think like beasts, which means you're missing the obvious."

"Enlighten us," I said, unable to keep a smirk off my face.

And so he did.

12

I held Eve's seed in my right hand. My left was coated liberally with fresh blood taken from the wound above my eye; no sense cutting open my palm when I had a perfectly good gash to choose from. Besides, the blood was only a key. What mattered most was what happened after I opened the door.

"Remember, focus on the message," Eve said, speaking over my shoulder in the hushed voice reserved for church or libraries. "If the hound is right, if you can convince her there's more to live for, she may bond with you willingly."

I raised the pip, curious. "And this?"

"Think of it as a fail-safe if things don't go the way we hope they will."

"Well, that's reassuring," I said sardonically. Still, I squeezed the seed in reassurance, replaying Cathal's words in my head for the dozenth time as I prepared myself for what I was about to do.

"She's lost her young," he'd said, speaking with the authority of someone who'd experienced something similar. "The only way to get over that is to find something else to care for. Another pup to take care of. If you can give her something like that, her instincts will take over."

Once he'd explained his reasoning, I had to admit Cathal's solution was obvious—perhaps even more so than he knew. It all came back to Wendy and James Hook, to the memories I'd been privy to. What if Neverland had fixated on those two instances not because she'd concerned herself with Peter's trajectory, but for some other, subconscious reason? Looking back, I realized she'd never shown me images of Peter interacting with his family, though of course she must have witnessed them. Had the older, more sophisticated Peter simply repulsed her, or had she kept those moments to herself as she'd kept her thoughts from Eve?

My own memories inevitably flashed back to those quiet moments in Peter's house, though they kept veering back to the little girl who'd been playing by the Hangman's Tree, who'd squealed with joy whenever Peter took her in his arms. Little Wendy. And then there was the boy who helped set the table, the child with his father's face watching me from behind his glasses. Little James.

Convinced of what I had to do, though I had no idea how I was going to pull it off, I thrust my hand against the withered bark of the Hangman's Tree. Nothing happened. The bark felt ashen beneath my hand, as if I could push harder and watch the whole thing turn to dust. After several seconds, I began to feel a bit silly; maybe drawing out Neverland with the taste of my blood wasn't going to work, after all.

"So, now wha—" I began.

And that's when Neverland tried to drown me.

It was nothing like before. There was no sense to it, no direction. Though I'd experienced the tremendous power of a hurricane once before, the sheer intensity of being buffeted to and fro—the brutality of having my mind whipped about—was far more overwhelming. And yet I felt I could read her thoughts; Neverland had asked me to kill her, and instead I'd tried to lure her, to initiate the bond. I'd come to dominate her, not to ease her suffering. She felt betrayed, momentarily overcome with rage, her grief forgotten. I would pay.

But that wasn't why I was here; I fought through the vertigo, shouting mentally with everything I had. Unable to produce coherent thoughts, I focused on one word, screaming it over and over again even as she assaulted me with everything she had. I could feel my sanity slipping under her barrage. I was losing myself, piece by piece. Neverland gnawed at my memories, consuming my mind in bite-sized chunks, much as she had Peter's childhood friends—a trick she'd learned to keep the other children docile, to make sure they continued to play with Peter even as their companions bled and died in the name of fun. For some reason, that knowledge—the horror of what she'd done to keep Peter happy—brought me back to myself. I was able to stand still in the eye of the storm, if only for a moment. At last, the sound of my voice reached my own ears.

"Children!" I screamed. "Children! Children!"

Neverland hesitated. I could sense her confusion, her caution. She'd been caught before by the words of a mortal, a man who'd spun such wonderful lies she'd practically rolled over before she knew what had happened, before she felt the leash close round her throat. That's why she'd always loved Peter; he'd been brutally, unapologetically honest. His moods were wildly unpredictable, but he'd never said anything he hadn't meant. The question she had to ask herself—the question roiling about in that tumultuous space which might have been called her mind—was whether I was like Peter, or like the man who'd chained her to this island.

Unfortunately, as I looked deep within myself, I realized the answer was neither.

Once, not so long ago, Peter Pan and I had shared similar traits; impetuous and unyielding, I'd prided myself on being untamable even when it contradicted my own self-interests, even as it ruined the few relationships I'd hoped to cultivate. And yet, though I'd become arguably wiser and there-fore better equipped to manipulate situations to suit my needs, I clearly lacked the crucial ambition, the necessary cruelty, to do what my father had done; I simply couldn't deliver false hope, couldn't offer empty promises. Whoever or whatever I'd become—goddess or godling or something else altogether—I was at least someone who valued her word above all else.

And so I gave Neverland my word. I gave her images. I gave her emotions, my emotions. I let her see, let her feel, what I was proposing. I held in my mind a vision of what we would create, of what would be born from our bond. I proposed not domination, but patronage.

Finally, I showed her Little Wendy. I explained she was to Peter what Peter had been to Neverland—that to love her was to love a piece of him. I fixated on James' face, on the way he held himself—in so many ways a cross between the Boy Who Wouldn't Grow Up and the dastardly Captain James Hook. What a man he might become, I thought, if only he had a place to call home. Using them, I painted one reality after another, each with Neverland in the backdrop, supporting Peter's legacy. And, since I couldn't keep my horror at what she'd done at bay, I leaned into it, insisting there were better ways to show her affection. That what she knew of joy and love were mere facets of much larger, much more valuable jewels.

Still, she resisted. It quickly became clear that my hunch was right; she'd always sensed there was something special about the girl, something unique about the boy. She'd felt drawn to them from the beginning, though she'd never spoken with them as she had Peter—by then, she'd been too busy fending off time. But the notion that they would fill the void Peter had left behind was not something she could comprehend, not something she could tolerate.

Nothing could replace Peter.

With that one thought, Neverland dismissed my visions of the future and prepared to lash out at me once more. Her will was even clearer to me, suddenly: she hadn't wanted this, but after consuming my power, she would escape this place. She would wander, would travel to those exotic places Peter had flown to without her. Maybe there she'd find someone who could end her existence there. If not, she suspected she'd go mad. Part of her regretted the harm she'd do, while another relished the idea of casting off the chains of consciousness—shackles which had never fit her to begin with.

In my mind's eye she rose up like a tidal wave, her malevolence replaced with sorrow and pain. In moments, she'd crash over me, taking away everything I was. Everything I could be. I'd gambled big and lost. I felt a surge of panic, but it wasn't my own; it was there in my hand. A pulse of frantic energy, waiting to be unleashed. But that couldn't be right. I had no hands here. No body. Before I could dwell on it, however, the wave descended.

I pinched my eyes shut, praying it wouldn't hurt.

*I*t hurt. It hurt a lot.

"Son of a bitch!" I screamed, my right hand throbbing with nerve-searing pain.

"Don't let go," Cathal said.

I blinked past tears to find the faerie hound standing not three feet away, his hackles standing straight up, teeth bared in a show of ferocity. But, if I could see him, it meant I'd returned to my body. But how? I turned to stare down at my poor hand only to find it pressed against the Hangman's Tree, Eve's seed caught between my palm and the bark. The pip was glowing white hot, and the stench of burning flesh rode the air.

"What's happenin'?" I demanded. I searched for Eve, only to find the Tree of Knowledge hugging the Hangman's Tree from the side. Everywhere she touched, the same white light shone, though in her case there was no smoke. And yet, based on her twitches, her pitiful moans, I knew she burned as I did.

"She's doing what she thought to do before," Cathal replied. "I told her you wouldn't like it, but it's her choice. Whatever you do, don't let go of her core. If you do, you'll kill them both."

I shook my head, breathing shallowly, the pain severe enough to give me the shakes. "What the hell are ye talkin' about?"

But there was no time for explanations. The light pulsed brighter as the seed sunk into the flesh of the Hangman's Tree. Eve did the same; the larger tree appeared to swallow her in increments, though I could tell she was the one fighting to merge. I realized that, somehow, she must have taken my place. That the pip had served as a sort of lifeline—a method to switch my consciousness for her own. Which meant that even now she was battling for control.

A fresh wave of agony crashed into me, and I dropped to my knees. Cathal barked at me, telling me to pick up the seed, to put it back. I swiveled my gaze, overwhelmed, and saw that Eve had caught fire; her bark burned where it touched the Hangman's Tree. Without my help, it was clear she'd go up in flames, taking Neverland with her. I fumbled in the dirt, feeling for the kernel. I had to do this. I wasn't sure what Eve's plan was, but I had to trust her—even if she hadn't trusted me enough to share it. At last, I managed to wrap my hand around the pebble-sized pip; it was surprisingly cool to the touch. I gritted my teeth, slapped the seed against the trunk, and pressed my head against the back of my hand to keep it in place.

And then I screamed.

I screamed until my throat hurt as bad as my hand, screamed until my gut ached. More than once, I felt my consciousness fade to black, the edges of my vision tunneling. I had no idea how long it went on, only that Cathal was close by; he yipped at me whenever I began to waver, whenever it seemed I might blackout. Then, at last, nothing. No pain, no sensation at all, really, beyond the sting in my throat. My hand no longer burned.

Suddenly, Cathal was at my back. The faerie hound took me by the scruff of my top and dragged me away from the tree, pulling my hair in the process. It hurt, though the pain was a distant thing. I thought to reach up to swat at him but barely managed to raise my arm; when he finally released me, it was all I could do to lift my chin and survey my surroundings.

What I saw left me speechless.

The Hangman's Tree was on fire. Lit from within, green flames flickered out from beneath cracks in the massive trunk, coiling upwards, licking their way towards the uppermost limbs. I tried to sit up, to yell Eve's name, but my throat was ruined, and my body battered. Perhaps sensing my desire, Cathal used his head to prop me up, though if he were concerned about Eve, he didn't show it.

"Have to...save her..." I whispered.

"Too late for that now."

I wanted to look back at the faerie hound, to see the expression that went with that gruff tone, but a low, keening sound stole my attention. I focused on the noise. It was coming from the Hangman's Tree, and it was growing louder. No longer a mere hum, it raised to an uncomfortable decibel. Soon, it was all I could do not to cover my ears. And then—with a crescendo I could only describe as ear-shattering—it got louder.

Provoked by the obscenely high pitch, I finally managed to clamp my hands over my ears, blinking through another bout of tears to find Cathal howling over my shoulder, joining his voice to the din. The combined result was deafening—a piteous harmony that seemed to have no end.

And yet, there seemed to be some purpose behind it.

The air changed; a gust of wind pressed at my back, the atmosphere no longer listless as clouds began flying by at an alarming rate. I felt the ground beneath my feet tremble, then shift—its impossibly dry, hard surface offering the slightest give where before there had been none. The wail ceased, abruptly. I cautiously removed my hands only to catch the sound of running water. No, not running, I realized. Rushing. I glanced back over my shoulder, forced to crane my neck past Cathal, just in time to see a wall of seething water speeding towards us from the bay; the massive wave broke through the shelf of rocks in a torrent, spewing along the path Eve had carved in the soil. It surged past Cathal and me and crashed into the Hangman's Tree with enough force to make me wince. The bark was stripped away in an instant, blasted to bits by the deluge.

The Hangman's Tree was destroyed.

In its place, however, stood something else—something new and yet familiar.

I found myself gaping at this new apparition even as the water pooled, forming a pond at first, only to continue onwards towards a distant mountain line, snaking inexplicably upwards in utter defiance of physics. Finally, silence descended in earnest, interrupted only by the gurgle of running water and a distant crack of thunder. I rose slowly, conscious of the river running not twenty feet to my right, not to mention the moat of water surrounding Eve.

If it was Eve.

The Tree of Knowledge, only a few feet taller than me when we'd arrived in Fae, stood perhaps three times that height, her sides so swollen I'd have to walk a wide circle to see her from every angle. Freshly cleansed, her bark —once a ruddy shade of brown—gleamed copper even in the gloomy afternoon light. Her leaves, meanwhile, remained gold, though they were no longer the slender, dainty things they'd once been. Instead, they hung, frond-like, their tips sickeningly sharp. And yet, it had to be her; cast smooth and superimposed, it was obviously Eve's visage splashed across the trunk.

"Eve?" I asked, tentatively, reaching out as though I might touch her. "Is that ye?"

A flash of annoyance rode the air.

"Not Eve," the tree replied in Eve's voice, though it boomed in comparison to what I was used to, almost as if it were coming from above rather than from the tree itself.

"Neverland?" Struck by the possibility that Eve had lost, that we'd suffered for nothing, it was all I could do to keep my voice steady. I took an involuntary step backwards as a fresh emotion surged—elation this time. Cathal padded up beside me, and I noticed the ground was greener than it had been a moment before. Tiny sprouts had begun poking up between the cracks in the dirt.

"Neverland...no. Neverland is gone. Only we remain."

"And who are ye?"

Confusion. Wonder. Comprehension. The sensations passed over me one after the other, and I realized I could perceive the changing moods the way you might feel a rise or dip in temperature. The thought alone made the hair on my arms stand on edge. I glanced at Cathal, but he didn't seem to be picking up any of what I was sensing; he'd sat back on his haunches, staring at the tree with his head cocked, one ear pointed skyward.

"Name us," the tree said, at last. "Eve was a name chosen by a child. A joke in poor taste. Name us, Quinn MacKenna, and see our covenant made."

I opened my mouth, determined to ask more questions, but found Cathal shaking his head at me in an oddly human way. I scowled, struggling to think past my exhaustion. Not Eve. Not Neverland. A bit of both, maybe? And she didn't want to be called Eve, anymore. In hindsight, I could admit the appellation had been a mistake—a cruel reminder of what her predecessor had gone through in the Garden of Eden. Eden, the false paradise. Neverland, the island of horrors. My head pounded, making it hard to think clearly. I touched my ear, gingerly, with my right hand and came away with blood.

"Name us, Quinn MacKenna," the tree reiterated.

"NeverEden," I replied, weakly. "Your name is NeverEden."

Relief. Determination. Pride.

"So it is," NeverEden replied.

14

*C*athal and I lingered on the bank of the pond, unable to ignore the sudden greenery spreading beneath us, the vegetation blossoming with every passing moment—like watching a video of grass growing on fast forward. I'd had to sit down, wrapping my arms around my knees, head burrowed. Every inch of me hurt. The gash above my eye had closed, and I bore no mark from the seed which had seared my flesh, but my whole body ached, sending pain signals every time I so much as twitched. What I needed—aside from a week-long soak in a hot bath and a full body massage—was sleep. Instead, I found myself arguing with the faerie hound, too exhausted to muster more than a mildly annoyed tone of voice.

"I can't just leave ye here," I insisted, for the third time.

"You're being stubborn," Cathal replied.

I raised my head and glanced sidelong at NeverEden, as I'd dubbed her. Since our initial interaction, she'd refused to speak, to answer any of my many questions. What had Eve done? And why? How was I able to sense her emotions? What was this covenant business? Of course, there were other, less tactful questions I'd left unspoken—like what the hell was she? Or, to put it even more bluntly, what sort of threat did she represent? Cathal, it seemed, shared my concerns; he'd volunteered to stay behind and keep an eye on her.

"What if somethin' happens?"

"You can take care of yourself."

"Not to me, ye idgit. What if the tree..." I drifted off, unsure how much NeverEden could hear. Best to assume everything, I decided; her roots might already have spread everywhere. I made a motion with my hand as if to imply the worst.

Cathal huffed, clearly amused. "I'm sure I can take care of myself."

"Like the time ye got caught by slavers and had to be rescued by yours truly?"

"Says the girl I saved from being poisoned."

I glowered at the hound but couldn't argue his point. We'd both screwed up. Both risked our necks to protect the other. Maybe that's why I was so reticent to let him stay; having him at my back was something I'd come to rely on. "Fine," I said, at last. "Stay here if ye must. But don't expect me to be happy about it."

"Quinn," Cathal replied, suddenly quite serious, "where you are going...it's not meant for me, for my kind. The Otherworld is my home. This realm shares similar air, a similar feel, but the odor that sometimes follows you, the stench on your clothes and those things you call guns and the place you call home...I don't believe I could survive there. One day, the same may be true for you."

"Ye mean the mortal realm?" I asked, frowning.

"Yes."

"What's wrong with the mortal realm?"

"It stinks."

"Constructive criticism," I replied, smirking.

"You aren't listening. It smells sour. Rotten. Not as bad as the Blighted Lands, but there are hints of that. Traces." Cathal shook his shaggy head from side to side. "There's something wrong with your world. Something sick."

I grunted, unsure what to say to that.

"There are other worlds like yours, other realms in decay. New worlds, too. This place," Cathal sniffed at the air, his nostrils flaring, "will become one. It smells different than before. Reminds me of home." He sneezed, muzzle wrinkling.

"How so?"

"Can't you sense it?"

"Sense what?"

"Life." Cathal pawed at the ground, nails digging furrows in the soil until I could see what lay beneath; thin, pale roots swarmed below like worms. The gouges disappeared in a matter of seconds, swallowed by eager dirt. I sighed and rose, wincing, wondering all the while what Eve—or NeverEden, rather—would do with this island. Would she return it to the way it was, or reshape it? I'd based the name on Eve's antipathy, while simultaneously honoring not what this place had actually been, but what it had meant to all those who'd been inspired by tales of Peter Pan and Captain James Hook. To be honest, I wasn't sure I wanted to know.

"I wish ye were comin' with me. Ye and her." I gestured vaguely at the copper tree, though in my heart I meant Eve. Now that she was gone, or at the very least so changed I didn't recognize her, I realized I would miss her. Not only for her wealth of knowledge, but for her opinions, for listening when I had no one else to talk to.

"Sometimes the only way to fill your own shoes is to walk the world alone."

I cocked an eyebrow at the faerie hound. "The hell d'ye get that from?"

"My Master. He said a lot of crap like that. Seemed appropriate."

I waggled my hand and shrugged.

"Quinn MacKenna."

Cathal and I flinched and turned as one to look at the gleaming copper tree. NeverEden swept her branches from side to side as though imitating a breeze that wasn't there—displaying the locomotion of a living, conscious being. A leaf fell from one limb, crashing into the water below before floating back to the surface. NeverEden bent, dipping one branch into the water, and nudged the leaf toward the bank where I stood.

"Take this," she said.

I swallowed nervously but did as she asked. The leaf was surprisingly heavy and as thick as a dinner plate; I had to resist the urge to bite it to see if it were made out of real gold. Be worth a small fortune if it were, I figured. "What am I supposed to do with it?"

"When the time comes, use it to find me. The piece always longs to become whole again. Remember that, Anu. Do not fight your nature."

I opened my mouth to say something else but was interrupted by a sudden shifting beneath my feet. I wobbled, unsteady, my muscles screaming with the effort to stay upright. But the quake—and that's what it was—only seemed to be getting worse. I fell to all fours, still clutching the leaf. "What's goin' on?" I yelled.

"I don't know," Cathal whined, sounding piteous as he fought to stay upright. Had I not been freaking out myself, I'd probably have enjoyed the sight; he reminded me of a dog trapped in a moving car.

"Quinn MacKenna, Eve releases you from your vow."

The voice descended as if from the heavens, louder now than it had been before. I felt NeverEden's emotions on the wind, each flavor unique. Nervousness. Resolve. Joy. She'd made a decision, something to do with the earthquake, no doubt. I leapt to my feet, prepared to confront her, to demand she tell me what was happening. I no longer felt sluggish. Indeed, it was as if the quivering ground held no sway over my equilibrium at all. I took an eager, impossibly quick step forward, determined to get my answers...and that's when I finally processed what she'd said.

Released from my vow.

I reached for the skin above my eye and found it whole—nothing but smooth skin, no sign of the gash that had been there only a moment ago. My body no longer rebelled, no longer ached. If anything, I felt energized. Pent up. I raised one hand, marveling at the sensation, and saw that the leaf I'd been given had folded in on itself. The result: a dense triangle of pure gold, heavy as a paperweight.

"You must return to your ship now, Quinn MacKenna," the copper tree said, bringing me immediately back to the moment at hand. "Without you, they cannot hope to survive. Your guardian will remain and await your return. So, do not dally."

"But—"

The ground heaved, shuddering so violently even my well-honed, Fae-like reflexes couldn't keep me entirely balanced. Damn it all. I had more questions! And yet, something told me I wouldn't get the chance to ask them even if I outlasted these ridiculous tremors. Cathal, looking miserable, bumped into me with his shoulder.

"Quinn, go! She's taking to the sky!"

"She what?" I gaped at the hound, but a quick survey of our surroundings proved he was correct; the horizon line was changing, the mountains in the distance brushing the tops of the clouds, much closer than they'd been only a few minutes before. NeverEden was making the island float. But why? And how high would she go? I gasped and spun, remembering the crew aboard the *Jolly Roger*; they'd probably have fled to the sea by now. If I waited any longer, it was possible I'd never make it aboard; I wasn't certain how much juice Tinkerbell had in her, but I doubted it would be enough to chase us into the heavens.

"I'll come back," I insisted, grabbing the faerie hound's face, fingers wound into the fur coating his cheeks. He jerked a nod, amber eyes flashing, the druidic marks on his body flaring to life. Only the flames were green this time—like those that had licked along the Hangman's Tree not so long ago. Unfortunately, I didn't have time to question the change; the clouds were closing in from above. I needed to run.

Now.

15

*C*ursing my choice of footwear, I charged towards the distant shoreline. Or, at least, where the shore should have been; the rocky shelf we'd climbed over earlier sported a gaping hole where the wave had struck, so I aimed for that, praying the Neverlanders remained on the other side. The landscape passed by in a blur, my quick, certain strides so powerful I covered in seconds what before had taken me minutes. Despite the circumstances, I had to admit it was exhilarating—there was nothing quite like running for your life to get your blood moving.

And yet, even as I indulged in my renewed strength and stamina, I couldn't help but wonder whether or not I'd regained access to all of my abilities. Eve may have released me from my vow, but that wasn't the same as saying I'd fulfilled it. Would my mother's powers return, as well? Would I know what to do with them, if they did? I'd been so sure of myself when I'd stepped into the shadows in that cosmic hallway, when I'd molded darkness to my will. It had felt like driving a car after a long hiatus—unfamiliar at first, but easy once I recalled where to put my hands and feet. Now, however, I suspected it would be more like flying an airplane; I knew I was supposed to fly the damn thing but had no clue which buttons to push or which levers to pull.

I burst through the gap at a full sprint, not even sweating, though I had to dodge more than a few dislodged boulders as I passed. The quakes had stopped, replaced by a steady quiver. Once I caught sight of the edge, I realized why; the island had cleared the sea altogether. Hundreds of feet below, perhaps thousands, waves frothed, surging from all sides into the cavernous pit the island had left behind. In a way, it was breathtaking—the sort of thing you never expected to see with your own eyes. But I couldn't stop to marvel. I scoured the sea, searching in vain for any sign of the *Jolly Roger* and its crew. This high up, however, it felt like searching for a speck of dirt in a haystack.

"Shit," I muttered as I gauged the distance I'd have to cover. If I were human, the fall alone would kill me. I'd hit the water as though it were a slab of cement, my bones turned to jelly. Even as I was now, I wasn't certain I'd survive; I'd tested my durability before, but never thought to try something as improbable as leaping off the edge of a flying island. Still, the longer I dallied, the further I'd have to fall.

Screw it.

"Cannonball!" I screamed as I launched myself into the open air, limbs splayed. My heart leapt into my throat as I fell, faster and faster, the wind whipping against me with enough force to take my breath away. The white caps grew more distinct with every passing second, the shape of the waves more discernible. Any moment now.

"Happy thoughts! Think happy thoughts, you idiot!"

The cry came from my shoulder, but I couldn't turn to look. I wasn't sure whether I wanted to laugh or cry, whether I should pray or curse. Instead, I did what the tiny, buzzing voice said and focused on all things joy. It proved even more difficult than I expected; memories of laying against Cathal as he slept were overridden by those of our recent goodbye, visions of Eve replaced by NeverEden, my time amongst the Curaitl pitted against what I'd seen in the Blighted Lands.

"Hurry!"

I doubled down, going even further back, but found only more pain, more suffering. Christoff cradling his head in his hands. Ryan's agonized howl, his tears frozen on cerulean cheeks. Othello and her cousin standing over fallen friends. Robin, Hilde, and the others shot to pieces while I watched. Max, bleeding. Blair, bleeding. Dez, bleeding.

Dez.

A memory rose, unbidden, of the night I'd snuck in from a rock concert. Well, the morning, really; me and a few boys from the neighborhood had driven down to New York to catch the show and had only just got back in town. I knew I was busted, but I'd had a couple beers on the ride home and was too buzzed to care. So what if my aunt grounded me? She was already livid I'd been kicked out of St. Jude's, always judging the friends I'd made since I'd switched schools. Anyway, it had been worth it. I'd moshed so hard at one point I'd forgotten my own name, forgotten everything but the beat and pulse of the music—caught up in the rush of adrenaline, I'd taken shove after shove, laughing all the while.

But Dez wasn't waiting for me when I got in. The cops were. Dez was huddled at the foot of the stairs in her robe, mopping at her eyes with a tissue. Certain she'd called the police on me, I nearly bolted, but Dez got there first. She wrapped her arms around me, pulling me down into an unsolicited hug, saying she was sorry, so sorry. That she'd listen more, that she'd try harder. The officers ducked out as fast as they could, clearly discomfited by this blubbering mess of a woman. I learned later that she'd pulled all sorts of stunts to get them there, including ringing up Father McKinley in the wee hours of the morning. After that, things changed between us. I opened up more, played it safer. Dez stopped harping, picked her battles with greater care. Even now, falling from the sky, I could recall the weight of her arms around my neck, her head burrowed in the crook of my shoulder, the scent of her hair, the way she trembled and sobbed. Loved, that's how I'd felt. Loved.

At last, I slowed.

"Too late, now!" Tinkerbell shouted from a few feet away, gesturing at the impossibly close surface, her pink glow reflected in the water below.

Well, shit.

I slammed into the sea and promptly blacked out.

16

A firm shake—followed almost immediately by a pail full of briny sea water splashing across my face and chest—sent me spluttering to my side, gasping for air. I groaned as the world around me writhed, the contents of my stomach threatening to come back up. Mainly candy, I'd expect, given my previous accommodations.

"Tink, not like that!" A hand crossed my field of vision, then again. "Are you alright?"

Both the hand and the voice belonged to James; the young man's eyes, pastel blue in the dwindling afternoon light, were wide and pitying. I frowned before I could help myself, unsure of my answer. Was I alright? I sat up a bit, struggling to recall how I'd gotten here—wherever here was. I stared past the young man, taking in the furled sails and loose rigging. The deck of the *Jolly Roger* was empty aside from the two of us, though I swore I could hear someone chattering away on the other side of the ship—a man's voice carrying somehow over the sound of waves lapping against the hull.

Memories came flooding back, haphazardly. Crashing into the frothing ocean. Eve's transformation. Green flames. Peter Pan, Wendy, and the man who'd called himself Killian Jones. The earth shaking beneath my feet. Running. Leaping. Falling. Tinkerbell's voice in my ear. My not-so-happy thoughts. I grunted, shook my head, and choked out a laugh.

"I've been better," I admitted.

"I wouldn't try and move too fast," James said. "You hit the water hard."

"How long have I been out?"

"A few hours."

His response sparked a series of questions. Where had the island gone? Where were we? Who remained onboard? I unleashed them in a barrage, firing off one after the other as each occurred to me. Even as I spoke, I rose, shrugging off James' attempt to help; despite the fall, I felt perfectly fine, albeit a bit wet. "And whose brilliant idea was it to pour water on me, anyway?" I asked, at last.

"That would be Tinkerbell. She thought it would revive you. Guess she was right." James made a motion, showcasing me as evidence. "Neverland is gone. Tinkerbell wanted to follow it, but worried she wouldn't be able to find us, after. Luckily, she spotted you on the edge just before you jumped." James hesitated, clearly waiting for me to fill him in on why I'd leapt, or perhaps what had happened on the island in the first place. When I didn't, he flushed red and continued. "Well, anyway, the ugly one Tiger Lily kept calling Lord left right before the island started to fly. Your other two companions are still here."

James said the last as though he were less than happy about it. Following his gaze, I realized the man's voice I'd heard earlier belonged to Narcissus; I couldn't tell what the Greek was saying, but it sounded unsurprisingly pompous. It seemed he'd taken over the Crow's Nest, high above our heads, though I wasn't sure who he was speaking to—not that there were many candidates left to choose from. James, Tinkerbell, Tiger Lily, Helen, and Narcissus. I wasn't shocked to learn Oberon had cut and run; from what I'd seen, the Goblin King had a knack for being elsewhere when shit went sideways.

Maybe one day I'd ask him to teach a seminar.

"And where are we?" I asked, again. "Ye can't have stayed put, what with the tides and all. Unless Tinkerbell got ye floatin' again."

"Doing the whole ship is really tough on her," James said, shaking his head. He opened his mouth to say more but apparently thought better of it. Instead, he gestured to the Crow's Nest. "We've been following his directions. Well, their directions. The woman doesn't talk as much."

"I've noticed," I replied, thoughtfully.

"Are you sure you're alright? That was an awful fall…"

In response, I held out a hand and flexed my fingers one by one, analyzing the sensation. Admittedly, it was hard to distinguish between how I felt now and how I'd felt earlier that day; while I could move faster, even hit harder, it was the increased durability which registered most. Frankly, it was as if I'd forsaken the aches and pangs one associated with being human. My hips and back—sore from days spent sleeping in a chair in a nightmare house designed to lure in curious, starving children—for example, no longer twinged with every movement. My bum knee no longer complained when I put too much weight on it. Even the stiffness in my neck had vanished. If anything, I felt uncommonly capable, as though something frenetic lurked beneath the surface—a latent, violent energy swirling in the empty air between my fingers. I smiled as I dropped my hand to my side.

"I feel better than I have in days," I replied, honestly, glancing up. This time when I met James' eyes, however, I caught a flicker of uncertainty in them—though I had no idea why. Was it that I'd survived the fall, or was it something else? The young man looked away, blushing again, before I could ask. Had I embarrassed him? I quickly took stock of my appearance, afraid something was showing that ought not to have been, but nothing was out of place, merely wet. "What's the matter, James?" I asked, finally.

"You're the first woman around his age who he's ever seen."

I turned to find Helen eavesdropping on us from the forecastle deck, still swaddled in her cloak, sitting atop a barrel. I frowned, wondering how long she'd been there. Not for the first time, I felt a tingle of suspicion working at my gut, telling me there was more to this woman than met the eye. "That's ridiculous. There were plenty of women his age in the village."

"Don't talk about me like I'm not here," James interjected, vehemently. He glared up at Helen, displaying a level of hostility that I found familiar, albeit disconcerting. "Anyway, she's awake now. It's time for you to fulfill your end."

"What's goin' on?" I asked, looking back and forth between the two.

"I made a deal with the boy," Helen explained, slipping off the edge of the barrel. She descended the steps to the main deck, flashing a pair of pale, slender legs in the process. "I swore I'd tell him where we were sailing once you woke up, provided he set the course I gave him and didn't ask too many questions. I wasn't interested in wasting time."

"She also said you'd tell us what happened to Neverland," James added, hands balled into fists at his side, spine unnaturally straight. "Tink has enough dust left to keep the ship running without a crew, but watching our home fly away wasn't exactly what we had in mind when we asked you for help. If you lied to us, you'll all walk the plank, and we'll return to our people."

I held up a hand, trying to calm the increasingly tense situation. "I'll tell ye what happened on the island, James, I promise. But I'd rather tell all of ye at once, so I don't have to tell it twice." I quickly shifted my attention to the Greek demigoddess. "And what's this about our course?"

Helen perked up a bit at my tone, almost as though she were offended. "You were unconscious, and the boy wasn't sure what to do. I simply pointed him in the right direction."

"And which direction would that be?"

"Land ho!" Narcissus cried from above, before she could answer.

The three of us turned as one, following the Greek's outstretched arm to find a speck on the horizon, almost imperceptible from this distance. That Narcissus had noticed it at all probably meant he'd been looking for it. Which also meant it was likely our intended destination. James and I turned back to face Helen, who continued to study the landmass.

"I thought you'd have figured that out, by now," she said, clearly responding to me despite her apparent disinterest. "We've taken our first steps on Odysseus' Path. Or we will, once we pass beyond the temple and cross the veil between this realm and the next."

"The veil?"

Helen tilted her head a bit, gesturing through her cloak. "We'll encounter it, soon. In fact, we should prepare ourselves while we still have time. The rest can wait."

I cocked an eyebrow, wondering why Helen was so determined to put James and I off; the island Narcissus had spotted was a ways in the distance, which meant we should still have had plenty of time to gather everyone and go over what had happened since I'd left the ship, not to mention discuss our next steps—all of which hinged upon the Greeks and their willingness to help us.

"Ye can't mean that island, there?" I asked, squinting. As we sailed closer, I thought I could make out a Greek temple sitting atop the tallest hill. The shape was distinct, though even from this distance I could tell the structure was made of wood, not stone; the light caught the inferior material differently.

"No," Helen replied, "the veil lies beyond Gaia's Temple. To get to the other side, however, we must first survive the storm. While avoiding the realm's guardians, of course."

"There's no storm brewing," James insisted, one hand planted above his eyes to block the glare as he studied the sky. He was right. Despite the dwindling daylight, there wasn't a cloud in sight. Still, I didn't doubt Helen's word; I'd seen an entire landmass take to the heavens like a helicopter only a few hours before, its surface miraculously rejuvenated, piloted by a talking tree. A storm sounded downright prosaic, by comparison.

"What sort of storm are we talkin'?" I asked. "And what guardians? Why didn't ye tell us any of this, sooner?"

"You didn't think we'd simply be able to stroll into this realm, to sail across seas that have remained undisturbed for millenia, without facing some sort of obstacle, did you?" Helen asked, voice deadpan.

Truthfully, I hadn't given it much thought; planning that far ahead hadn't seemed prudent, given everything else I'd had going on. In hindsight, however, I had to admit it made sense. I'd spent decades trying to find an entrance into Fae, after all, only to plummet from the sky the instant we sailed across the threshold. My first trip to the Otherworld had involved deep sea diving through scalding waters without so much as a pair of goggles. Hell, years back I'd seen a wizard slit a man's throat to gain entrance to a peculiar pocket of the afterlife. Indeed—now that I'd visited a few realms—I had to admit I approved of the heightened security.

"Alright, James, let's do as she says, for now. Find Tiger Lily and Tinker-bell, would ye?" I offered him a thin-lipped smile before giving Helen the full weight of my gaze. "Once this is over, ye and I need to have a word."

"Very well."

"Don't forget to include me, as well," James added for good measure before spinning on his heel to leave, only to accidently clip Narcissus as he scampered down from his lofty perch. The Greek danced away, rubbing his shoulder, but the son of Captain Hook hardly seemed to notice; he spared Narcissus little more than a glance before continuing on his way.

"My, he seems wound up. Was it something I did?" Narcissus asked.

"No, it wasn't," I said, still glowering at Helen.

"Oh, don't spare my feelings," Narcissus replied, gesticulating with one hand. "I'm sure whatever it is I've done to upset the poor boy, he'll come around. I'm really quite approachable, you know." Narcissus beamed at us both until—after perhaps a full minute of sullen silence—his gleaming smile at last began to wilt about the edges. "So, how about those sirens? Isn't it just revolting what that lot does with all their luring and drowning and what not? Personally, I wish they'd give it up, already."

If possible, I gave Helen an even dirtier look.

"I t'ink I'll have that word now, instead."

"Oh dear, now I've gone and done it," Narcissus said, dramatically. "Guess the nymph's out of the bag!"

17

The storm Helen had predicted hit before we could have our much needed one-on-one. Judging from the roll of the ship and the howl of the wind outside, I doubted very much whether a typical sailing vessel would have survived. Thankfully, Tinkerbell's dwindling supply of dust kept us from capsizing; we skimmed the surface of the choppy water, slipping over each massive swell with but a slight bob. Meanwhile, we'd gathered in the captain's quarters, located below the poop deck—an unfortunate descriptor if ever I heard one—per Helen's advice. Initially, I'd hoped to take the opportunity to catch the Neverlanders up on current events, perhaps even talk strategy, but Helen put a stop to that almost immediately; she passed out earplugs while Narcissus browbeat us all into shoving them into our ears. Mainly by refusing to shut up.

"Sirens, fellow shipmates, are half-bird, half-human creatures," he said as he sashayed about the cabin. "Not sure which end is which, having never seen one myself, but reports suggest they are quite repulsive. What we want to avoid here is overhearing their song, which is reputed to be quite lovely. Though, of course," he added, nudging Tiger Lily with one elbow, "they'd hardly hold a note next to yours truly. Apollo himself once crowned me karaoke champion, you know."

"Don't touch me," Tiger Lily growled.

"Wait, I thought the sirens were located elsewhere?" I asked, dimly recalling my tenth-grade reading of Homer's second most-famous work behind *The Iliad*. For some reason, I thought they'd be further along in our journey. "Why would they be here?"

"Did you already put in your ear plugs?" Narcissus asked, clucking his tongue. "I told you, dear, sirens are half-bird. They migrate. Anyway, what was I saying? Oh, yes. You'll want to wear these earplugs until the storm is over, just to be safe. Any questions?"

I ran my tongue over my eye-teeth, casually weighing the pros and cons of throwing Narcissus out into the storm. I doubted he'd die; I wasn't and never had been that lucky. "James," I said at last, "if Narcissus calls me 'dear' one more time, I want ye to make him walk the plank."

"With pleasure."

"So sensitive!" Narcissus cried. "That's alright, we can't all be thick-skinned. Or smooth-skinned for that matter." Narcissus ran his hands tenderly up and down his slender arms. He flashed us all a beatific smile, blew me a kiss, and slid his own earplugs home. Helen quickly followed suit, her hand dipping in and out of the shadows of her cowl. After a moment's hesitation the Neverlanders—though clearly baffled by the foam devices they'd been given—imitated the Greeks.

For a brief moment, I considered leaving my own ears unplugged. Hadn't Odysseus done something like that? From what I recalled, he'd had his crew tie him to the mast so he could hear the song without succumbing to it—curious to a fault. Indeed, the notion struck me as profoundly unwise, however clever his execution had been. Frankly, I wasn't interested in trying my luck, no matter how incredible an experience it might prove to be. In that sense, I supposed Eve had been right on the money: the bottom line was the only unit of measurement I cared about. Which meant if we had to sit in a cramped cabin for several hours waiting for a supernatural storm to die down while ignoring the calls of mythical creatures hoping to lure us to our deaths, so be it.

Unfortunately, it seemed it wasn't going to be that easy; the ship suddenly shuddered with enough force to send us all sprawling. I collapsed onto the captain's desk, spilling a bottle of ink and several sheets of parchment onto the floor in the process. Helen and Narcissus tumbled against the far wall, taking out maps that had been pinioned there by daggers—the pirate equivalent to thumbtacks, I gathered. The Neverlanders, on the other hand, kept their feet with enviable ease. James even had the gall to cock an eyebrow at us, as though we were children playing a silly game.

"What was that?" I yelled, my voice barely audible even to my own ears as I peeled away from the desk. Unsurprisingly, no one responded. Instead, the Greeks scrambled to their feet, watching the door as though it might explode inward at any given moment. A thread of noticeable tension filled the room. The ship took another blow, from the starboard side this time. I nearly stumbled, but found James at my side, keeping me upright. Helen— thinking quickly—grabbed hold of the rope that ran the length of the wall, but Narcissus wasn't so lucky; he tumbled over a chair and flipped head over heels to land in the inky stain I'd left behind moments before.

James gripped my arm, tight, his expression panicked. He waved a hand, seeming to indicate the ship as a whole, and shook his head. No more, he mouthed. I nodded, knowing what he meant even if he hadn't said it aloud; the ship wasn't built to take hits like these. Even with Tinkerbell's magic, if the hull sprung a leak, we'd be hard pressed to stay afloat, especially in a squall like this one. I hurried to Helen's side, convinced she'd know more about what was happening than I did. Unfortunately, with her hood up and earplugs in, I couldn't tell if she even knew I was there.

"What is it?" I asked, wheeling her about to face me. I pointed towards the door, jabbing my finger at it several times over. "What's out there?"

A hand on my shoulder brought me around. It was Narcissus, half his face smeared black like some football fanatic on gameday. He shouted, though I couldn't make out the words. Another blow—only slightly less violent—took us all out; I inadvertently tackled the Greek with Helen riding my back. We landed in a jumbled heap, and the volume skyrocketed.

"I'm going to die!" Narcissus was shrieking, pawing at his ink-stained chest. "I'm bleeding! Oh, I should never have agreed to this! I'm too lovely to die!"

I fought to stand, forcing Helen to grab hold of me lest she collapse to the ground. The storm outside had intensified, the spray slapping audibly against the hull from one direction after another. I'd lost an earplug. Fortunately, it seemed the siren's song had either abated or had never begun, which meant the only sounds I had to withstand were those of Narcissus' pitiful wails. I reached out and slapped the clean side of the Greek man's face.

"That's enough, ye crybaby! It's just ink!" I yelled. I motioned for

91

everyone to remove their earplugs. At this point it didn't matter whether the sirens called to us or not; we'd drown the ordinary way unless we figured out what was happening. Helen dropped from my back, pried the foam stoppers from her ears, and gripped my arm.

"This storm is unnaturally strong, and there is an energy to it that I've felt only once before. It has to be Typhon. I don't know who else it could be, not unless Oceanus himself is guarding passage into the realm."

"Who's Typhon?" James asked as he tossed his earplugs.

"The Father of Monsters," she replied, hurriedly. Helen turned her attention back to me as if willing me to believe her, to acknowledge the threat this Typhon represented. "You've probably heard of his offspring. Cerberus, the Nemean Lion, the Sphinx, the Hydra. They're all his. And trust me, at best, they're a pale imitation of their father."

"And ye knew he would be here?" I asked, yanking my arm free of her grasp.

"No! I thought it possible he'd be somewhere in this realm, but his being here makes no sense. Having him watching over this entrance is like...like..." Helen threw up both arms in exasperation.

"Like replacing the front gate with one of Daedalus' labyrinthes," Narcissus finished for her, idly rubbing at his injured cheek with one hand as he studied the ink-stained fingernails on the other. "But Helen, if it really is him, then he isn't trying to sink this ship."

"Yes," Helen replied. "Yes, you're right. Typhon could do that in an instant, if he wanted to. Which means this must be his way of trying to get our attention. But why? Why let us live?" Helen voiced the last two questions as though speaking to herself.

"Maybe he wants to talk," Narcissus suggested.

"Are ye actually insistin' that was Typhon's *knock*? Bit over-the-top, don't ye t'ink?" I let my incredulity show as I spoke, unable to believe what I was hearing. First a violent storm, then sirens, and now this? For perhaps the first time since I'd opted to chase after Ryan, I found myself forced to acknowledge the possibility that our voyage might end with my bones decorating the bottom of the sea. After all, if this was the gate, how on earth were we going to survive the yard?

"For a Titan," Helen replied, matter-of-factly, "I would call that extremely subtle."

*U*nfortunately—what with the immediate threat of being sunk and all—we didn't have time to play multiple rounds of rock-paper-scissors to decide who'd step out to have a chat with the Titan presumed to be ramming our ship. And, seeing as how I was all out of short straws, we did the only democratic thing I could think of: we played the pointing game.

"On the count of three, everyone points to who they t'ink should go talk to the Titan," I explained. "Whoever gets the most fingers loses. Make sense?"

Everyone nodded.

"Alright, then. One, two, three!"

I dipped my fist on each count before bringing it round to point at the person I felt best equipped to handle this Titan business, only to find all other fingers pointed at yours truly. I blinked rapidly, shocked to see that even Narcissus had chosen me as his representative. The self-absorbed son of a bitch spun his dirty digit in tiny, concentric circles, the way you might call attention to a mouthwatering dessert, a shit-eating grin nearly bisecting his two-toned face. My own finger, naturally, was aimed straight at Helen; it was obvious that the demigoddess knew a hell of a lot more about what was going on here than I did, which meant she most definitely had a better shot negotiating on our behalf. Once, perhaps, they'd have been forced to hold me back from going out there and shooting my mouth off, guns literally blazing. But I was wiser, now. Less petulant. Not nearly as eager to get myself and everyone around me killed.

"I must not have adequately explained how the game works," I said, clearing my throat. "Let me go over the rules, again."

"We understood," James interjected nervously before glancing at Tiger Lily and Tinkerbell for support. "We all think it should be you."

"But why?" I asked, surprised by the Neverlanders blind faith. "I mean, I know I survived that fall and all, but I'm not exactly immortal—" I bit back the rest of what I was going to say, realizing it could very well be a lie. Frankly, I had no idea what perks came with accepting my mother's sovereignty. That being said, I had zero interest in testing those limitations here and now; just because we were sailing Greek seas didn't mean I had to be a victim of hubris. "Listen, I've never even heard of Typhon until today. What if I go out there and accidentally insult his mother, or somethin'? Ye know how these deities are with their petty, inbred bullshit. No offense," I added, glancing Helen's way.

The Neverlanders stared blankly at me.

"Ah, right. Well, if ye lot ever meet one, you'll understand."

"I will go with you."

I turned from the Neverlanders to find Helen within arm's reach, the edges of her robe in hand, clearly prepared to venture outside. Now that surprised me—perhaps even more than the results of the pointing game had, if I was being honest. Why had Helen volunteered? Once again, I found myself questioning her motives, sensing an underlying ambition I couldn't account for. But, in the end, it didn't matter; if she wanted to step out into the squall with me and help ensure our safe passage, I certainly wasn't going to stop her.

"I appreciate it," I replied, cagily.

"I have no idea what he wants, which means we're still at a disadvantage," Helen said, completely ignoring my expression of gratitude. "And he won't want to hear from me. The Titans have no love for the offspring of Olympians."

"Olympians?" I echoed, struck by the title of those who'd lived and served on Mount Olympus, according to ancient myth. Narcissus twitched at the word, his face scrunched up in distaste. "I didn't realize Nemesis was an Olympian, that's all," I admitted.

"Oh, she wasn't, dear," Narcissus chimed in, the lines of his face smoothing away in an instant. "Nemesis was Helen's mother. Her father—"

Another brutal jerk of the ship sent us reeling before the egomaniac could finish his sentence. I fell into Tiger Lily's arms this time. Though significantly shorter than I was, there was a solidity to the brave, a lean muscularity which I couldn't help but appreciate—especially when she used it to keep me from careening across the room.

"How the hell are ye lot stayin' upright?" I asked, cursing as I disentangled myself from the Neverlander and stumbled back to my feet.

Tiger Lily snorted, then pointed to her feet. I scowled, squinted, and drew back rubbing the bridge of my nose once I realized Tiger Lily and James were floating inches above the cabin floor, entirely unaffected by the lurching ship. Tinkerbell took one look at my face and began laughing so hard she strobed a brilliant shade of scarlet, the din of her chortles eerily similar to those of an alarm clock. I glared at her.

"You're a cruel little bug, ye know that?"

Her laughter cut off abruptly.

"I am not a bug!"

"We don't have time for this. We have to go," Helen insisted, snatching my wrist and dragging me towards the door before I could flick the faerie across the room for holding out on the rest of us. "If Typhon gets impatient," Helen continued, "he'll destroy us. The Titans aren't exactly rational beings, and Typhon was always more monster than he was anything else."

"And how d'ye know all this?" I asked, wondering under what circumstances Helen of Troy would have encountered Titans—certainly not in the tales I'd read. After Troy, maybe? I could see how that was possible; the historical gap between now and then included things like the rise and fall of the Roman Empire, the birth of Christ, two world wars, the moon landing, and the invention of the potato chip. And yet, Helen's intimate knowledge of our current assailant struck me as especially convenient. What were the odds we'd run into an old friend of hers this soon into our voyage? What if this was all some sort of trap? If so, had Oberon set me up, or was this someone else's idea? I hated not knowing.

Helen swung the door open without answering, inadvertently engulfing us both in ocean spray. I sputtered as she marched us out into the storm, still clutching my wrist. For a moment, I could barely see; the downpour was so intense it felt like I was being pelted with pebbles from above. In mere seconds, I was soaked for the second time in half as many days; my hair clinging to my shoulders and back like wet, tangled ropes, my leather boots all but ruined. I pulled away from Helen, planning to return to the cabin to find something to cover my head with when, inexplicably, the downpour abated, leaving little behind but the lightest drizzle.

Who wishes to sail across the Eighth Sea?

The voice seemed to ride the wind only to crash into me like a wave, the booming cadence of it swirling about the ship so that the final word grew louder and louder before fading. The effect was disorienting to say the least. Helen nudged me forward, pointing to the sky. I scowled at her but turned, though I was unable to make out anything beyond a seething mass of grey storm clouds which reminded me of writhing snakes. No, not snakes. Something winged. I ran my forearm across my face, flinging the water from my eyes, wondering when this Typhon character would show himself.

Suddenly, two smoldering orbs pierced the murky gloom. Then two more. Eyes. Four sets of eyes in the face of a creature from nightmares more terrifying than any I'd had before. I gasped, realizing what I'd mistaken for clouds were in fact the long, sinuous necks of winged dragons; hundreds of them sprouted from shoulders so broad that they took up half the sky. As one, the dragons began breathing fire, cutting through the post-storm gloom. My eyes traveled inexorably to and fro, finding a set of wings that rose above the clouds, hands with dozens of wriggling serpent fingers, and a pointed beard of cragged stone. Lava trickled from his mouth, running down his chin like drool.

The orbs, impossibly far away and yet each several hundred times as big as the *Jolly Roger*, seemed to fixate on us—on me. I could sense Typhon's attention, could feel it resting on me the way you might if you were being tracked by a vicious predator. I also realized he'd asked us a question. And yet, it was all I could do to stay steady on my feet in spite of the hideousness of this gargantuan monstrosity, this thing which made even the gods I'd encountered up until now seem ridiculously underwhelming, perhaps even comically pitiful by comparison. But it wasn't simply his size that put me off, it was the wrongness of him, the incongruity; he reminded me vaguely of another misshapen, malformed creature I'd encountered in the mortal realm—a surgically-enhanced version of Frankenstein's monster, crafted from body parts taken from members of Boston's Faeling congregation. A being created for one purpose, and one purpose only: to kill a godling.

"We do, Typhon," Helen replied, glancing sidelong at me.

A cacophony of sounds sent me to my knees, hands clasped over my ears. The cries of hundreds of creatures filled the air as if coming from every angle at once. The bleating of goats, the snorts of a boar, the moans of cows mingling with the screams of leopards, the howls of wolves, and the shrieks of eagles. I glanced up through watering eyes to see the heads of these creatures and more emerging from Typhon's throat, each of them voicing their displeasure before slipping back into the dark mass of his flesh.

We are not speaking to you, faithless wife.

Faithless wife? I shot Helen a look but she wasn't paying any attention to me. Anyway, it seemed to me that he wanted to talk, after all. I gathered myself to stand, knowing I had no choice but to see this through; potential goddess or not, I wasn't equipped to take on a being of this magnitude. Frankly, I doubted anyone was. Still, that didn't mean I had to meet his eyes while we had our little heart-to-heart; I kept my gaze locked on the deck beneath my feet, refusing to look up. I found if I did that, I could at least function—Typhon's existence was simply too much for my brain to comprehend.

"So, you're talkin' to me, then?" I asked as I inspected my poor boots, distracting myself with their sorry condition.

You are unfamiliar to us.

"If ye mean I'm not from around here, then aye, that's true."

Do you seek death?

I thought about that for a moment, chills running up my spine as I contemplated whether or not Typhon was threatening me. But it hadn't sounded like a threat, it had sounded like a legitimate inquiry. Like, did I have a death wish? Or was I seeking a manifestation of death, like Heming-way? Or perhaps a place associated with death? That was the trouble when dealing with obscenely powerful beings from different eras: their grasp of the literal and the metaphorical was remarkably intertwined.

"I'm not sure what you're askin'," I admitted.

Do you seek death?

The words were the same, and yet this time the tone suggested something else altogether; Typhon wasn't asking if I sought death in particular so much as he wanted to know what—if anything—I *was* seeking. I hesitated, unsure how much I should tell the Titan. Would he care about the details of our visit? I doubted it. If what Helen had said was true, Typhon wasn't the sort to concern himself with trivialities, or even nuances. The truth, then, and nothing but the truth, I decided.

Here's hoping he could handle it.

"I seek the deaths of others," I replied, at last.

Helen twitched beside me.

The deaths of our kind?

Our kind. That was a curious way to phrase it. Did he mean the Titans? Other monsters like himself? I shrugged, realizing the answer was the same no matter which group he was referring to. "Not unless ye lot get in me way. I'm lookin' for someone."

"Are you trying to get us all killed?" Helen hissed.

You hunt the Cold One.

"I do," I replied, ignoring Helen altogether, my pulse speeding up at the mention of Ryan—assuming that was who Typhon meant. Which meant he had come through this way. I frowned, aware that meant he, too, must have encountered the storm and its denizens. Had Typhon spoken with him, already? Had he survived?

Will you kill him?

Typhon's question this time was anything but casual; I could sense an undercurrent of animosity in it that reminded me of the tone he'd taken with Helen. And yet I sensed his anger wasn't directed at me; it seemed there was a grudge brewing between this Titan and my old friend. What the hell had Ryan done, I wondered, to provoke the Father of Monsters? And, of even greater interest to me, how had he managed to survive after having done so? I shook my head, wishing for the billionth time that I had more information to go off of.

"If I must," I replied, at last. "If I cannot save him from himself."

Save him?

"Aye. He was me friend, once, before he became a..." I bit off the word I was going to use and cleared my throat. "Before he became what he's become."

He is not worth saving. For what he has done, he must suffer.

"What has he done?"

You will see.

Before I could ask Typhon what the hell that meant, the weather shifted once more; the scent of burning ozone permeated the air for only an instant before the downpour resumed, the sudden onslaught forcing Helen and me to duck back beneath the eaves of the cabin's slim canopy. I had only just turned to ask her what she thought was going on when I felt the waves beneath us surge, catching the bottom of the boat and lifting it high into the air with such speed I fell back, pinned to the deck by the sheer force of gravity, my teeth gritted, my spine rigid against the deck.

Beside me, Helen screamed.

Which was the last sound I heard before I went blind.

*S*everal hours later, I stood on an unfamiliar beach, surveying the landscape, using my free hand to shield my eyes from the glare. The sun overhead was both uncommonly large and therefore uncommonly bright, which is what had blinded me; the rogue wave had carried us out of the storm and deposited the *Jolly Roger* so far inland that it sat moored, buried so deep that half its hull lay beneath the sands. That we'd survived at all was a testament to Tinkerbell's infusion of faerie dust—something she no longer had enough of to get us out of this mess.

"Quinn! It's time!"

I turned to find James waving from the ship's stern. The others were likely already in the captain's quarters where we were having a meeting to discuss our next step. Personally, I was counting on someone else to have a plan. I'd already wracked my brain for possible solutions and—barring a miraculous discovery of some sort—had no idea how we were going to get off this godsforsaken spit of land, especially with the *Jolly Roger* stuck a hundred yards out from the nearest body of water. Worse, I wasn't sure how we were going to survive at all without finding some nourishment soon; my throat was beginning to ache with a nagging thirst, my gut rumbling from hunger.

"Comin'!" I replied.

I took one last look at the bluffs which overlooked the shore, my eyes darting across the top, searching for any sign of movement. There was none. At last, I turned and made my way back to the ship, still pondering our circumstances and the bizarre events which had precluded them. Had Typhon sent us to this island on purpose? Had he known we'd survive, or had he intended for us to crash upon the shore and die? And how did Ryan fit into all this? I had too many questions and not enough answers.

"Do you need help up?" James asked once I reached the ship's ladder, offering his hand. I took it, though I could likely have leapt the ten or so feet. The Neverlander huffed as he drew me up but then quickly disengaged. While he'd been relatively cordial since we crash landed, James and his companions hadn't particularly cared for their home's origin story or my description of what had transpired on it. In hindsight, I could see why they'd balked: it must have been hard for them to grasp the stark realities I'd been shown, to hear the truth about the Hangman's Tree and its connection to Peter Pan. Of course, the fact that Neverland had somehow fused with my talking tree only to go rogue and fly off to heaven knew where hadn't helped.

"How's Tinkerbell?" I asked.

"She's alright. When we left Neverland with Hook and his pirates with the other survivors, the same thing happened. She'll feel better once she's rested."

I nodded, feeling for the Faeling—even if she was a bratty little shit. Since we'd arrived on the island, the pixie had grown visibly ill, her light dimmer than I'd ever seen it. If anything, I'd have said she was suffering from a bout of the flu. She had that tired, malaised look about her. Still, I had to admit part of me hoped to find out what pixie vomit looked like.

I was betting glitter.

"And Tiger Lily?"

James snorted. "She refuses to take it easy. Says she's fine. But she's suffering, too, even if she doesn't want to admit it. I catch her making pained noises under her breath when she moves about. Honestly, I'm not sure why I'm not affected. I'm from Neverland, same as them."

Except you're human, I thought but didn't say. Unlike Tinkerbell and Tiger Lily, who'd been on the island perhaps longer than Peter Pan himself, James had mortal parents. Hook and his mother may have spent centuries in Neverland, but that didn't mean they shared the same ties with the place that the Faelings had. I couldn't be certain, but it was entirely possible the severing of that connection was responsible for their sorry states, and—worse—that they wouldn't get better until we got them back home.

"So, ye want to feel like shit, is that it?" I teased, trying to lighten the mood.

"Of course not. I just...I wish I knew more about what was happening. We know you did your best to save our home, but this..." James drifted off, making a sweeping motion with one hand. "Will we ever see Neverland, again, do you think?"

"No. Not as it was, anyway," I replied, painfully aware of James' crestfallen expression.

"I see."

"I swear I'll help ye find it, James. The island, that is. When this is all over, once I've done what I came here to do, I'll help ye and your people find your home." Of course, that wasn't a difficult promise to make; the truth was that—assuming I resolved this crisis with Ryan—finding Never-Eden was at the top of my priority list.

She had my dog.

"And what is it you came here to do?" James asked.

"Ah, right," I said, nodding idly to myself. I waved for him to follow me to the captain's quarters. Together, the two of us strolled across the deck, accompanied by the sound of the surf and the thud of my new boots on the hardwood; I'd found a chest full of clothes and assorted gear in Hook's cabin, including flintlock pistols and a bevy of quality pirate attire that could have doubled for sexy roleplay. I'd swiped a black leather bodice to replace my soaking wet shirt, traded out my ruined shoes with a pair of ankle-high boots, and snatched up a marvelously tailored black leather coat with wonderfully ornate buttons and flowing sleeves, because fashion.

As we approached the cabin, I mulled over James' question and how best to answer it. Sure, I'd originally planned to chase Ryan down, recover what he stole from me, and ideally get him to rethink his vendetta against Nate Temple. If that meant sailing all the way to Atlantis, so be it. But now I had to ask myself how far was I willing to go? Encountering Typhon in all his awful glory had put into rather stark perspective just how little I knew, how little I'd thought this through or prepared for the journey ahead. What I needed was intelligence. Information. I needed to share my intentions with the Greeks and find out how much they knew before I started gallivanting around, putting myself and others in danger.

"I'll tell ye what, let's talk about this inside with the others," I insisted. "That way I don't have to go over it twice." Unfortunately, by the time we opened the cabin door, it seemed no one was much interested in discussing much of anything.

They were all too busy trying to kill each other.

"I warned him not to touch me," Tiger Lily growled, hoisting Narcissus into the air by his throat. Sick or not, the Neverlander clearly had the egomaniac outclassed; Narcissus kicked wildly, his lovely face turning purple, hands clutching at her wrist.

"Put him down, or this one will never fly again."

I turned to find Helen standing to the side with Tinkerbell caught in one hand, the pixie's wings pinched between two fingers as though planning to pluck them off. The pixie struggled lamely, beating her diminutive fists on the demigoddess' flesh, insisting she also be released. As Mexican standoffs went, I had to admit this one at least had a bit of flair.

"What is goin' on here?" I demanded.

"Tiger Lily, put him down," James snapped.

Tiger Lily snarled and tossed her hapless victim to the floor. Helen set the pixie down with much greater care before going to her companion's side. Neither of the females answered me. James, meanwhile, quickly waded into the room, gathered up Tinkerbell, and settled in alongside Tiger Lily.

"What happened?" James asked, squeezing her shoulder.

"I don't like him, that's all." Tiger Lily shot a glare at the Greek that would have done Medusa proud as she spoke. "He's vile."

"Nonsense," Narcissus croaked. "Everyone loves me."

"He reminds me of Peter Pan," Tiger Lily continued, as though the Greek hadn't spoken, "but he's no warrior. He is like a shallow pond who thinks himself an ocean. It is pathetic."

"I believe you've misspoken," Narcissus interjected, massaging his throat. He'd regained most of his color and managed to look indignant even as he sat propped up against Helen's legs, clutching at the hem of her robe like a child. "The word you're looking for is 'perfect'." He reached up to pat Helen's hand. "We really must help these savages with their grasp of the language, my dear. Remind me to give them lessons, at some point. I'm an excellent teacher, you know, when I put my mind to it."

"That's enough," I said as I stepped between the two parties, shielding Narcissus from view before Tiger Lily—who was indeed savage, though perhaps in ways Narcissus likely knew nothing about—gutted him like a fish and ruined what little goodwill I'd hoped to nurture between the two groups; whatever we decided to do, our odds of success were much improved if we worked together. Our odds of survival, too, come to think of it.

"I believe it's time we put all our cards on the table," I said, urging everyone to take a seat as I shut the trunk of clothes I'd found and plopped down on its gilded lid. "We're stranded on some uncharted shoreline with no food and water, very little means to protect ourselves, and no clear cut way to contact the outside world for help. Suggestions? Or would ye all prefer to slit each other's throats and call it a day?"

Helen cleared her throat. "I know exactly where we are."

"Wait, since when?"

"Not long. I had to check the other shore to be certain, but given what I found this has to be it. Narcissus, give me your map." Helen held out a hand imploringly. "I believe we're on an island, one of those Odysseus and his fleet encountered not long after his men betrayed him."

"You won't believe what I had to do to get this," Narcissus said as he passed over a bound scroll. "That sailor wanted me to..."

But Helen wasn't listening. Instead, she removed the ribbon and spread the map across one of the tables. I rose and loomed over her shoulder, staring down at the mass of squiggles and notations. The map was crudely drawn and matched no cartography I'd ever seen; I saw not one familiar shoreline. Granted, my knowledge of topography was shoddy, at best, but the fact that it all looked so odd meant we must really have crossed over into a strange new realm. What had Typhon called it? The Eighth Sea? Honestly, I'd hoped the hoary bastard had simply miscounted; easy to do when you have so many extra fingers with minds of their own.

"It's as I thought. Here." Helen pointed to an island shaped vaguely like a heeled boot, then to what would have been the toe. "We're on this stretch of shore, here. But if you climb the rocks like I did, you'll see the main shore-line." She slid her finger along the top of the shoe. "This is where you'll find all the other ships."

"Like a dock, ye mean?"

"No, not a dock."

"Then what?"

"A graveyard."

*H*elen was right. It was a graveyard. A graveyard of shattered ships, the debris piled up on the far end of the beach in mounds as tall as a person. I could make out the remains of even larger vessels in the shallows, their masts poking up from the waves like the tips of swords. The demigoddess and I stood a few feet apart on the tallest boulder we could find, overlooking the distant cove. From where we'd landed, that was all we could do; the two shores were divided by impassable stone and frothing sea. Indeed, had Helen not known to go searching for the wreckage, I doubted we'd have found it at all.

"They must have thrown their stones from up there," Helen said, pointing to the cliffs above the cove, several hundred feet high at least. "That Odysseus survived at all is a testament to his cleverness. He always was a cautious man."

"What d'ye mean they 'threw stones'? And who are 'they'?" I frowned at the distance between the sea and the cliffs above, then at the decimated ships. "Also, how are these ships still here? They look ancient."

"My apologies, I forget how few of you mortals know of Odysseus' journey. The Laestrygonians, a race of cannibalistic giants, were responsible for this. After they caught and ate one of his men, Odysseus and his fleet tried to escape, but the giants rained boulders down upon them. This is what's left of those ships." Helen huddled further into her cloak as a cold breeze blew across the water, her face still miraculously obscured beneath the shadows of her cowl despite the bright sunlight. "And, to answer your other question, they are still here because this realm was created not long after the age of heroes ended. They have been, it seems, preserved."

"The Eighth Sea," I said, echoing Typhon's use of the term.

"That is one name for it. There are others, though they all amount to the same thing..." Helen drifted off, shuddered, and gestured for me to follow her back down. "This realm belongs to the Titans. It was fashioned for them, in a manner of speaking."

Unlike the Father of Monsters, whose existence I'd never come across, I'd heard of the Titans. Precursors to the Olympians ruled by Zeus, the Titans were allegedly born from the coupling of deities who represented the primordial elements. Vast manifestations of earth and sky. From what I could recall, the distinction between the two groups lay in temperament and chronology only. The Titans were what you might call first generation gods, which meant they were older, rawer, and perhaps a tad more powerful than those who eventually overthrew them. The Olympians, meanwhile, were younger, cleverer, and far more melodramatic. Not so different, if you thought about it, from Baby Boomers and Millennials.

"Titans like Typhon," I suggested.

"Yes and no," Helen replied as we dropped from one boulder to the next, working our way back down to the beach. "Typhon is technically a Titan, yes. But he should not have been guarding the entrance to this place. Long ago, Zeus defeated him and cast him into the pit. Into Tartarus. From there he was able to bear his offspring, even to cause many natural disasters, but never to interact fully with the world. Indeed, the last time he walked the mortal realm, the seas boiled."

Now it was my turn to shudder. Having come face-to-face with the Father of Monsters, I was only too aware of how devastating his presence could be were it not restrained in some fashion. I'd heard of Tartarus—a make-shift prison for Titans felled by Zeus and his cohorts during the Titan War. "So, what, did he escape?" I asked.

Helen froze. "Gods forbid. No...no, it's far more likely he was released. He seemed a great deal more...reasonable than I'd expected." She adjusted her cloak. "Anyway, this is the realm we must survive if we wish to reach Atlantis."

"About that," I said as I dropped a good ten feet to the sands, unwilling to scurry the remaining distance, "I t'ink it's time ye and Narcissus filled us all in on what to expect."

"What do you mean?"

"Atlantis. How do we get there? What sort of trouble will we run into along the way? What does Odysseus' Path actually mean?" I gestured to Helen's breast where I'd seen her pocket the map. "Show me where Atlantis is so we can plot a route to get there, assumin' we ever make it off this island."

"But, I thought you knew…" Helen drifted off.

"Knew what?"

"There is only one way to reach Atlantis, and you will not find it on this map. On any map. To get there, you must speak to the dead. Only the dead can tell you the way. That's what kept it protected, even from the gods. That's why we came here." Helen descended to the beach alongside me and retrieved the map, brandishing it. "Odysseus' Path is not the one he took to return home to Ithaca. It's the one he took to reach the Underworld."

21

*T*he six of us were gathered in the captain's quarters once more, the two groups hotly debating our next move. The Greeks, it seemed, felt we should salvage what we could from the other shore to build ourselves a boat and sail away from this island of man-eating giants at first opportunity; their arguments were sound. Narcissus preferred the dangers of the open sea to the threat of being eaten, while Helen was clearly eager to move on to our primary objective. The Neverlanders, on the other hand, refused to leave their ship behind, insisting we find another way. Obviously, the *Jolly Roger* meant a great deal to them, and abandoning it on a foreign shore they were unlikely to ever see again was a brutal ask.

I, meanwhile, took the opportunity to mull things over while I looked about the cabin. We'd straightened everything up after the crash, returning Hook's quarters to how they'd looked before the storm—minus a few busted picture frames, a shattered vase, and an ink-stained rug. The walls were largely dominated by landscape paintings, the tables covered in maps pinioned at their corners by daggers from various eras. Warm light streamed in through the floor-to-ceiling windows which were bookended on either side by lush, red velvet curtains, illuminating the profile of a marble bust sitting atop an upright piano. The face was unfamiliar, and yet I found myself staring into the statue's blind, enigmatic eyes, struck by the notion that Captain James Hook had spent centuries in this room.

"Miss MacKenna, what do you think?"

I looked over my shoulder to find James and the others staring at me. The young man's hands were mottled where they gripped the captain's desk, his face flushed from the argument. The others seemed less affected; Narcissus studied his nails, Tinkerbell lay on James' shoulder, and Tiger Lily sat cross legged on the floor, fussing with her moccasins. Only Helen seemed to share the young man's fervor, though it was naturally hard to tell what she was feeling without being able to read her expression.

"Call me Quinn, please, James," I replied. I adjusted my chair so I could see everyone and steepled my fingers, weighing our options. After having studied the map, I knew precisely the path of least resistance we could take to reach the entrance to the Underworld—there were clear avenues that would keep us away from the greatest dangers Odysseus encountered. That being said, to get there we'd have to cross a fair distance, all while avoiding any unforeseen catastrophes which cropped up along the way. Except none of that accounted for our biggest problem: without readily available stores of food and water, we'd have no choice but to deviate from our planned route, which meant making landfall on some other island—many of which were perhaps at least as dangerous as this one.

"I agree with the Greeks," I admitted, then held up a hand before James could retort. "Gettin' off this island should be our main priority. I've seen what these giants did to that fleet of ships. We can't risk 'em doin' the same to this one." I shook my head. "But if we rush this, we may end up some-where even worse. So, I propose a compromise. At nightfall, we go look for supplies. Food. Water. Anything else we might need, we take. But if," I added, holding up a single finger, "we find the means to get the *Jolly Roger* off this beach, we have to try." I searched the faces around the room before I met the young man's gaze. "I don't want to leave the *Jolly Roger* behind any more than ye do, James, but this is the best I can come up with."

James bit his lip, a child's gesture, but eventually nodded.

"And does that work for ye?" I asked, swiveling to face Helen.

"It will suffice, for now. But you should know that you won't always be able to compromise, not if you intend to lead. There will be tougher deci-sions to make before this is through."

"Lead?" I waved that away. "No t'anks."

James coughed into his hand. "Actually, we've been meaning to talk to you about that," he said, shifting nervously from one foot to the other.

"This young man thinks you should be named Captain," Narcissus interjected when James didn't immediately speak up. "I did try to explain that I'd be a much better candidate, especially seeing as how it's my map we're using, but he's far too smitten to listen to reason."

"That's not true," James replied, hotly. "I mean, not the smitten part, anyway. Look, I just think we need someone in charge. Someone decisive." He scanned the faces gathered around the room, though he pointedly skipped over mine. "When the ship was getting hit, Miss MacKenna—Quinn—stepped in and got us working together. And I'm not sure where you two stand, but she's the only reason Tinkerbell, Tiger Lily, and I are here."

"She is a warrior, as Peter Pan was. But also a survivor, like Hook," Tiger Lily added, her tone decidedly neutral despite giving me all the eye contact James hadn't. "Of course, in this as in all things, we will support James." The brave gestured to Tinkerbell, who took the opportunity to raise a half-hearted thumbs up before slumping back down, shielding her face with her arms as she nuzzled up against the collar of James' jacket.

"I agree," Helen said, surprising me yet again. "If we are going to continue, we should be led by one voice, not several."

"Yes," Narcissus chimed in, nodding. "I vote we choose the voice with the most experience. Show of hands. Who here has actually sailed a real ship before?" Narcissus held his own hand up. James followed suit, though tentatively. "And who here has set a course without the help of a faerie? Navigated using maps? Ran a very profitable, extremely fashionable cruiseliner company?"

James dropped his hand.

"I thought so."

"Narcissus, that's enough." Helen reached out to lower her companion's arm. "I'm sure our new Captain will find you immensely valuable as a helmsman. Without your expertise, we're likely to go nowhere. But these Neverlanders do not trust us. Nor can we expect them to."

"You're bein' awfully understandin' about this," I said, suspiciously. "Don't ye want the job?"

Helen huffed a laugh. "No."

"Smarter than ye look," I said with a sigh. Helen straightened a bit at that, probably offended by the implication. I shook my head, waving that off. "Sorry. Look, I don't want the job, either. So, let's table the Captain talk until we have a ship to sail, alright?"

"Alright," James echoed, though I could tell he wasn't pleased about it.

Narcissus twitched for the second time before leaning towards his companion, one hand shielding his mouth from view, though when he spoke it was more than loud enough for us all to hear. "You know, for someone who doesn't want to be the boss, she's awfully bossy."

"Narcissus…" Helen cautioned.

"Teasing, my dear. Only teasing."

22

I'd left the cabin following Narcissus' catty comment, opting to get some fresh air before I really did throttle the smug bastard. The problem was, he wasn't wrong. I always found excuses to take charge in groups, even when I didn't objectively want to. There was simply something about other people's way of doing things that rubbed me the wrong way. In any case, what I'd told James was the truth. I hated the thought of being Captain; I'd seen the price of authority firsthand and had no desire to lose any sleep at night wondering if I'd made the right choice—if I'd said the right thing or chosen the correct path. Unfortunately, I disliked the thought of anyone else being in charge at least as much.

With all this swirling around inside my head, I decided to go for a walk. I leapt off the side of the ship, landing easily in the sand, and strolled towards the sea. The tide had come in a fair amount since we'd arrived, the sun several hours from setting. The island was chillier than I'd thought it would be, especially with the breeze coming off the waves; my hair whipped about in ginger tangles, occasionally flitting across my vision so that I literally saw red. Above the sound of the surf, I could make out footsteps crunching towards me, accompanied inevitably by the drag and swish of a cloak.

"My husband used to stare out at the waves much as you are, now," Helen said as she came up behind me.

I cocked an eyebrow. "Paris?" I asked, recalling the myth that had made her infamous.

Helen spat indelicately, a gob of spittle emerging from her shadowed cowl to stain the sands. "No. My husband was always Menelaus. Paris and I never married."

I wasn't sure what to say to that; Homer's description of events, from what I could recall, had included a torrid love affair spawned by interfering gods, complete with abduction, bloodshed, and—supposedly—romance. Of course, it was entirely possible my memory was tainted by alternate, tele-vised renditions; Hollywood had a way of skewing one's perceptions of literature towards gratuitous sex and violence.

"It was not Helen of Sparta's choice to become forever known as Helen of Troy," she continued. "Menelaus was a hot-tempered man, but honorable in his own way. Fierce, passionate, but loyal. Paris was nothing but a child. A naive child, cursed by his own choice. And don't get me started on Menelaus' brother, Agamemnon, that power-hungry cretin..." Helen bit off her tirade, stepped up alongside me, and waved all that away. "Forget it. Ancient history."

"I had no idea. Sorry for bringin' it up."

"I'd love to say times have changed, but I'm afraid the days of men taking what they want, of doing whatever they please, are not as numbered as I'd prefer." Helen turned to face me, the shadows beneath her cowl taking on an ominous element in the harsh light of day. "You seemed surprised that I sided with the others against Narcissus' wishes. Would you like to know why?"

Though I sensed a trap of some sort, I nodded.

"Do you know what the Greek word 'pathos' means?"

"No."

"It was a term coined by Aristotle. I expect you've heard of him."

"The philosopher?"

"Yes, though he was far more than that," she replied. "Aristotle was a man who turned our history into fables, who made myths out of our tragedies, our realities. He and his predecessors kept us alive, in many ways." Another gesture of dismissal. "Anyway, the word translates directly to mean 'suffer-ing,' though what it typically refers to are the emotions that can be drawn out of an audience."

I nodded along, unsure where Helen was going with this little lesson;

until now, she'd gone out of her way to compartmentalize information, to share only when it was required. In fact, it was that reluctance on her part which had bothered me from the start. What was she hiding? Or, more importantly, why was she hiding it?

"Alright," I prompted, "so what's your point?"

"You may not know this, but we Greeks are famous for our tragedies. Our heroes have a tendency to make questionable judgment calls, our gods to behave like spoiled children. In this respect, we are the perfect display of pathos and all its trappings. Aristotle's lessons were meant to guide humanity, to underscore our failures so that they wouldn't repeat our mistakes. And yet..."

"I don't understand," I admitted. "I mean, I appreciate the history lesson. But what's any of this got to do with me bein' Captain?"

Helen waved that away.

"Tell me, Quinn MacKenna, what are you?"

"Excuse me?"

"I can sense it in you, bright as the sun above our heads and hot as the sand beneath our feet," she said as she held out her hand, letting it hover just a few feet from my gut the way you might before pressing it to the bulge of a pregnant woman's stomach. "The spark of divinity. Ever since we fetched you out of the water, it's been there, flickering. Except it's different from others I've encountered. Less certain. Unaffiliated, perhaps."

"Unaffiliated?"

"You will have choices to make," Helen said, as though I hadn't spoken. "Decisions that will determine the sort of being you will become. Who you will answer to. Who you will condemn, or save."

I found myself covering my stomach with both arms, shielding the so-called spark Helen had referred to as if there were indeed a child growing in my belly. "It's not mine. It's me ma's power," I admitted, liking less and less the way this conversation was going. "Her essence. Spirit. Whatever."

"Just because it's inherited it doesn't mean it isn't yours." Helen snorted a quick laugh that was anything but ladylike. "Don't you see what this means?"

"No," I replied, defensively. "So why don't ye explain it to me?"

Helen let her hand fall back to her side.

"I've overstepped. I apologize."

"No, it's time ye say what ye came to say. But be quick about it, because

I'm gettin' tired of the runaround." I fought to keep the frustration out of my voice, but it wasn't easy; part of me desperately wanted to flee before I had to confront yet another uncomfortable truth. But then, no matter how much I'd changed of late, I supposed deep down I simply wasn't the sort of person to avoid confrontation.

"You are the first of your kind to emerge in millennia," Helen replied after a lengthy pause. "The first since the Old Ones abandoned the mortal realm. Haven't you wondered what that means for our future?"

"For *our* future?"

"It means," Helen continued, "that the old magic is returning. The old forces. Perhaps the Old Ones themselves."

"Now hold on a minute—"

"I agreed with the boy," Helen continued, cutting me off, "because I believe you have a destiny to fulfill, and because I want to see what you will do with your newfound power. It's possible you will succeed where others have failed. Perhaps you will become an unblemished, untainted deity destined to rise and never fall. Or perhaps you will make the same mistakes which ruined so many before you. Only time will tell."

"Oh, golly, ye really t'ink so?" I asked in a child's voice, eyes comically wide, making a mockery of her bold pronouncement.

"Would you like to know the real reason I agreed to help you? The reason I agreed to come along on this journey?" Helen asked.

Even though I'd suspected Helen's motives, I was surprised to hear her admit it; the demigoddess didn't seem the type to give up her secrets willingly. If anything, she struck me as a strikingly premeditated person. Perhaps that was why all I could do was wonder what purpose her sudden candor served. I gestured for her to continue, fighting to keep the skepticism off my face.

"It was foretold, long ago, that I join you on this quest of yours."

"Foretold by whom?"

"By someone who insisted the fate of us all depended on you and your allies—or your enemies, depending on the choices you make."

That sounded too familiar. My mother had said something similar, perhaps more than once. Others, as well. But I only knew of one prophet who'd decided to meddle in my affairs, lately. "I swear if ye say Merlin put ye up to this..." I said, eye twitching at the mere thought that my father might have been involved in recruiting Helen as well.

"Merlin? No, not at all. I've never even crossed paths with him. No, the prophetess I spoke to died long before you were born. We knew her as the Pythia, though many refer to her now as the Oracle at Delphi. It was she who told me that I would be sought out by a wounded god, and that through him I would be introduced to a child who belonged to two worlds. At first I thought she meant a literal child, but now I realize she meant a child in relation to someone who has survived the ages. Regardless, the Pythia insisted I should follow that child to the edge of death and back if I would see my greatest wish fulfilled."

"Your greatest wish?"

Helen hesitated. "To awaken my mother, of course. As I said."

"Of course," I said, pretending I hadn't noticed the pause. "And how long ago was this, exactly?"

"Several thousand years, give or take a century."

Unable to decide if Helen was being glib or not, I was forced to seriously consider the fact that, at some point in the ancient past, she had indeed met with the infamous prophetess—a fortune-telling priestess who'd pointed her in my general direction. It wasn't a pleasant notion; it spoke to the nature of predestination, suggesting the trajectory of my life was already determined.

"Does everyone know what me future looks like besides me?" I wondered aloud.

"It doesn't work like that," Helen replied. "Prophecies are vague, open-ended things which tend to make sense only after the fact. Even with the Pythia's guidance, even after spending centuries preparing myself for this journey, I don't know anymore than you do about what's coming, or how it'll come about. I can't even tell you how we'll make it off this island, for example, or whether we'll all survive."

"Well, aren't ye the life and soul of the funeral."

"The Pythia did give me one clue, however," Helen said, ignoring my jibe. "And this is why I voted for you, why I believe you are the one I was meant to follow."

"Oh? And what's that?"

"She called the child 'Captain.' She spoke it in English, which is why I remembered it. Your language hadn't even emerged yet, and so the word was not easily forgotten."

Even better, I thought. According to Helen of Troy, it seemed I'd been inadvertently appointed Captain by a prophetess thousands of years before —a predestined promotion, as it were. I wished the idea were laughable. Unfortunately, despite my misgivings, it appeared the insidious influence of destiny was already at work; if fate decreed I was to become Captain, I doubted there was much I could do about it. I turned my back on the sea and started towards the ship.

"Gather everyone on the main deck when the sun goes down," I called over my shoulder. "And have the others keep an eye on the cliffs, just in case."

"Very well. And what will you be doing?"

"I'm goin' to see if Hook kept any booze on that damn boat."

23

*U*nfortunately for me, it turned out Hook was a teetotaler. Either that, or he was a hell of a lot better at hiding his alcohol than he was his leather fetish. Regardless, I spent the few hours leading up to sunset aimlessly wandering the ship before returning to the cabin to meet with my would-be crew. My thoughts churned as I ran my fingers along the wooden railing, occasionally reaching out to swing around the taut ropes, relishing the sensation of being alive. The breeze had picked up, the sky darkening beneath rows of stratocumulus clouds rolling as if to reflect the surface of the churning sea. My own emotions were similarly disturbed. After my stilted conversation with Helen, I felt oddly unsteady. Uncertain.

When this all began, everything had revolved around Ryan. Whether by stopping or saving him, the outcome would be the same; I'd end his plotting and make the world a safer place. But now I wasn't so sure. To find Atlantis, we'd have to seek out the entrance of the Underworld to speak with the spirits of the dead. But which spirits? Who would come calling if and when we engaged in this seance? What more would I have to endure, what new secrets would come to light? To be honest, I wasn't sure I wanted to know; I had an ominous feeling about this journey, a sense of foreboding that sent chills up my spine. And yet, with nothing concrete to go on, there was still work to be done.

So, I headed for the cabin at last and laid out my plan for the evening's activities.

"It's a simple scout and report job," I said. "Tinkerbell, ye and Narcissus will take the northwest. Ye keep an eye on everythin' from above and keep the Greek from gettin' into any trouble. If ye two t'ink there's any danger, double back and wait for us here. But make sure ye aren't followed. No sense doin' all this sneakin' around just to get caught and turned to jelly when they start tossin' boulders at us."

"Why do I have to go with him?" Tinkerbell asked, her face scrunched up in distaste.

"Because if he finds a mirror, I worry he won't ever make it back."

Narcissus opened his mouth to say something, thought about it, then closed it. He nudged Helen, smirking. "It's like she knows me."

"James, I want ye and Helen to go north. Same rules apply. Ye won't have anyone lookin' out for ye from above, so you'll have to be extra careful." I glanced sidelong at the demigoddess. "That little trick when ye take off your hood, is it useful?"

"Are you asking whether or not the sight of my face would make a cannibalistic giant think twice before eating me?"

"Aye, that."

"Haven't tested the theory," she replied, deadpan. "But probably."

"Good. James, if things go sideways, be sure to look away until she tells ye otherwise. Wouldn't want ye gettin' caught in the crossfire."

Helen snorted indelicately.

"I wish to go with James."

I wheeled to find Tiger Lily standing in the corner of the room like some sort of poltergeist, her painted face even eerier in twilight. She slipped silently out from the shadows, her animal skins barely rustling. As I'd suspected, the Neverlander could move like a damned wraith when she wanted to.

"Yes, I know, but I want ye with me," I replied. "The two of us are goin' northeast, which means we have the largest stretch of island to cover before dawn. If the others run into trouble, they can at least get back to the ship quickly. We may not have that luxury."

What I didn't say aloud—though I hoped the Neverlander compre-hended on her own—was that Tiger Lily and I were the only two fighters aboard. The only two who could handle ourselves if we ran into real trouble; despite the sword at his hip, I had no idea whether James could hold his own, and Tinkerbell still wasn't feeling well, even if she was worth her weight in gold as air support. Sadly, the way Narcissus had freaked out during the storm told me everything I needed to know about his combat experience. As for Helen, well, the demigoddess was proving to be an enigma wrapped in a mystery wrapped in an absurdly gorgeous, shockingly intelligent box.

What I needed was someone who would have my back, not stab it.

"So, none of these splits are meant to get us working together?"

The question—which I'd honestly expected from Helen—came from James. The young man half-sat, half-stood with the majority of his weight on Hook's desk. Once again, I was struck by the intensity, the watchfulness, behind his eyes. At times, the Neverlander reminded me of every awkward teenage boy I'd ever met: one half hormones, the other half...more hormones. Indeed, his crush on me, I suspected, was merely circumstantial; I was the only grown woman he'd ever met who wasn't his mom, his sister, his thumb-tall companion, or his father's childhood partner-in-crime. Helen, whose face he'd never seen, didn't count. And yet, despite all that, I had to admit the kid had an air of maturity about him that I'd come to rely on—not to mention rather keen instincts.

"If I'm goin' to be your Captain, I have to see how ye follow orders," I replied, begrudgingly. "If we do this and nobody ends up eaten, great. If ye all end up workin' better together on top of that, I'll consider it a bonus."

Before I could even finish speaking, however, Tiger Lily and Tinkerbell turned to their young charge, obviously waiting to see what he'd have to say about this arrangement. James exchanged glances with both before giving his tacit consent, and it was in that moment that I realized I'd never be Captain aboard the *Jolly Roger*. Why? The answer was simple.

Because she already had one.

Though young and somewhat untested, it was clear that James had already earned the respect of his fellow Neverlanders, and that—between the two of us—he had a far better claim to the *Jolly Roger* and its fortunes. Sure, I was older and more experienced in a crisis, but that wasn't what made a leader great. Charisma, the ability to recognize and implement good advice, and being able to command authority—these were the defining features of a good Captain. Did James have them? Perhaps. Perhaps not. But there were ways to find out, ways to elevate him to the status he'd already achieved in the eyes of Tiger Lily and Tinkerbell.

To my surprise, the thought came as a complete relief.

And yet, I shared my thoughts with no one as we prepared to leave the ship, knowing deep down that the Neverlander's ascension would have to wait. That my momentary authority, however dubious, had to suffice for the time being; once James was ready to take over and felt he'd earned the role, I'd step down. But, until then, we had immediate problems to solve.

Like not dying of starvation or getting eaten by cannibals.

he six of us split up shortly after using a pinch of Tinkerbell's dust to get us over the cliffs, sparing only a few brief minutes to secure ropes we'd found among the rigging to serviceable trees. We'd spent about the same amount of time saying our goodbyes, after which I reminded everyone of their roles, impressing upon them once more the need for stealth.

"Remember," I'd said, "we're lookin' for food, water, and anythin' we might use to move the ship. Levers, pulleys, ye name it. If ye can't move it, make a note of where ye saw it, and we'll come back."

"Did she say 'bully'?" James had asked.

"A leaver?" This from Tinkerbell.

"My, how the education standards have fallen since my day." Narcissus had said with a pat on James' shoulder, his amusement palpable. "Don't worry, Helen will explain it to you on the way. Come on, lightning bug. Work to do."

Perhaps an hour later, Tiger Lily and I ended up creeping inland under the cover of darkness, my face coated in the same black varnish as her own —though admittedly I'd asked for a less garish pattern than the skull mask she'd gone for. Not everyone can pull off the Day of the Dead look. The island of cannibals was surprisingly quiet and eerily still, remarkably devoid of the wildlife I'd have expected to find. Of course, maybe that was for the best. Giant man-eating boulder-throwers were bad enough without running into any equally large, equally carnivorous animal counterparts.

We moved slowly beneath the light of the moon overhead, though I found the pale glow more than enough to see by; the night seemed inexplicably bright, like a television screen turned to its highest setting, the deepest shadows only the slightest shade of grey. Indeed, as we slipped from one copse of trees to the next, working our way across the landscape, I was surprised to find it was I who had the surer footing. And I wasn't the only one.

"You move like you've been here before," Tiger Lily commented, speaking for the first time since we'd left the others behind.

"I t'ink me eyes got an upgrade, that's all." I held a hand up, displaying three fingers. "Can ye see how many fingers I'm holdin' up?"

Tiger Lily squinted. "Three."

"How about those weird shapes over there, to our left? D'ye see those?"

"No."

I pointed for clarification, but Tiger Lily still struggled to make out the bizarre silhouettes poking up from the opposing hillside; she shook her head, expression troubled. I reached out, squeezed her arm, and adjusted our trajectory. To get there, we'd have to pass through a tree-filled valley and emerge on the other side, which meant we'd have cover, but would also be exposed if anyone or anything called the valley home. Luckily, we'd already found a fresh water source not far from the beach—a frigid stream that trickled down from the north. Provided we found a few serviceable containers, at the very least we weren't going to die of thirst.

"Alright, keep your senses sharp. We'll see what's over there. Maybe we'll get lucky and it'll be food. But if it's nothin', we'll go a little further, then head back." I waited for her to respond, but the Neverlander simply fell in step behind me, trailing like a shadow. "Listen, I know you're worried about James, but I'm sure he's fine."

"I am not worried about him."

"Then what's wrong?"

"I don't know. Something is in the air, here. I came expecting to smell death. Meat. Blood. But this island does not feel like such a place. The air is clean. The forests untouched. It reminds me of our home as it was before the Manlings came."

"Before Peter Pan, ye mean?"

Tiger Lily scoffed. "Peter was never a Manling. He was something else, a child with his hands in two worlds, taking what he desired from both. When he wanted playmates, he rallied Tinkerbell and his Lost Boys. When he wanted an ally, he called me. When he wanted a fight, he picked one with Hook. And when he finally wanted love, he found that, too." Tiger Lily's voice was tinged with bitterness, but I could tell it was an old wound, scabbed over. "Do you know why I'm not worried about James? It's because he does not take what he wants, but gives."

"How d'ye mean?"

"Have you not seen it for yourself, yet?"

I paused beside a tree trunk, pressed flush against the bark, eyes scouring the darkness for movement besides our own. Nothing. "Noticed what, exactly?"

"The way he...Look!" Tiger Lily hissed, pointing at the hillside I'd indicated earlier, just visible beyond the tree line. There, the silhouette of a figure emerged, too distant for me to make out. But I could tell it was huge. Not quite a giant, in truth; I'd met a frost giant as well as a Norse goddess, both of whom would have dwarfed this thing. Still, it was larger than any man or woman I'd ever met, closer to nine feet than eight.

"Good eye," I replied. "Come on, let's get a closer look and see what it's doin'."

A dagger of carved bone I hadn't seen before flashed in Tiger Lily's hand.

"Don't attack unless there's no other option," I insisted. "We don't want to draw attention to ourselves, and we don't know how many of 'em there are."

"I've played this game before."

Tiger Lily's painted face betrayed none of her emotions, but I recognized the cool detachment of a killer in her words, in the set of her shoulders. How many pirates had she killed on Peter's watch? How many others who'd stood against her tribe? And what about me? My hands were so soaked in blood they could have named a ruby red nail polish after me. And yet, here I was, counseling her to rein it in—the irony was almost enough to make me laugh.

"Fair enough," I said, at last.

We pressed onward, ducking from tree to tree until we made it to the base of the valley. Here, I paused. The slope was bare, which meant we'd have no cover to speak of; if the giant had even modestly good night vision and looked down at any point, we'd be busted. It was a risk—one I'd have urged the others not to take. But we needed food. Real food. Already my stomach was aching from the lack of it; I'd survived our stay in the ginger-bread house by plucking candy from the wall whenever hunger struck, riding roller coaster sugar highs and lows. On this journey, however, I suspected my body would need something more sustainable. Vegetables. Protein. Sustenance. If we couldn't find any on our own, then perhaps the giant would lead us to some.

Preferably nothing man-made, of course.

I took a deep breath, let it out slowly, and began ascending the hillside. We moved quickly, using our hands as well as our feet so we could stay as low as possible; Tiger Lily looked like a four-legged wolf running uphill in all her animal skins. The giant's silhouette was no longer visible from this angle, so I skirted to the left, hoping to pop up out of its line of sight. But Tiger Lily stopped me before I could peek over the edge, latching onto my arm and drawing me flat to the earth with enough strength to drive the air from my lungs.

"What the hell was that for?" I whispered, glaring at the Neverlander.

"The smell. It's different."

I scented the air, trying to discern what had changed. Tiger Lily was right, there was an odd aroma on the wind. But it wasn't an unpleasant smell. On the contrary, the peculiar odor made my mouth water. There was a floral, earthy quality to it that reminded me of the produce section in a grocery store. Like sticking your nose up against the rind of a watermelon. I exchanged puzzled glances with Tiger Lily, shrugged, and began crawling forward the last few yards. What we found when we got to the top, however, explained the smell but left me with a whole host of new questions. Tiger Lily nudged me, eyes so wide with surprise that the skull over-laying her face went from terrifying to comical.

"What is this doing here?" she whispered.

"I...have no idea."

And so the two of us turned back, our bodies pressed flat against the earth, and continued staring at what could only be described as a garden. Except, of course, it was unlike any garden I'd ever seen; fruit trees as tall as sycamores had been planted in neat rows, their branches laden with every-thing from volleyball-sized apples to basketball-sized oranges. Between the trees, asparagus rose out of the ground like corn stalks, each easily as tall as a man. Pumpkins big enough to carry princesses to balls sat below dozens of cucumbers that could have doubled as billy clubs. Broccoli rose out of the ground like Bonsai trees. Ripe strawberries that reminded me of human hearts spilled out from their planters, left to dangle in the wind.

And of course, perhaps even more eye-catching, were the giants themselves; there were at least six of them from what I could tell, each remarkably well-formed and proportional from the tops of their heads to the bottoms of their feet. And I knew that for a fact because each of them milled about the garden naked as the day they were born, or were hatched, or were molded from sea foam and spit. In any case, it took me a minute or two to look past their nudity and realize that each of the approximately ten-feet-tall Leastrogynians wielded a gardening utensil of some sort. Were they all here cultivating their crops in the middle of the night, in the freaking dark, for a reason? Unfortunately, I didn't have time to solve that mystery; I felt a presence emerge from behind a moment before I heard the all-too-familiar cadence of a masculine chuckle.

As one, Tiger Lily and I rolled to our backs, only to find an obscenely large, remarkably well-endowed giant looming over us, his beefy arms folded across a hairy, barrel-like chest. Amusement glinted in his eyes, and a toothy smile appeared within the maw of his bushy beard as he spread those arms wide.

"Well, well, looks like we've found some rats in our garden."

$\mathcal{T}$iger Lily and I, operating purely on instinct, made to break away in two opposite directions only to be brought up short by two more nude Laestrygonians appearing from each side of the hill. Both female, this time. It seemed we'd walked right into an ambush—with extra emphasis on the bush. But how the hell had they known we were coming? Had they spotted us earlier and waited to spring their trap, or had we given ourselves away when we'd left the forest for the hillside? Sadly, I knew it didn't matter; our only priority right now was to make a break for it and pray we could outrun the bare-skinned bastards.

I whirled, hoping to see Tiger Lily doing the same, but instead saw that she'd been caught in a net fashioned from vines tossed by one of the gardeners; she struggled, using that dagger of hers to try and slice her way out, but the giants were closing in too fast. Another net appeared in the periphery of my vision, arcing towards me, but I was able to avoid it by diving headlong to my right. I scrambled back to my feet, trying to think past my throbbing pulse, to predict where the next strike would come from.

I felt the hairs on the back of my neck rise. Behind me. I ducked and rolled just in time to see a pair of tanned, finely muscled arms sweep the air where my upper body had been; the giantess who'd cut off my escape route must have closed the distance—at least a dozen yards—while I'd been focused on Tiger Lily, apparently hoping to snatch me up from behind. Which meant she was fast, maybe even as fast as I was.

The Laestrygonian recovered quickly, laughing as she lunged for me a second time. She moved well, her reflexes far quicker than I would have imagined given her size and weight. Weren't there supposed to be laws against that? Like, you know, mass and acceleration and all that Newtonian shit? Fortunately, she wasn't the only one whose abilities defied reason; I danced out of reach using my own improbable speed, arms pinwheeling to keep from tumbling backwards down the slope.

Unfortunately, it seemed that not only had the laws of physics betrayed me, but time was no longer on my side, either; two of the gardeners came for me, charging from both sides with their arms thrown wide as if planning to tackle me. Had they been my height, they'd likely have gone for my legs. But as it was, to evade them all I had to do was crouch. The two giants collided with one another and careened past, rolling down the hillside in a jumble of naked limbs. Sadly, the momentary victory was short lived; the giantess, clearly more agile than the third-string linebackers had been, lunged for me once more.

Except this time she caught me, crushing me to her ample chest with a cry of triumph. I struggled, of course, but found it difficult to breathe, let alone escape. It wasn't simply her strength, but my lack of leverage; she held me a foot off the ground, which meant no matter how hard I kicked and screamed, I was well and truly stuck. Damn it all. After I'd gone and warned everyone to stay out of trouble, after preaching caution at all costs, I'd gone and gotten myself and Tiger Lily captured. All because I'd been too damn confident, because I'd underestimated our enemies.

"You dodged well, little one," the giantess said as she adjusted her grip, raising me to eye level. I took the opportunity to take in a deep breath, fighting back the tunnel vision that had been slowly creeping in. For a moment, she and I looked at one another eye-to-eye. She was an arresting creature, big-boned and broad-featured enough to be considered borderline masculine—the bulge of her cheeks a little sharper, the cut of her jaw a little squarer than most women could pull off. Still, it was an attractive face.

It was a shame I had to break it.

I reared back and fired my forehead into the Laestrygonian's face with all the force I could muster. Given the angle and my lack of mobility, it wasn't enough to knock her out, but it was enough to loosen her grip; I broke free as she stumbled back, clutching at the right side of her face. My own head pounded from the blow, but my blood was up, my adrenaline pumping too hard for me to care. In that instance, my thoughts turned animalistic, primitive. Tiger Lily. Escape. Those were the only two things I cared about, the only goals that mattered. I took a step back, preparing to launch myself past the giantess, tear the net off Tiger Lily, and run for all I was worth.

Except my heel met nothing but empty air.

I cried out in frustration and shock as I fell backwards, having completely forgotten how close to the edge I'd been only moments before. This was it. Once I tumbled down the hillside, the giants could collect me at their leisure. Hell, given their speed, they might even be able to catch me at the bottom. I threw out one hand in what felt like slow motion, watching the summit disappear, replaced by the night sky. I pinched my eyes shut and hit the ground.

Hard.

For a moment, all I could do was lay there, the breath driven from my lungs. But, when I realized I wasn't rolling downhill, I opened my eyes. The night sky had changed, the stars swiveling to form altogether different patterns. I got to my feet, slowly, my head still pounding from using it as a weapon, only to find myself standing but a dozen feet away from the thrashing Tiger Lily, my body hidden amidst the shadows that lay outside the torchlight held by the two kneeling giants who held her down. I must have made a noise of some sort—likely of surprise—because her two guards immediately wheeled towards me, their faces slack.

We stared at each other like that for at least three heartbeats before all hell broke loose; the giantess yelled that they still hadn't found my body at the base of the hill, followed by a series of other shouts declaring the same. Which meant they had no idea I'd ended up here, or how. Not that I could blame them—I hadn't the faintest notion how I'd done it, either. One of the guards released Tiger Lily and turned towards me with his arms held wide as if to gather me in a hug, while the other prepared to shout.

But neither ever got the chance.

Tiger Lily, currently held by only one of the giants, contorted herself to bring her dagger across her captor's hand even as I launched myself at the nearest assailant, firing off a flying punch that connected with the big bastard's jaw. He fell like a stone. The other opened his mouth to wail, clutching his bleeding appendage, but Tiger Lily was already behind him, pressing the tip of her dagger against the soft flesh of his throat. Though little more than a needle by comparison, I knew that Tiger Lily could pierce the giant's carotid artery, knew that the Laestrygonian would bleed out in a matter of minutes.

"Quiet!" she hissed.

The giant shut his mouth, though that didn't put a stop to his pitiful whimpers.

"How did you know we were coming?" she asked.

The giant gasped but didn't respond.

"Tiger Lily, we need to go," I insisted. As much as I wanted answers, there was simply no time; once they decided to stop searching and return to the summit, we'd be nearly as worse off as we were before. From where I stood, it seemed a hell of a lot better to retreat with no answers than to get caught.

"Fine. Should I kill this one, then?" Tiger Lily growled.

But before I could answer, as if on cue, the giant fainted. Tiger Lily, unable to hold up his weight, let him collapse face first. The Neverlander sheathed her dagger, shaking her head in disgust.

"This was no warrior."

I felt inclined to agree. When I took everything into account, it struck me that these Laestrygonians were not only incompetent fighters, but rather inept ambushers, as well. Had they come at us as one, in a coordinated effort, we'd never have stood a chance. Instead, they'd employed nets and—when that didn't work—chased me around the hilltop as if we were playing tag. Still, there was no point putting their resolve to the test. If we were going to flee, now was our chance.

I gestured for Tiger Lily to follow, and together we hustled down the opposing slope, staying as low as we could afford to without sacrificing speed until at last we found cover among the bushes of a nearby valley. There, we paused to catch our breath. I listened for the tell-tale shouts, expecting Tiger Lily's captors to be found at any moment. But there were none. Instead, the search for me seemed to have spread; I heard cries echo back and forth from the other side of the hill as torches were lit.

"It looks like we're in the clear," I whispered. "Let's get back to the ship."

"They'll come looking for us. Not tonight, perhaps, but by morning."

"Then we'd best not be there when they show up."

"Please, we cannot leave the ship behind," Tiger Lily insisted, her expression tortured. "It's all we have left to remember our home by. All James has left to remember where he comes from."

I sighed, sensing the underlying context of what Tiger Lily was saying: without the *Jolly Roger*, the Neverlanders might help me, but they'd never forgive themselves for leaving the ship. In time, they'd come to resent me, too. And I wouldn't blame them. The homes we carve out for ourselves in life are often even more precious than those we are born into—the difference between something earned and something given.

"We'll see what the others have to say," I replied, mentally crossing my fingers. "Maybe they'll have found a better solution, one that gets us *and* the ship off the island."

Tiger Lily's hand on my shoulder surprised me. For a moment, I thought we were about to have a little heart-to-heart, but then I realized her eyes were locked a few inches above my own. She examined the skin above my right eyebrow, squinting.

"You're bleeding."

"Probably from headbuttin' the giantess," I replied. "Don't worry, I'll live."

"If it gets worse, they may be able to track us."

Damn, I hadn't thought of that. Realizing Tiger Lily was right, I tacitly agreed that it would be foolish to keep running until she'd bandaged my wound. The Neverlander reached into the lining of her animal hides, retrieving a small leather pouch full of an ointment that smelled of peppermint. She dabbed its contents onto my forehead, murmuring words in a language I didn't recognize. The tincture was cool against my skin, then hot.

"What is this stuff?"

"Pixie lactation. Don't worry, it will be healed by morning," she said. Then, with almost deliberate slowness, she slipped each of her fingers—still coated in the gunk she'd smeared across my wound—into her mouth, sucking them clean one at a time. Once finished, she turned to me as if she'd done nothing out of the ordinary. "There is still something I don't understand, aside from how they knew we were coming."

"And what's that?" I asked, choosing to ignore the hygienic implications of what she'd just done, although I did resolve to wash my face as soon as inhumanly possible. Oh, and never to drink after the Neverlander.

That's how you get cooties.

SHAYNE SILVERS & CAMERON O'CONNELL

"How did you sneak up behind them?" Tiger Lily asked.

It was a good question, and one I'd given thought to ever since I found myself on the opposite side of the hilltop—lingering in the back of my mind like a subconscious tickle. How had I done it? Was it even me? Or had someone else plucked me from midair and deposited me behind enemy lines? The truth, unfortunately, was even less pleasant to say out loud than it was to think.

"I really have no idea."

$\mathcal{T}$iger Lily and I returned early, able to make it back well before sunrise at a brisk trot that seemed to tire her more than me; I was coated in a light sheen of perspiration for my trouble, while Tiger Lily seemed somehow diminished, the bones of her face more prominent beneath her morbid mask, her eyes sunken. Together, we sat huddled against a large boulder that let us keep an eye out for the others while also keeping us relatively hidden, just in case the Laestrygonians did somehow manage to track us from the garden to the coast. Unfortunately, I put our chances of remaining undetected somewhere between slim and none. At best, I figured we had the remainder of the night and maybe a few hours of the morning before they searched for us in earnest, scouring the island's shores for signs of life other than their own.

Then again, it was entirely possible I was simply being pessimistic. After we'd flipped their ambush and taken out two of their own, they'd be foolish to come after us without knowing the full extent of our capabilities. Indeed, they might not hunt us down at all if they thought we were a viable threat. Also, there was still the question of their vegetable garden and all its gargantuan splendor. What sort of cannibals went around growing carrots the size of baguettes?

"It's James!" Tiger Lily cried, leaping from the shelter of our rock and sprinting like a demon in the dim light of dawn towards the two figures who hobbled towards us. I rose but didn't chase after the Neverlander, opting instead to scan the uneven terrain for signs of Narcissus and Tinker-bell. I'd expected both to be back hours ago. But the horizon was empty—nothing but a pale purple blush backlighting motionless silhouettes.

Several minutes later, all three returned, the two Neverlanders cradling a limping Helen between them. As far as I could tell, there was no blood, no sign of an external injury. And yet she leaned heavily on both for support, wincing as if each step were causing considerable discomfort.

"Twisted my ankle," she explained once she was within earshot, voice laced with pain.

"Demigoddesses can twist their ankles?" I asked.

"She saved me," James added, helpfully. The Neverlander lowered Helen to sit, his hand loitering on her shoulder even as he sought out my face. "There was a pit, and I almost fell in, but Helen pushed me out of the way." There was something in his voice, a tone of admiration, even fondness, that I found disconcerting. Only several hours back the two had been at each other's throats over whether or not to leave the *Jolly Roger* behind. What had changed?

"It was dark," Helen insisted. "I saw it before he did, that's all. It was nothing."

"It wasn't nothing. If I'd have fallen, it would have been a lot worse than a twisted ankle." James rose, rolling his stiff shoulders and neck. "There were rocks at the bottom of the pit. Sharp, jagged ones."

"Sounds more like a trap to me," Tiger Lily said, voicing my own thoughts.

"Maybe. But it was a huge pit. Deeper than it had to be, and big enough to take twenty of us out, maybe more." James plopped down at Helen's side, letting the demigoddess lean on him for support, one arm coiled across her shoulders. A suspicion—something I should have considered but hadn't—flickered to life. Was it possible Helen had revealed her face to the boy? Intentionally or not, that could account for his suddenly smitten behavior. Of course, it was also feasible that the act of saving the young man's life had endeared her to him in a way that arguing he abandon his ship had not. Either way, I'd have to have a word with the young man in private, time permitting.

"Look, there," Tiger Lily urged, gesturing to a dim, thready glow headed this way—hardly visible against the backdrop of dawn. I almost let out a sigh of relief before I realized it was coming from the northeast, from the direction Tiger Lily and I had gone. Which made no sense.

"Is that Tinkerbell?" James asked, gawking at the weaving, strobing light.

This time it was I who took off; sensing something was amiss, I tracked the pixie's unsteady dips, her laconic flight pattern. By the time I reached her, she was in a tailspin. I lunged for her, cradling the pixie in the palms of my hands, and drew her close. She looked exhausted, her once bubblegum pink skin as pale as a hollyhock. But at least she bore no wounds that I could see. Unfortunately, I didn't have time to let her recover; Narcissus was still nowhere in sight, and the pixie's flight trajectory suggested she'd been coming from entirely the wrong direction.

"Tinkerbell," I said, speaking softly, my breath rustling her hair. "What happened?"

The pixie groaned, curling into the swell of my palm as though she'd fall asleep—something I simply couldn't allow. Though I felt like a real jerk for doing so, I shook the poor creature. But the motion, coupled with her fatigue, was apparently too much for her; the pixie puked. Fuschia glitter spilled all over my hands.

Heh. Nailed it.

"I'm sorry, Tinkerbell. But ye have to tell us what happened," I insisted. By this point, the others—even Helen with her limp—had joined us. I let them crowd around us, let them see that she was alright, if a bit debilitated. "Why were ye flyin' from the northeast and not the northwest? Where's Narcissus?"

"Caught." Tinkerbell moaned, wiping glitter off her chin. The pixie glared at me over her shoulder as if I'd done far worse than give her motion sickness. "The Manling you sent me with told them everything."

"Told who?" James asked.

"I don't know. They were naked. Big. Bigger even than you all are. The one who got me jumped so high." Tinkerbell shook her head. "I've never seen anything that couldn't fly get that high."

Tiger Lily and I exchanged meaningful glances. So, the Laestrygonians had captured Narcissus and Tinkerbell. Not good, not good at all. James caught us eyeing each other and demanded we tell them what we knew. Together, Tiger Lily and I explained what had happened on our end, though I left out a few details—like precisely how I'd managed to slip away and rescue Tiger Lily. Still, the simple fact that I'd come back for the Neverlander seemed to mollify the young man. Even Tinkerbell seemed less resentful towards me, by the time we were done filling them in.

"They sent me to tell you to come," Tinkerbell said. "They sounded...excited."

I glanced at the others in alarm—finding my own anxiety reflected in all faces but Helen's— until a prick of something sharp brought me back around with a hiss. I found Tinkerbell holding a sewing needle like a miniature sword, a bead of blood welling at the tip of my thumb. Guess I'd misread her change in mood.

"They don't want us," she insisted. "Just you."

"Why just me?"

"Because they want your help. They described you. They said you'd done something impossible and that you had to come."

I shook my head, trying to comprehend what on earth the man-eating giants would want from me. What had they seen me do? Sure, I'd managed to evade their clutches and eventually escape from right under their noses, but how could something like that help them? No, the far more likely scenario, unfortunately, was that this was a trap of some sort. Perhaps the cannibals simply wanted a scrumptious pairing, something that would appeal to the true connoisseurs among them. I doubted Narcissus alone would satisfy anyone's palate; the Greek was so full of himself I doubted he'd fill anyone else.

"Did they say what they wanted help with?" James asked.

"I didn't ask," Tinkerbell replied, weakly. "They kept me in a box. But I could hear them talking. Asking the Manling questions."

"Surprised they didn't eat him, instead," Tiger Lily said in a way that made me wonder whether she'd have been bothered if they had. Tinkerbell's head shot up in what I would have described as a twitch at that, except the motion proved far too much for her and ended with her convulsing in my hands as another wave of glitter spewed from her mouth. The stuff was quickly getting everywhere, twinkling obnoxiously whenever I moved.

I was no longer amused.

"They told me," Tinkerbell managed, her voice thready and pained, "to tell you that they won't eat him. They won't eat any of us. They made me repeat it over and over until I got it right."

"Made ye repeat what?" I asked, utterly baffled by the news.

"Vegetarians. They called themselves 'vegetarians'."

he decision to take the Laestrygonians up on their offer was easy to make; no matter how much Narcissus got on my nerves, I wasn't about to leave him stranded. It'd been my plan, which meant it was my responsibility to ensure his safe return. Surprisingly, I hadn't had to fight Helen on staying behind with Tiger Lily and Tinkerbell; she'd let James fuss over her before wishing us good luck. James had clearly preferred to stay behind as well, but I wasn't eager to let the young man spend any more time with Helen of Troy. Her face might have launched a thousand ships, but I wasn't sure I wanted her floating his boat.

"How far is it?" James asked, stifling a yawn.

I frowned, only just realizing we'd all been awake for at least twenty-four hours. Ordinarily, fatigue alone would have clued me in, but for some reason, I felt as well-rested as ever. In fact, even the pangs of hunger I'd felt earlier had faded, my thirst no longer clawing at my throat. Adrenaline, maybe? The aftermath of surviving the Laestrygonian assault? I couldn't be sure.

I considered James' question, measuring the distance to the garden in my mind. Images of perfectly sculpted flesh flashed in quick succession against my will, prompted by the brief reflection. Was it true, I wondered? Were the Laestrygonians really vegetarians? Did that make them...Vegiants?

"To the garden Tiger Lily and I saw? A couple hours at this pace. Less, if ye t'ink ye can run."

"I can run." James shook himself, craning his neck back and forth. "But are you sure you'll be able to keep up in those?"

I glanced down at my muck-covered pirate boots. Ordinarily, he might have had a point. But, with my increased durability and reflexes, I hadn't even paused to consider my footwear; twisting my ankle was about as likely as snapping my thigh bone in two. Which, frankly, was what bothered me most about Helen's injury. Shouldn't a demigoddess be more durable than that?

"No, that's alright. You'll have trouble keepin' pace with me as it is," I replied, shrugging.

"Is that so?" James asked, eyes glinting with amusement. "Race you!"

The Neverlander took off at a brisk clip, one hand pinning his scabbarded sword in place to keep it from lurching about. I watched the young man for a moment, admiring his long gait; though not yet fully grown and still gangly, James moved remarkably well. In time, and given the right stimuli, he'd be what I'd call athletic. Which, if I'd been your average, ordinary woman, meant I'd probably have struggled to beat him in a race of any sort. As it was, however, he might as well have been crawling. I took off at a sprint, tearing gouges into the earth with every stride, pumping my arms so fast my jacket squealed from the friction.

I blew past the Neverlander in seconds.

His cry of surprise caught up to me as I headed for the nearest copse of trees and the shade they offered. I'd barely worked up a sweat, my breathing even, my muscles fresh. James reached me nearly two minutes later, huffing, his shirt covered in a mantle of sweat, his hair wild and windswept. The young man bent over, chest heaving so hard I thought he might keel over. Then I realized he was laughing—or at least trying to.

"Stand up and put your hands on your head," I insisted. "Let the oxygen flow. It'll help. Oh, and next time ye plan on challengin' someone to a race, make sure ye can win."

James straightened and took deep, shuddering breaths. His expression was pained and yet faintly amused as he clutched a stitch in his side, his other hand resting on the pommel of his sword. "Can everyone move as fast as you where you're from?"

"What d'ye mean 'where I'm from'?"

"You know. Home."

"Oh, right. Some can, I suppose, but not most," I said. "Boston has a few characters, but most of its citizens are ordinary, average humans. What we call 'Regulars'."

"Humans? You mean Manlings?"

"If ye like."

"But, I thought...I mean Helen said..." James drifted off.

"Ye thought what? What exactly did Helen say?"

"She said you were like Tiger Lily. Like Tinkerbell. That you were one of the Fae. She said that's how you were able to survive falling from Neverland."

"Did she, now?" I asked as I mulled that over. Why would Helen have told James I was a Faeling? It wasn't entirely inaccurate, but it certainly wasn't the whole truth, either. Did she truly have no idea what I was, or had she lumped me in with James' companions for some other reason? Noting we were finally alone, I decided to press the issue. "James, did Helen show ye her face when ye were alone together?"

The young man's reaction was both immediate and telling; he flushed, his already red cheeks flaring bright scarlet. His grin, however, wasn't the least bit ashamed. "No, but I did see it. Her hood slipped when she saved me," he added, hurriedly. "You've seen her too, right? Isn't she just so..." James seemed to grope for the right word. "So..."

"James," I said, choosing my words carefully, "has it occurred to ye that it didn't fall the whole time we were in the cabin, gettin' tossed about?"

"What do you mean?"

"I'm just sayin', why would it have fallen when she was savin' ye and not on the ship?"

"I don't know," James admitted, scowling. "Maybe she...no..."

I patted his arm. "Don't worry about it. I'm sure it was an accident, like she said. She knows the effect her appearance has on people. I doubt she wanted ye to follow her around like her slave, or anythin' like that. I mean, why would she?"

I turned away and started jogging at a normal pace towards the garden and the city which, according to Tinkerbell, lay beyond it. If I felt any guilt about implanting the idea that Helen was manipulating James, I kept it to myself; what I'd done just now was perhaps just as bad, but until I knew what Helen's agenda was, I couldn't risk the young man getting blindsided by her scheming. At least this way he'd have a chance to reflect on his own feelings. Still, I had to wait several minutes before I heard James come puffing up behind me.

"Let's hurry up and see what these Vegiants want!" I called back over my shoulder.

James said nothing.

wo of the Laestrygonians met us as we surmounted the hill upon which the garden sat. The gargantuan fruits and vegetables gleamed in the bright morning light, though it was a testament to James' rumbling stomach that he deigned to notice them at all; the two giants were female, their assets on full display. The one on the left sported a sizeable bruise which marred her otherwise lovely face. Had to be the one I'd head-butted. I thrust my arm out to warn James, halting the two of us on the edge of the garden, anticipating another tussel—or at the very least a standoff. But, to my surprise, the giantess I'd assaulted merely grinned, revealing a pretty but otherwise ordinary smile free of fangs or filed teeth. Indeed, were she not nearly ten feet tall and built like a brickhouse, I'd have said Tiger Lily looked far more capable of eating someone than she did.

The giantess waved for us to follow and set off with her companion through the garden, taking a stone-lined path I hadn't spotted in the moon-light. James and I fell in behind them, though we maintained our distance, prepared for an ambush. I'd already discussed the possibility with him; he'd been decidedly reserved since I poked at his feelings for Helen but had agreed to follow my lead when and if the time came to run or fight.

The city that lay beyond the hillside spread out along a massive cliff overlooking the coast, its cragged surface littered with white marble dwellings topped with red clay roofs which appeared to catch fire in the light. It was a sprawling metropolis, complete with a stunning temple which dominated the cliff's edge, looming over the rest of the city like a sentinel. And yet, the actual number of residents seemed relatively few; I spotted only a couple dozen milling about, their nudity evident but far less objectionable from so far away. Most seemed to be moving to and from the outskirts of town where clouds of dust spewed into the air to the tune of hammers falling. Even from this far out, I could tell there had been some damage; there was a broken aspect to the city's edges which spoke of a natural disaster of some sort.

The giantess turned to me, still smiling, and bowed at the waist, her hands steepled together between her breasts. "Peace be with you, mortals."

I ogled the giantess for a long moment before responding with a half-hearted greeting of my own. James followed suit, even going so far as to bow as well, mimicking her. We eyed each other, likely both wondering different versions of the same thing: what the hell was going on?

"We told the chickie we only needed your help," the giantess said as she rose, her voice deeper than you'd expect from a woman, more rumbly. "Who's the meat?"

"Ye mean him?" I asked, jerking a thumb at James. "He's the Captain of the ship that got me here. He thought it best he come along to see what you've done with a member of his crew."

James twitched but managed not to betray my half-truth in front of our escorts—assuming that's what they were. Honestly, I had no idea what any of our roles were at this point; the Laestrygonians had captured Narcissus, attempted to capture Tiger Lily and I, and sent a beleaguered Tinkerbell as their envoy—and yet it seemed they weren't the least bit interested in eating us.

"Bit young for a sailor, isn't he?" the giantess asked, squinting. "But I guess I can dig it. I could never really tell with you mortals, anyway. You all look like ankle biters, to us."

"And how old are you?" James asked.

"Older than the trees. Younger than the stones."

"Sounds like something Tiger Lily would say," James muttered.

"So," I interjected, deciding I'd had enough of the idle small talk, "what is it ye want with me?"

The giantess ran a hand through her hair, mussing it as though she hadn't given any thought to that question. "You know, I never asked." She turned to her companion, who appeared equally uncertain, then giggled. "Well, I guess we'll all have to find out together. Let's book."

"Wait, ye really don't know?"

"Don't flip your wig, sister. I like to hang loose, dig?"

James shot me a bewildered look, but all I could do was shake my head.

"So who would know?" I asked.

"Our Queen. She's over there." The giantess gestured with one massive finger towards the damaged section of the city. The dust had begun to billow skyward, hovering over the city like a rain cloud. "Stay close. Oh, and don't bug out if anyone stares. Most of us haven't seen a mortal in like forever." She cringed suddenly, studying our seemingly frail, diminutive forms, then her own surprisingly dainty—albeit still massive—feet. "And hey, be careful when you're truckin', alright? Wouldn't want any of us stepping on you by accident. Bad for karma, stepping on cats."

Our two escorts turned and began loafing down the side of the hill towards the city, allowing James and I to trail after them should we wish it. I eyed the city, wary of its tight confines and its potentially hostile population; no matter how bizarrely chill our escorts behaved, I couldn't forget that they'd tried to capture Tiger Lily and me the night before. Unfortunately, there was nothing we could objectively do about it. We had no leverage, nothing we could use to free Narcissus and escape unscathed, which meant it was up to the two of us to sort this whole mess out. I turned to say as much to James, but the Neverlander spoke first.

"They aren't big enough to step on us, are they?"

"I doubt it, but I wouldn't test the theory, if I were ye."

James sighed, swiping idly at an errant lock of hair. The Neverlander was drenched in sweat from our run, but his eyes were bright, the wheels in his head churning. "Are you sure this is a good idea?"

"Not really," I admitted.

"Then why are we following them?"

"Why d'ye t'ink?"

James thought about it, then shrugged and shook his head. "I'd say for Narcissus' sake, but he obviously set you and Tiger Lily up to get caught. Plus, I can tell you don't like him. Honestly, apart from Helen and Narcissus himself, I don't think anyone likes him."

"Oh, Narcissus has his fair share of friends," I said, thinking back to the first time I'd met the Greek on his cruise ship. "Anyway, he did me a favor once. I owe him for that." I sighed. "You're right, though. I don't like him. But I can trust Narcissus to do whatever serves his own best interests. In that sense, he's extremely dependable. Which is more than I can say for most."

"And you aren't sure if you can depend on us, is that it? Tiger Lily, Tinkerbell, and me?"

"I don't know," I answered, honestly, hoping my answer would soothe the hurt lingering beneath the Neverlander's claim. "Me memories of ye lot are too jumbled. Tinkerbell aimed to kill me when I saw her last, Tiger Lily was on the warpath, and ye were a boy living in Peter's house, in his shadow, with no idea who your father was. I'm still gettin' to know ye, that's all."

"I knew who my father was," James said after a moment of silence. "Back then, I knew."

That was news to me.

"Since when?"

"Hook came to visit, once. I think he was looking for Peter, planning to confront him for the last time. I'm not sure. It was before you showed up. Hook took one look at me and left. When I asked my mother about him, she said he was an old friend of Peter's. But she was strange after that." James fidgeted with the sword at his hip. "I knew Peter wasn't my real father. We were too different. He was still a kid himself when I was growing up. Always wanted to play, even when I didn't. The man, the father he became after Hook left Neverland, after you left, was better. He really tried to understand me, and I loved him for it."

I reached out to squeeze his shoulder, but James slipped away and began descending the hillside. Clearly, he had no desire to be comforted. Frankly, I could understand; I kept everyone at arm's length, if I could help it. "To be clear, it's not an issue of trust with the three of ye," I said as I drew up alongside him. "We're all still strangers to each other, that's all."

"Is that why you haven't told us everything?"

"What d'ye mean?"

James flicked his eyes to me, then away. "You told us you're chasing someone. An old friend. And that to find out where he's going, you needed Helen and Narcissus. You needed their map and their experience."

"Aye, that's pretty much the gist of it."

"So how do we fit in? Why get us to help you? Was it only because we had a ship? If so, surely you knew others you could ask. Other Fae or Manlings you could depend on." James shook his head vehemently. "Why put my friends in danger?"

The words were bitter, accusatory. I realized in that moment that James hadn't wanted any of this. That—had I not technically saved Neverland and fulfilled the conditions promised by the time-traveller—he and his two companions would even now be headed back to his sister and the remnants of the Lost People. Honor, not desire, had governed his actions thus far. And now I—by questioning his dependability—had inadvertently questioned his honor.

"You're right," I admitted. "It wasn't fair of me to ask ye to come."

James didn't stop walking, but the tension in his shoulders lessened.

"I'd planned to ask your fathers, originally. Hook and Peter Pan, two of the fiercest adversaries I'd ever met...it was those two I hoped to do this with. I thought if I could get 'em to work together, to sail with me, that we'd have little trouble findin' Ryan and puttin' a stop to whatever he's plannin'. But, when I found out they were dead, I latched onto ye and your friends like ye were a lifeline. It wasn't right for me to do that. I see that, now."

When James looked at me, there was a surprising amount of resolve in his face. Not sadness. Not anger. Just an iron-clad determination visible in the bunching of his jaw and tightness around the eyes. "You told her I was the Captain. Why?"

"Because that's what ye are." I met his gaze evenly. "James, your people already know it. Tinkerbell and Tiger Lily look at ye like you're their savior, because that's what ye are to 'em. Helen saw it, too. Which is why she's tryin' to get close to ye, to gain your affections." I held up a hand to his protests. "I could be wrong. It's just what I feel is true."

"But...why would she bother with me? Why not you?"

Fortunately, I'd already considered that. "I t'ink she has been, in her own way. She volunteered to go with me to speak to Typhon. She's counseled me, given me unsolicited advice, even supported me when she thought I was the frontrunner to become Captain. But me guess is at some point last night she finally realized she's been courtin' the wrong person, all along."

"What do you mean?"

"She's lookin' for a child who belonged to two worlds. She thought that meant me because she knows I've traveled between realms. But she missed the obvious. What was it the time-traveller called ye when he claimed I'd come to save Neverland, d'ye remember?"

"Captain Shake Spear."

"Shakespeare," I corrected. "One word."

"What about it?"

"What are you two doing up there lip flappin'? Come on, if you snooze, you lose!" The giantess and her companion waited at the base of the hill, watching us while performing intricate and altogether cringeworthy stretches. I did my best to ignore them.

"Listen," I said, focusing all my attention on James for just a moment longer, "I'd say Helen was a little slow on the uptick, is all. A mortal child who belongs to two worlds, who will one day be called 'Captain' by his peers...sound like anyone ye know?" I left James to sort that out as I hurried to join the Vegiants, confident he'd reach the same conclusion I had. "We're comin'!" I called down.

Here's hoping we wouldn't regret it.

29

The Laestrygonians split up as we entered the city, leaving us with just the one who'd snatched me up only hours before. She showcased the city as we wove our way through its wide thoroughfares and shaded alleys, pointing out signs of the city's prosperity as we went, as though we'd signed up for a tour. To be fair, there was a lot to admire; even disregarding its naked inhabitants, James and I found plenty to ogle. The whole city seemed to bask in the sunlight, the white marble so bright it glared, the clay pots in the windowsills painted iridescent shades of green and blue, the walls coated in vibrant, flower-laden trellises. Indeed, though we passed all manner of dwellings, we never once caught the faintest whiff of the foul stenches that so often plagued this sort of metropolis; had I shut my eyes, I'd have said we were standing in the middle of a cultivated garden, surrounded by trees and flowers. Honestly, I found the duality disconcerting. Cities were supposed to stink. Why else would anyone move to the suburbs?

"Telepylus, that's what we call this place. It's a gas, for the most part," the giantess was saying, basking in the glory of the city, arms thrown wide. To me, she looked like she was posing for a lead role on The Buff and the Beautiful. She craned her neck. "Oh, thank Gaia. We're nearly there."

Gaia. The name struck a chord. That was the namesake of the temple we'd passed before encountering Typhon. The name given to the mother of the first batch of Titans, if memory served. The deity who personified earth —indeed, Mother Earth herself. Did that mean the Laestrygonians worshipped the Mother of Titans? Or was it her aspect they revered?

"So, is that why ye stopped eatin' meat? For her sake?" I asked.

"What? Oh, no way Jose." The giantess actually looked embarrassed for a moment, her broad cheeks flushed. "That happened after our island was pulled into this realm. We weren't privy to the details. But, after that, sailors stopped coming to our island...." she drifted off. "We chowed down on the local game, first. But that hardly did the trick, dig? Anyway, then the mortals started complaining. So we ate them, too. Eventually, there was a war between us as brother and sister tried to...well...you know."

"Cut each other up and have a barbecue," I suggested, helpfully.

"What's a barbecue?"

I waved that away. "What happened, then?"

"A mortal arrived. Little, like you. At first, our king planned to make a meal out of him. But the mortal used some far out magic to escape. Eventually, he convinced us that there was another way, a more harmonious way, to live. He showed us how to make things grow, how to live off what Gaia provides. It took time, but we've become the flower children he always claimed we could be."

Flower children? Really? Part of me wanted to stop the conversation right then and there and demand someone explain what was going on here. Had we seriously stumbled on some sort of hippie commune in the middle of the Titan realm?

"I thought you said we were meeting a Queen? What happened to your King?" James asked before I could voice my own concerns.

"Oh, right," she replied, cheeks burning even redder this time. "King Antiphates wasn't interested in seeking enlightenment. He wasn't fond of the idea of discovering inner peace. Or outer peace, really. Anyway, we decided to remove his chakras and send his negativity out to the sea."

"His what?" James asked.

"They cut him up and tossed his body to the sharks," I whispered.

"Anyway, that's all behind us, now. We've accepted our place in the universe as Gaia's chosen since then. We are now the harvesters of the earth. We don't even care who shags whom, anymore. That's how hip we are." She giggled and shot a glance back at James and me, her eyes burning with a little something more than altruism and goodwill. "Say, have either of you ever made it with a giant?"

"Made it?" James asked.

The Laestrygonian flashed me an eloquent look.

"Ye still haven't told us what any of this has to do with us," I said, choosing to ignore her overture and focus on the task at hand before James got sucked into a conversation he might never survive. As the old adage said: if you had to ask, you probably didn't want to know. No sense traumatizing the poor Neverlander. "Or what ye plan to do with our crew member," I added.

"I told you, that's Queen Adonia's bag."

Fortunately, it seemed we didn't have long to wait to find out what Queen Adonia had to say on the matter; she came into view only a few moments later as we finally cleared the urban sprawl, stepping out among the remains of what appeared to be a devastated section of the city—decimated renditions of the marvelous architecture we'd been privy to up to this point— shattered as though they'd been hit by a hurricane.

The queen, pale-skinned and fair-haired, stood among the rubble. Unlike the vast majority of her subjects, she was not entirely nude but more...tastefully decorated. She wore a laurel wreath upon her head, her arms and legs encircled by golden bracelets, her breasts and hips hidden behind seashells woven together by silken threads. Still, even without the adornment, I'd have recognized her; standing perhaps a foot taller than our escort, she displayed the regal bearing that only true sovereigns ever seemed to manage. Provided they aren't ugly, of course. Ugly royals are still ugly.

"That's it, put it there!" she cried, waving one gilded arm from the far end of the site to the other. Four male giants moved as one to accommodate her. A pillar as long and thick as a mast lay mounted across their backs. Each of the Laestrygonians were coated in enough white dust and moved with such eerie grace that it nearly took away the novelty of seeing four naked males carrying a phallic symbol across a courtyard at the behest of a woman in charge.

Nearly.

"My Queen!"

Queen Adonia spun around, saw us, and held up a hand for us to wait. "Put it up next to the others, then go report to Obelius!" she instructed.

The Laestrygonian she gestured towards stood about a dozen yards away, helping a crew salvage what they could from a building that appeared to have been shorn in half. He was as large as she was, if I had to guess, but twice as thick; his muscles strained with the effort of holding up an entire wall as we watched, his skin ripe with bulges. It took me a moment, but I recognized him as the first giant who'd snuck up on Tiger Lily and I.

The workers nodded and wandered off without so much as a word, their grunts lost amidst the general din of construction. A column like the one they'd carried rose to our right, hoisted by a series of ropes and pulleys. Indeed, the general level of engineering seemed not so different from what you might expect to see in a developing nation; there weren't any jackhammers or power drills, but there were plenty of tools I recognized. Still, this whole section of the city seemed to have sustained a catastrophic amount of damage—far more than what simple tools could fix in any sort of reasonable time frame.

"Earthquake?" I asked, once the queen was in earshot. I gestured vaguely at the mess, unsure what else to make of it. A hurricane would have meant water damage and would have left behind things like trees and rocks in its wake. But there was nothing like that here.

"What, this?" The queen made a disgusted noise in the back of her throat and bade us to follow her to the edge of the worksite, where we might hear her better. Her voice was softer than our escort's, but far sterner; there was none of the playfulness in this one. "No, Polyphemus is certainly a walking disaster, but not a natural one."

"I'm sorry," I said, "Poly what now?"

"Polyphemus. A Cyclops. A son of Poseidon, the god of the sea who usurped Lord Oceanus." Queen Adonia gave me a funny look, as though I'd said something inexplicably dumb, or at least socially reprehensible. "The dumb brute should never have been relocated with the rest of us, but that's what happens when you let a bunch of glorified bureaucrats handle—"

"My Queen..." our escort interrupted, her tone clearly urging a little restraint.

"Oh, give it a rest, Ismene. The Olympians were to blame for this, and we all know it. Giving us our own realm like we wanted their charity, then leaving us to rot. Thank Gaia for the Stranger, or we'd have devoured each other and there'd be nothing left."

"For real, but I still wish you wouldn't sweat it." Ismene coughed into her hand. "My Queen."

Adonia rolled her eyes. "You'll have to forgive my daughter. She's really bought into this whole clean living, clean eating lifestyle we've adopted. She prefers not to dwell on the past."

"Live in the now, because the present is a present, you dig?"

"Yes, like that," Adonia said, rolling her eyes. "Meanwhile, I wish I still had some meat in my diet." The queen patted her taut stomach with a discontented sigh, drawing my attention to her body in a way it hadn't before. She, like Ismene and so many of their race, seemed almost improbably fit. To be honest, I had to admit it was a nice change; in my experience, attractive giants were harder and harder to come by these days.

"Wait," I said, holding up a hand as my brain finally caught up to the full content of our conversation, "d'ye say a Cyclops did all this?"

"That is exactly what I said," Adonia replied. "The bastard sneaks onto our island once every couple months to take one or more of us, usually while they're sleeping. He never subscribed to the Stranger's teachings, though this is the first time he's actually attacked us. Obelius and a few others were able to chase him off, thank Gaia, or the damage would be far worse."

I glanced back and forth between the mother and daughter as I tried to process what they'd insinuated. Polyphemus, a one-eyed Cyclops, had been sneaking onto the island of man-eating—excuse me, formerly man-eating—cannibals to snatch and, in turn, devour them. Until, apparently, he'd changed tactics and leveled a whole city block. Talk about a vicious cycle. Good thing Charles Darwin had stumbled on Galapagos and not this island, or he'd have written an altogether different theory of evolution.

On the Origin of Sustenance by Means of Unnatural Selection.

Yikes.

"Alright, so what is it ye want from me, then?" I asked, at last. "Your daughter couldn't tell me what this is all about."

"I thought that would be obvious," Adonia replied. "I want you to kill Polyphemus, of course."

$\mathcal{W}$e retired as a group from the ravaged edges of the city to the temple overlooking the sea. The air was crisper this high up, briny and salt-laden. Birds called to each other from the gardens that lay outside the temple grounds, audible just above the purr of the surf below. A breeze drifted across my skin, light as gossamer.

It really was a beautiful day to talk about murder.

"Killing him would be ideal, but blinding Polyphemus would suffice," Adonia said as we left the outdoors for the cool recesses of the temple proper. Terrifically ornate columns stood in rows a hundred feet high on our left, casting long shadows across the pool that ran the length of the temple. Adonia reached out to brush her fingers along each as we passed, muttering a blessing as she went. "Ismene and Obelius tell me you managed to evade our welcome party," she continued. "By magical means, to hear Ismene tell it."

"She was there one second and gone the next," Ismene said, grinning widely. "We booked it to the edge, but there was no one there. No one at the base of the hill, either. She totally bearded us."

"And then, of course, there were the gardeners you attacked," Adonia added, not the least bit fazed by her daughter's rampant and occasionally erroneous use of 60's slang. "They say you appeared out of nowhere, despite the fact that they'd thoroughly checked the area when they captured your companion." The queen's gaze drifted over to James. "Not this one, though, I think. You don't seem the type to threaten to slit someone's throat."

"Tiger Lily?" James asked me.

I nodded, then shrugged as if to say "what else was she supposed to do?" Truthfully, I still wasn't sure whether or not I'd have let her kill the gardener who'd fainted. In hindsight, I was really glad she hadn't; I doubted we'd have received this level of hospitality if we'd have cut one of their people's throats. Hell, they might even have done the same to Narcissus as punishment.

And, speaking of Narcissus...

"Quinn! And James!" the Greek shouted, waving merrily from his perch —an alcove carved into the wall, its recesses layered in cushions of all shapes and sizes. A very nude Narcissus lounged across them, popped a grape the size of a walnut into his mouth, and grinned at us with one bulging cheek. "Do you like what I've done with the place?" he asked, gesturing to his little nook. "It was so drab before. Excellent builders, these giants, but their interior decorating could use some work. Thank the gods I came along."

"Is this mortal truly yours?" Adonia asked, eyeing Narcissus skeptically. James and I exchanged a look; neither of us were eager to claim the indolent bastard, but we'd come this far already. At last, I nodded.

"Unfortunately."

"Good. Please take him back."

I sniggered but didn't immediately agree; there were answers I needed to questions I'd yet to ask. Better to find out more about the role they wanted me to play before I agreed to help them. And besides, if I could use Narcissus' extremely grating personality to my advantage, I would gladly do so. It was about time our self-centered liability did something useful.

"First, can ye tell me why ye t'ink I have a chance of blindin' Polyphemus when ye lot can't even stop him from wreckin' half your city?"

"We gave you the skinny, already," Ismene insisted. "What you did was unreal. If you can do that again, you could sneak onto his island. You could beard that Clyde like Odysseus did."

The instant she mentioned Polyphemus and Odysseus in the same breath, I was able to recall the legend that linked the two—or at least part of it. From what I remembered, Odysseus and his men had ended up caught by Polyphemus, who'd eaten them two at a time for several days before

Odysseus got the Cyclops drunk, stabbed his eye out, and escaped by impersonating sheep. The only thing that had saved Odysseus from being killed by the other Cyclopes on the island was the fact that he'd told Polyphemus his name was "nobody." It was a clever trick, until the infamous veteran had gone and shouted his real name for all the world to hear—including Poseidon, who'd taken a real disliking to the mortal who'd blinded his son.

"Wait, so what happened to his eye? Shouldn't he still be blind?" I asked, confused.

"Poseidon replaced it with an eye given to him by Helios," Adonia replied. "The other Cyclopes left the island long ago, and since then he's even grown worse. He's more a monster now than he ever was. Which is why we were hoping you'd be able to do what we could not. Stealth is what our people lack, not speed or strength."

I bit my lip, considering her request. Unfortunately for us all, I had no idea how I'd managed to teleport myself from one place to another. A theory gnawed at me—triggered by the faintest memory of stepping from my mother's cosmic hallway to the inner sanctum of the Winter Queen. But back then I'd operated purely on instinct; I'd wanted to travel between worlds and somehow knew exactly how to get there. This time I'd done it reflexively, like running across a tightrope at full speed without thinking. The question was, could I count on my reflexes to kick in when facing a creature powerful enough to level a city block? I doubted it. As for relying on cleverness alone, well...let's just say Odysseus went through a lot of epically awful shit before he ever made it home.

"I don't know if I can help ye," I admitted. "What I did was more by accident than design. And I doubt Polyphemus will fall for the same trick a second time."

"I see." Adonia lowered her gaze to meet mine. "I should tell you, we know all about the state of your boat."

I shot a glare at Narcissus, but the Greek was too busy admiring his naked reflection in the temple's pool to notice. James, however, flinched. He'd heard it, too—the underlying threat in Queen Adonia's statement. Would she send her people to destroy it if we refused? Were there Laestrygonians in place already, waiting to rain boulders down upon the *Jolly Roger*?

"What about it?" I asked.

"If you help us, our people will move the boat for you. We will make sure it's seaworthy, that it is stocked with all the food and water you will need for your journey, and we would consider any other request you would make of us."

"I told them you'd be hard pressed to say no to a deal like that," Narcissus added, running his fingers lovingly along the contours of his face, his reflection beaming back at him. "Seemed like the best we could hope for, am I right?"

"Aye, it's not a bad offer," I replied, thoughtfully. In truth, Adonia's terms were the best we could have hoped for. Provided we survived Polyphemus, this was easily the most efficient course of action; with the Laestrygonians' strength and engineering skills, we could likely return the *Jolly Roger* to the sea intact. Plus, with enough food and water to survive our whole journey, we wouldn't have to make landfall anywhere else, which meant it was possible we'd reach Atlantis and secure Lugh's Spear well before Ryan. If so, he'd be out of options and far more willing to talk. Or at least I hoped so. "But ye know," I added, fixing my attention on Narcissus, "if I'm goin', then so are ye."

"Who, me?" Narcissus finally looked away from the water, his eyes wide, mouth gaping. "Oh, well of course I'm flattered you'd want me along, but—"

"Stow it," I barked. "From now on, where I go, ye go. That way I can keep an eye on ye and make sure ye keep your trap shut." I turned my attention back to the queen of the Laestrygonians, struck by the terms of her offer. "Alright, let's say I agree, how does this work?"

"If you agree, I will send you and whomever you wish to Polyphemus' island in my fastest ship. I'll also send my greatest warrior, Obelius, and my best crew. Obelius will confirm you did as you promised, or that you were slain in the attempt. I'm afraid I must insist that none of my people aid you directly. That is not a risk I wish to take. Too many lives have been claimed by Polyphemus already."

So, we'd be on our own, then. I had to crane my neck to study the queen's face, and even then I wasn't entirely sure I could accurately read her expression. Regardless, I felt I understood where she was coming from; her people were under siege and, despite their superior numbers, unable to stop what amounted to a plague on the society they'd created. She wanted peace restored but was unwilling to pay the price of losing any more of her people. In that sense, this was a gamble with considerable upside; if I killed or maimed the Cyclops, great. If I died, but still managed to wound him, great. If he simply ate me and mine, then at least his appetite would be diminished. The only notable risk lay in Polyphemus seeking retribution for bringing us to his island. But then, what else could he do to them that he hadn't already?

I opened my mouth to speak but was interrupted by the raucous gurgle of James' stomach. The young Neverlander blushed and clutched at his gut, mouthing an apology. I smiled, glad for the brief easing of tensions. "Very well," I said, "I agree to your terms. But first, can we please have some food?"

31

*A*fter pigging out on everything but pigs, we headed for the docks, descending a narrow footpath that led along the winding cliffs to the beach below. Had I not known it was there, I'd never have thought to follow it down—or up—assuming the cliffs insurmountable without a contraption of some sort. Such was the design of the Leastrogynians, apparently, who clearly enjoyed their relative isolation from the outside world. Indeed, were it not for Polyphemus' nightly assaults, I believed they'd have had everything they needed to thrive as a society. With that in mind, as an additional condition, I'd asked Adonia to send some supplies back to the rest of the crew, along with news of what we planned to do. I'd tried to send James back as well, but the Neverlander had refused.

"I'm the Captain," he'd declared, boldly. "And I won't let you go alone."

"Ah, there, see?" Narcissus chimed in while slipping back into the clothes I'd insisted he wear. "Looks like you won't need my remarkable services after all. I'm sure young James here will do a decent job."

"So, you're volunteerin' to be the one to tell Tiger Lily, is that it? After sellin' us out to the giants?" I clapped the Greek on his shoulder hard enough to make him wince. "Brave man. But you're right, I'm sure she'd love to hear it from ye, directly."

In the end, that's all it had taken; Narcissus had opted to tag along with us.

The Greek was self-centered, not suicidal.

"We don't have the means to fashion many weapons on the island," Queen Adonia said as we reached the beach. Here the sand was coarser, less glittery. It crunched hard beneath her bare feet as she marched towards an array of moored boats. Now that I'd been amongst the Laestrygonians for a stretch, I could admit I found their nudity far less disconcerting than I had upon arrival. Not that I could see the appeal, mind you; sand tends to get in all the nooks and crannies, and I had no doubt the Vegiants would be shifting uncomfortably before long. "But," she went on, "I've asked Obelius to bring any you might use aboard this ship."

The vessel she showcased was of a design I'd never seen before. Low and sleek, it had a single sail and a dozen oars on either side, reminding me of pictures I'd seen of Viking longships with their long, narrow hulls and tapering prows. But it was the figurehead which struck me most of all: a three-headed crow. I froze the instant I saw it, staring, until the others were forced to slow and turn.

"Everything copacetic?" Ismene asked.

"Huh?" I shifted my focus from the ship to the giantess. "No. I mean, yes. It's nothin', really. it's just that ship...it reminds me of somethin', that's all."

"It belonged to the Stranger." Queen Adonia cast an appraising eye over the vessel, clearly admiring its clean lines. "He left it here with us, taking a larger one for his own after he taught us how to cultivate the land."

"You've mentioned him before," James said. "The Stranger. Who was he?"

"We aren't sure. In ancient times, we would have called him an Oracle. Many of us believed him a bastard son of the gods, perhaps even a god in disguise. But we never could unmask him, and he never gave us his name."

"And the name of the boat?" I asked. "Did he give ye that?"

"He called it the Crow Boat, said it reminded him of an old lover," Ismene replied helpfully, her voice bubbling with restrained laughter. "He talked jive like that all the time. Dude was downright funky."

"Ismene and many others practically worshipped him," Adonia added.

"And ye?"

"He was a strange creature, Oracle or not. He often talked in riddles, saying things none of us understood. He was ferocious when angry, but a patient teacher. Had he been here when Polyphemus' raids began, he'd have ended this madness long ago." Adonia shivered. "My husband always feared the Stranger's magic. His prophecies. Even I have to admit, looking back, there was something about him that unnerved me."

"What was it?" James asked.

"A feeling, that's all. He reminded me of so many of the Titans who fell to Zeus and his Olympians, in the end. Doomed. That's how I think of him, still. He was a doomed creature, and I think deep down he knew it."

I turned to stare at the ship once more, unable to believe it sheer coincidence that a man with the ability to see the future had shown up, given the Vegiants the keys to their survival, and left a boat with a three-headed crow behind. Was it seriously possible my father was the Stranger they spoke of? And, if so, what did it mean that I was following in his footsteps? The unanswered questions swirled and multiplied, leaving me with nothing but a headache for all my trouble.

"Let's meet our crew," I said.

While the others may have been perplexed by my abrupt desire to end the conversation, they asked no questions. A dozen Laestrygonians greeted us as we approached, their heads bowed in deference to their queen. They began to introduce themselves at Adonia's bequest, but I only had eyes for the largest of them.

"Ye move pretty well for a big fellow, Obelius."

The giant who'd snuck up on me smirked but said nothing.

"Sister, don't let this cat fool you; he's boss," Ismene insisted. "When Polyphemus saw him coming, he totally beat feet. Even that dip knew better than to mess with Obelius."

"I couldn't have chased him off alone, Ismene," Obelius insisted. The Laestrygonian had a robust voice, booming, with an edge of hostility to it that paired seamlessly with his obscenely muscular frame. "If I could have, we wouldn't have had to ask for help from mortals."

"Aww, don't be a drag, you big hunk."

"I am not a hunk. I'm a Laestrygonian."

Ismene rolled her eyes but refused to stop grinning at the larger, more imposing giant. Indeed, I sensed a sort of playfulness in their repartee which suggested she enjoyed baiting her mother's fiercest warrior. Sort of like kicking your playground crush in the shin and running away—counterintuitive, perhaps, but undeniably memorable.

"Perhaps we should get on with this," Adonia suggested.

"Yes, my queen." Obelius bowed and showcased the ship. "All aboard."

We began embarking until only I and a few crew members were left. James was there to help me up, steadying me with a hand on my arm that lingered no longer than it had to. This time when he met my eyes, there was nothing shy in them, but neither was there any heat. It seemed whatever feelings he had for me had undergone a profound shift, though it did seem as if something connected us. The tenuous beginnings of friendship, perhaps? I wasn't sure; excluding my identity crisis in the Otherworld, I'd always had a tough time making friends. Keeping them, sadly, had proved even more difficult. For now, I decided not to pick at it; we had more important concerns to deal with.

"Ready to sail, Captain?" I asked.

"As ready as I'll ever be."

Obelius bellowed a command, and the crew members on the shore heaved themselves against the prow, thrusting the longboat into the sea with nothing but the strength of their bodies. James teetered, off balance, and this time it was I who steadied him. We stayed huddled for a moment as the crew members leapt aboard.

"Listen, James," I said, keeping my voice low so as not to be overheard, "don't get yourself eaten, alright? I'd hate to survive this only to have Tinkerbell and Tiger Lily cut me into a thousand pieces."

"I'll do my best. Though the same goes for you, First Mate MacKenna."

I cocked an eyebrow at that. First Mate—an amusing title to say the least —was the second highest rank aboard a pirate ship. In lieu of the Captain's presence aboard the ship, it meant I was essentially in charge. But still, as gestures went, it was a considerate one. I smiled, squeezed his shoulder, and stepped back only to bump into an eavesdropping Narcissus.

"Watch it!" I hissed.

"What about me?" Narcissus asked, his thick lips pursed in a petulant frown.

"What about ye?"

"Aren't you going to tell me to be safe?"

James and I exchanged glances.

"I best check with the crew and see what to expect when we get to the island," the Neverlander said, leaving me alone with the Greek while he worked his way among the Laestrygonians.

Coward.

Fortunately, I didn't have to respond; Queen Adonia and her daughter called to us all, bidding us goodbye. Standing together like that, I could at last see the resemblance between the two. Not in their features, per se, but in the way each stood, in the way they waved. I returned the farewell, uncertain whether or not I'd see either of them again.

"Good luck, mortals!" The queen yelled. "Obelius, return safely!"

"As you wish, my Queen!" Obelius waved back, though the set of his shoulders bore a tension I hadn't seen before. Nerves, maybe? Was he worried about leaving Adonia and Ismene behind? Whichever, I found myself at his side as we slid through the waves, the ship bobbing unpleasantly up and down in a way it hadn't, and I'd taken for granted, when on the *Jolly Roger*.

"Ready for this?" I asked.

Obelius grunted.

"Mortal, I've been ready for this for longer than you can imagine."

I opened my mouth to ask a follow-up, but the Laestrygonian turned abruptly on his heel and left, leaving a sense of foreboding in his wake. I glanced at James, who was chatting up one of the Vegiants at his oar, the Neverlander's hands weaving as he spoke. Narcissus, unsurprisingly, had decided to take this opportunity to sunbathe; he sprawled across one of the benches, posed like a Pin-Up girl. Dear Lord, I found myself praying, please let us carve up this cyclopic son of a bitch and survive this shitty ass realm.

Amen.

32

The island of the Cyclopes, which supposedly Polyphemus alone inhabited, was a cragged, steeply angular thing which rose up from the depths of the sea like the horn of some primordial god. It's funny, I thought as I stared at our destination, how I used to enjoy metaphors like that. Of course, that was back before I'd actually encountered deities. Since then, I'd lost all sense of size and scope, my appreciation for the natural wonders of the world irreparably altered by the mere existence of the unnatural. Take the young, handsome man on my right, for example: a twenty-something whose lineage could be traced to a storybook villain I'd found oddly charming, even as a child. Or the Laestrygonian looming to my left: a giant whose very existence called into question everything I'd ever read in a history textbook. I gazed out upon the rest of the crew, knowing deep down that I'd never see the world as I had only a few years before—not with these eyes, at any rate.

"We're getting close," James offered.

I nodded, unwilling to break the silence I'd cultivated since we left the island of the Laestrygonians behind. Instead, I watched that sword-tip land-mass grow, expanding until I could make out nothing of the sky beyond. Somewhere on that foreboding island was a creature I'd never thought to see: a one-eyed Cyclops. The son of a sea god. A unique breed of giant who supposedly dwarfed even the Leastrogynians. I had to admit, it was a strange world—a serendipitous existence—I'd found here in the Land of Titans. How had I gotten here of all places? How had I managed to sail across an uncharted sea on a boat that may have once belonged to the man I thought to call my father? How had I survived Boston, New York, Moscow, Salem, the Otherworld, and Neverland?

And now, this place. Would I make it out alive here, as well? Or would this be my last adventure? I wanted to tell myself that wasn't the case, that I would triumph here as I had in those other places. But I couldn't. I wasn't that naive—not anymore. I'd seen too many people die to think myself, or anyone else, invincible. The question, then, was whether or not it was worth dying here. I wasn't sure about that, either. Frankly, I had too many unanswered questions. Too much to worry about and not enough time to think of a better solution. And it seemed what little time I might have had was up.

"There," Obelius said, pointing to a gap in the rocks which stood like sentinels between us and the shore. The other Leastrogynians adjusted their strokes, turning the prow at an angle until we sailed perpendicular to the beach, barely squeezing through the narrow opening. For a moment it seemed as though the three-headed crows moved before my very eyes, jostling one another, but I knew it was merely a trick of the light; overhead, the midday sun blazed. Though a breeze drifted across the water, I felt its oppressive heat press against the back of my neck, across my shoulders. Indeed, it seemed we'd left a temperate climate for an inhospitable one; I felt as though I were being baked the moment we landed on the shore. What sort of masochist would choose to live here, I wondered? Our vessel ground to an abrupt halt, jerking us all forward.

"Are we sure this is the only way to get the *Jolly Roger* off that beach?" James asked after he'd regained his footing. "I don't like the look of this place."

Truth be told, neither did I. It wasn't just the sun bearing down on us like a domineering parent, either. There was something about the rocky shoals, the pebble-laden beach, the steep crags, that made me think of a stone oven. But then, it wasn't the island we'd come here to deal with. Our objective was Polyphemus. Take him down, flee, and we'd have all our needs met the moment we returned—provided Queen Andonia kept her word. Of course, if she didn't, there was nothing we could do about it. The Queen of the Vegiants had us between a cascade of rocks and a hard place, and she knew it.

"We don't have a choice," I replied. "Come on, let's go."

"I'll be coming with you." Obelius motioned to his fellow giants, who quickly passed him a heavy wooden shield and spear as though they'd been waiting for the declaration. A snap of his fingers saw James and I presented similar options. "The crew will take the boat to the other side of the island, where Polyphemus lives, but stay out of sight until we've dealt with him."

"But I thought Queen Adonia wanted us to do this on our own," I said as I took the most serviceable weapon I could find—a long-shafted, leaf-tipped spear with a spiked bronze butt to keep it balanced.

"My queen asked that I ensure the mortals fulfill their end of the bargain. This is me doing so." The Laestrygonian curled his lips in contempt, his fists clenched so tightly around his weapons I could hear wood creak under the strain. "Polyphemus has grown too dangerous, too bold. I won't let him return to our island to take anyone else from us." Obelius hesitated then, and I heard something in his voice that I should have expected, but hadn't considered until now: grief. He'd lost someone. Maybe more than one person. Even before his rampage, Queen Adonia had made it clear that Polyphemus had been a terror, a monster who abducted Laestrygonians in the night. No wonder he'd been so eager to sail to this island. His was a vendetta to rival anything I'd ever known: an individual determined to end a genocide by any means necessary. "I mean no disrespect," he added, "but I don't know if you can succeed, and I will not risk failure."

"None taken," I said, lightly. "But when we report back to your queen, I want your word you'll see our bargain honored."

Obelius locked gazes with me for a moment, then nodded. It seemed we had an understanding; I wouldn't get in his way, and he wouldn't get in mine. Frankly, I was glad to have the giant on my side. Stealth was great in theory, but it always helped to have brute force available in a pinch. Which left only one loose end to tie up.

"I'll leave Narcissus with your crew, as well."

Obelius frowned.

"He's a liability, Obelius. I think we both know that. There's no sense in draggin' him along into a fight. Besides, if we fail, someone will have to tell Queen Adonia what happened. What better messenger than Ms. Chatty Cathy?"

Obelius barked a laugh

"Very well."

"Did I hear my name up there?" Narcissus yelled from the other end of the boat.

I grimaced but quickly moved to confer with the Greek, one arm wound around his slender shoulders. "Listen, I'm not sure what your real motives are, or what Helen truly hopes to accomplish on this little adventure of ours, but I know you're not a fighter. Helen was right. We do need ye as a navigator. Ye know these waters, you've studied that map, so keepin' ye alive is a priority. Which is why I want ye to stay here."

Narcissus flashed me his characteristically gorgeous smile, though this time it went all the way to his eyes. "You can count on me. I'll keep an eye on these giants, make sure they don't try to run off and leave you stranded on the island as bait."

Shit. I hadn't thought of that.

"Good man."

"Listen Narcissus," James interjected as he came upon us, "if we don't make it back, I want you to tell Tiger Lily and Tinkerbell...tell them to find our home. I worry about what will happen to them if they stay here too long."

"If we don't make it back," I added, putting strong emphasis on the first word of that sentence, "then tell Helen to send them home and request aid from Queen Adonia. She may not be inclined to give it, but I believe the Laestrygonians are kinder than they seem. I doubt they'll leave ye stranded indefinitely."

But Narcissus was already shaking his head. "I've studied that map for decades. Although it only made complete sense to me once we got here, I've always known one thing for sure. There is no exit."

"No exit..." James echoed.

Narcissus twitched.

"What d'ye mean, 'no exit'?"

"I mean," Narcissus drawled, "that we knew where to look for the entrance. Past Gaia's temple, following the sun until we reached the storm that never moves. But the map says nothing about an exit. If you leave the archipelago, you'll find nothing but open sea. Helen thinks its possible we'd simply circle back somehow, but I'm not so sure. I think we'd find nothing but open sea."

James turned to me, panicked.

"Don't worry. We'll just have to find one," I reassured the Neverlander, reaching out to squeeze his shoulder. "Ye and I will get back to the others, one way or the other. Then we'll take another look at Narcissus' map. I'm sure he and Helen missed something."

The Greek raised a finger as if planning to refute that, but I jabbed him in the gut with an elbow before he could say a word. Inwardly, of course, I was as upset as James to learn we'd booked a one-way ticket. Not that I was surprised; shit like this always seemed to happen to me. But no, I reassured myself, everything was fine. After all, all we had to do was take out Polyphemus, journey to the Underworld, find Atlantis, stop Ryan, and get the Neverlanders home before they keeled over.

No sweat.

"It's time," Obelius called from the shore, reaching out with both hands for James and I to join him. We passed over our weapons first, then took them, our own hands like those of children in his massive paws. Thankfully, the Laestrygonian maintained his grip even after lowering us to the shore, or I'd have toppled the instant my feet hit the ground.

Because something was very, very wrong here.

$\mathscr{I}$t was in the air—that something. A chill that left me shivering, my breath pluming. If the others noticed, however, they kept it to themselves; James and Obelius surveyed our surroundings as if nothing was amiss even as I leaned against the hull of the Crow Boat. I watched the Vegiant making gestures in slow motion, moving his hands as if taking a measurement—relating the height of the Cyclops we were tasked with stopping to himself. A flash of fingers. Three. Three times as tall as a Laestrygonian? Three times as wide? I wasn't sure. All I knew was that Polyphemus was a monster big and strong enough to break through solid walls with the sheer mass of his body. A being capable of snatching up giants like you might a child, dragging them off into the night with the savage efficiency of a serial kidnapper.

But at the moment, none of that mattered. What mattered was the air. The sensation of wrongness that permeated the soil beneath my feet. I'd felt it before. I'd sensed it on the street that had once housed the corpses of eight mutilated women, recognized it despite the London Fog roiling outside my mother's cosmic window, even tracked it from behind the barrel of a gun. Later—after I thought it gone forever—I'd caught a whiff of it in a blood-soaked shack in Boston, felt its presence among the labyrinthian hallways of a mad doctor. But it hadn't been as strong, then. It hadn't reeked of mass murder, of undiluted evil, of brutal malignancy.

And yet, there was no mistaking this. I wasn't sure how I knew, not when I'd been so blind to it before, but I knew with a certainty that literally chilled me to my core. Jack Frost, the Winter Queen's personal assassin, her henchfae, and once a dear friend of mine...was here. On this island. Now.

"Is something wrong?" James asked, his face coming into view in bits and pieces, blurry at first, then exceedingly clear. I realized the Neverlander had a faint scar on his chin, a tiny mole below his left eye. He was so young, his skin smooth and pliant in a way mine no longer was and perhaps would never be again. Immortal I might be, but young? After everything I'd seen, everything I'd done? No. Never that.

"Ye have to get back in the boat," I whispered.

"What?"

"Both of ye, back in the boat." I locked gazes with him, then Obelius, willing them to believe me. "There's someone else, somethin' else, on this island. Somethin' worse than Polyphemus."

"There's nothing worse than that monster," Obelius replied, sounding outraged.

"I'm not arguin' semantics," I said, though I was already shaking my head. "Let's just say Polyphemus isn't the only monster here. I'm not sure why or how, but the person—the creature—I've been chasin' is on this island. Which means it's possible this could be a trap."

"How do you know? Did you see someone?" James scanned the horizon, then the shore, and finally the distant cliffs for signs of life other than our own.

"No, not that way. I can feel him, that's all. Can ye not sense it?"

"Sense what?"

"The cold," I insisted, waving my hand about, my fingers brushing the frigid air that seemed to have settled over the island like a fog.

"Is she crazy?" Obelius asked, cocking an eyebrow at James.

"Not that I've seen," he replied, sounding skeptical. "No, Quinn. I don't feel cold. If anything, it's extremely hot."

"Enough of this. I refuse to waste this opportunity." Obelius began striding towards the rocks. "I'm going to find Polyphemus. If you two want our help, you'll join me. If not, then at least stay out of my way."

James shot me a pleading look and plodded after the Laestrygonian. Unable to come up with better justification than "I feel it to be true," I snatched up my spear and joined them both, thrusting my free hand into my jacket pocket, fighting not to shiver. I began to scan my surroundings as James had only moments ago, searching for signs of life—any life. But, as we hiked, the chill diminished and the sensation faded, leaving me feeling silly for having overreacted. Maybe Obelius was right, and I was simply being paranoid? Or maybe Ryan had been here, but wasn't anymore. Whatever the reason, by the time we left the beach for the foothills, I could at least breathe again.

"Better?"

I found James at my side, looking concerned. I nodded, flashing a reassuring smile. He seemed relieved; the young man stepped away, rejoining Obelius at the front. They made an odd pairing—the former a ten-foot-tall, naked giant with tan, rippling muscles, the latter a pale, gangly young man in a billowy shirt tucked into leather breeches. Like a day at the Renaissance Faire meets the men's locker room at Gold's Gym. And here I was, the odd woman out, subconsciously waiting for the other shoe to drop.

Obelius turned and shielded his eyes, watching as the Crow Boat—crewed by his fellow Laestrygonians and a waving Narcissus—worked its way along the coastline. Soon, they would disappear around the bend and, from there, find a cove on the other side of the island where they'd presumably wait for Obelius' signal. Whatever that was.

"So, any ideas about how we stop this thing?" James asked, directing the question to the both of us.

"Polyphemus?" Obelius grunted. "He's not the smartest, or even nearly the smartest, of his kind. He's easily riled. The only reason we haven't taken care of him already is because we couldn't be sure his father wouldn't seek retribution. Queen Adonia worries he'll visit this realm and wipe us all out if we slay his son. I'm the one who convinced her to let you try. As strangers to this realm, Poseidon would be hard pressed to find you, let alone punish you."

"Then why are ye here?" I asked, confused by the obvious contradiction his presence presented.

"Truthfully, I don't share the queen's beliefs. I think Poseidon and the other Olympians have forsaken their children. I believe Polyphemus is on his own. And, now that the queen is not here to command me otherwise, I plan to slit that one-eyed bastard's throat, myself." Obelis turned to look at us each in turn. "If you want to help, then distract him, somehow. Give me

169

time to set a trap, to find an opening. If you cannot manage that, then the least you can do is stay out of the way."

I frowned, uncomfortable with the risk Obelius was taking. Of course, the notion that our actions might come with such unforeseen consequences didn't sit well with me, either; nearly all of Odysseus' troubles had started when he'd pissed Poseidon off, and I wasn't eager to repeat his mistakes. Still, could we really let Obelius attempt this on his own? What sort of welcome would we receive if he failed and we returned to Queen Adonia empty-handed and a Vegiant short?

"Let's see what we find when we get there, first," I insisted. "We won't leave ye to do this alone, though, no matter what happens."

Obelius shrugged but didn't disagree with me, which was the best I supposed I could expect. Instead, he pointed towards another bluff in the distance. "Polyphemus lives in the cave that sits at the base of that cliff. Once, before the grass gave way to stone, he and all his kind lived here. Sheep grazed all over this island. But it's said that Helios got distracted while driving his chariot one day, and that the heat of the sun turned the lush fields to ash. Eventually, this drove the other Cyclopes away. They took their flocks and left blind Polyphemus behind. To appease Poseidon, Helios gave Polyphemus a new eye of molten gold. A gift to replace his missing organ."

I studied the island from our new vantage point, noting the inhospitable beaches, the frothing seas. It really was nothing like the island we'd left behind, despite being only a few short hours' away by ship. A thought struck me, then. "How does Polyphemus get to ye?"

"What?"

"To your island," I clarified. "Does he use a boat?"

"He can breathe underwater and walks the bottom," Obelius replied, his voice laced with disgust. "That's why it's so hard to stop him. He can strike from any direction and always waits until nightfall to attack. We laid traps all over the island, but we believe his new eye is gifted with Helios' prophetic sight, which means he can see through any of our ambushes. The worst are the nights when Selene refuses to sail the sky, when we are forced to send out sentries with torches…" Obelius drifted off, unpleasant memories playing themselves out behind his eyes. "We don't know what he does to those he takes, not for sure, but he taunts us with their fates. Sometimes he'll leave their bones scattered on our shores. It was these our people were searching for when they found your crewmates. It's something the families of those who've lost someone do routinely."

"And did ye lose someone?" I asked, gently.

Obelius jerked as if I'd slapped him.

"That's enough talking," he insisted. "Let's go."

James and I exchanged looks, but eventually followed in the giant's exceptionally large footsteps; I had to pick up my pace considerably to keep up with him, which meant James was basically jogging behind us both. Still, we made good time; we reached that distant bluff in perhaps an hour. There was no footpath this time, which meant—if we wanted to sneak down unnoticed—we had to follow the slope, each of us keeping our eyes peeled for signs of the Cyclops we'd come to maim. But there was no sign of anyone or anything, no indication that a living, breathing creature had made this place his home. Not, that is, until we stepped onto the beach below and heard the screams.

The ear-piercing, tortured wails mingled with the pounding of the surf against the shore as we huddled together behind one of the boulders strewn along the beach, staring at the cave's gaping mouth from which the sounds emerged. The bone-numbing, discomfiting chill I'd felt earlier was back, only this time I wasn't the only one to notice it; frost-coated pebbles gleamed beneath the sun in a swath around the cave entrance as though they'd been soaked in liquid nitrogen. James and Obelius rubbed at their arms, emotions rippling across their faces. Confusion, anxiety, even fear.

"Who is that screaming?" James asked.

"It sounds like Polyphemus," Obelius replied.

Indeed, the screams were horrifically loud—far and away more sonorous than what a human throat could produce. And yet, they were so full of pain, so tormented, that the notion they came from something as dominant as the Cyclops boggled my mind. What the hell was going on? Now that the sensations had returned, I felt I knew the answer. Or at least part of the answer. Ryan was here. Not merely on this island, but on this very beach, inside that very cave. Somehow, he was responsible for the noises coming from within, just as his predecessor had been responsible for the harrowing screams of his victims. The real question was why. What possible motive could Ryan have for attacking Polyphemus? Sadly, there was only one way to find out.

"I'm goin' in there."

Obelius blocked me like a mother guarding her children from running into the middle of the street, his face contorted with unease. I sidestepped his stiff arm and shuffled towards the cave entrance, bobbing from one boulder to the next, keeping my eyes peeled for signs of life. The screams stopped as abruptly as they'd begun, leaving an eerie, pregnant silence in their wake. I paused just outside the mouth of the cave, listening. Scuffling sounds from behind brought me around, panicked, only to find James and Obelius hustling towards me. I groaned inwardly, waited for them to join me at the entrance, then gestured for us all to huddle up.

"Let me go in alone," I insisted in a hushed whisper.

"Are you sure?" James asked.

"Aye, trust me. If it's who I t'ink it is in there, then I'll have the best chance of stoppin' him."

"Don't be foolish," Obelius said, his eyes dancing wildly back and forth from James' face to my own. "Whatever is in there will be dangerous. Deadly. I never thought to hear Polyphemus make such sounds."

I sighed. In a way, I pitied the poor Vegiant. He'd come here, certain he'd at last have a chance to settle things with his people's greatest nemesis, only to be confronted by the possibility of a bigger, badder fish. And he was right; in a straight fight, superior numbers were an asset. But our goal had changed the instant we stepped onto the shore. What we needed now was information, not conflict. To get that, we needed someone who could move well in the dark, who had at least a vague idea of what to expect, and who wouldn't flinch when the time came to make the tough call. Granted, I'd experienced a lot of uncertainty lately: an identity crisis, trust issues, and even a crisis of faith or two.

But pulling the trigger was, and always would be, my specialty.

"Your queen sent me here to do one t'ing," I said. "I'm here because I can sneak about with the best of 'em. Which means ye would only get in me way."

"I would not—"

"Ye would."

Obelius snapped his mouth shut and glared at me.

"She's right," James said, tapping the Laestrygonian's bulging forearm.

"We should signal the boat and wait, just in case we need to leave in a hurry."

"Good idea," I acknowledged. "And keep an eye out for other ships, while you're at it. If the...monster I'm lookin' for really is in there torturin' Polyphemus, then he had to get here somehow. And he'll have to leave, eventually."

Obelius flinched and began scanning the horizon, one beefy hand shading his face. James, however, only had eyes for me; the Neverlander studied my face as though it were some sort of riddle he could solve if only he had the right clues. At last, the young man cocked his head.

"You promised you'd take us home."

"That I did."

"Well then, don't get yourself killed and break it."

"Aye, aye, Captain."

Fingers crossed.

The yawning entrance to the cave gaped like an open mouth—its cavernous maw as tall and wide as the side of a six-story building. Skin-prickling cold leaked forth from its stone lips, visible as a sort of listless fog. That chill grew worse as I stepped from the harsh light of day into its dark recesses, almost as if I'd crossed the threshold of a walk-in freezer. The smell, however, was not that of flash-dried ingredients but of freshly carved meat mingled with a stale musk. The stench clung to the back of my throat, so thick I thought I might be sick. But I wasn't. Instead, I crept forward, keeping to the deepest shadows, relying on my improved night vision to move silently despite the uneven ground below and the deadly spikes above. The cavern was massive, and yet difficult to navigate at first; twice in as many minutes I had to retrace my steps, to work around a knotted tendril of stone which ran directly from ceiling to floor.

Eventually, however, I began to see patterns in the stone where it had been cut away, where it had been widened or raised—stalactites scraped clean from the ceiling to leave apertures like teeth fallen from a child's mouth. I also found refuse strewn about, discarded remnants of bygone times: bent and rusted swords buried amongst shattered shields, snapped footwear, threadbare rags, and broken spears. I gripped my own tighter, aware that I alone would be hard pressed to kill the Cyclops if it turned out my supposition was wrong. And yet, I was inexplicably certain those screams had belonged to Polyphemus. What were the odds of another crea-ture his size being tortured on this island? Slim, I decided. Which left only the question of what had been done, what damage inflicted, to incur such piteous wails.

The answer, I suspected, would be clear the moment I found Ryan. I could sense him still, stronger now than ever. It was almost as if we were tied together at the navel; his presence tugged at the core of me, my guts practically writhing with each step that drew us closer. It wasn't merely the cold, nor was it the repulsive sensation I'd picked up when I'd first stepped foot on the island. No, this was something more symbiotic. A recognition that left my bones aching, my flesh pebbled, my breathing shallow.

After perhaps ten minutes of walking, at last, I heard something other than the scuffle of my own steps, the occasional dribble of water, and the low moan of glacial air wafting past. A voice, hissing and fierce with anger. A voice I recognized.

"I can't get it out!"

I froze, picturing the speaker immediately, though I'd not had cause to think of the Faeling in ages. In my mind, I saw Mabel, Ryan's former lover and my would-be assassin, with her perfect, sun-kissed skin, bright eyes, and blonde hair. What was she doing here?

The Faeling cried out in frustration before I could dwell on that. Up ahead, a dim blue light shone, rippling across the stone. The cold was even harsher here, somehow, the ache that much worse. It practically hurt to breathe.

"The eye was put there by a god," another said. "I doubt it will be so easily removed."

This voice was Ryan's, though there was nothing in it of the warmth and playfulness I'd become accustomed to over the years we'd spent in each other's company. Nothing human in it at all, really. I slipped forward, moving carefully, until I could see what was happening through a gap in the cave walls. I bent forward, pinning my face to the frigid rock, trying to make sense of what I was seeing.

The blue light belonged to Ryan. It spilled from his cerulean skin, flick-ering across his face and hands like eels beneath a frozen lake. I watched those brilliant strobes for a moment, mesmerized, until Mabel stole my attention with another agonized grunt. I turned to find her straddling Polyphemus' neck, her arms drenched in gore to the elbows, her upper body perched over the Cyclops' enormous face. And it was enormous; as tall as the *Jolly Roger* was long, the rest of his body extended so far into the darkened cavern beyond that all I could make out was his chest and shoulders. Standing, his head would have brushed the ceiling, making him even larger than Obelius had suggested. But then, the Cyclops wasn't standing.

He was dead.

A pool of blood had crystalized on the floor beneath the corpse—a frozen liquid surface disturbed only by slender footprints. Mabel's footprints, if I had to guess, from when she'd crossed to mount the body, unmindful of the frostbite which clearly blackened the Cyclops' chest and throat. And so Polyphemus, son of Poseidon, had died screaming, hoping to force air through windpipes that no longer supported life. It was a horrifying way to go, even for a ravenous monster who abducted peace-loving giants in the middle of the night. And Ryan had been the one to do it—I was certain of it. Unfortunately, as I looked on at what he was capable of, I was equally certain of something else: Ryan had grown stronger since we'd last met.

While the title of Jack Frost came with its fair share of perks, I doubted Ryan's predecessor had ever been capable of anything like this. The former Jack Frost had needed all sorts of rituals to invoke his will, and yet there was nothing like that here. No sacrifice. No ceremony. Merely a display of raw power, of force. To kill the son of a god, to send him squealing to the floor, had seemingly taken nothing; Ryan stood as he always had, relaxed and poised. Framed as it was by the light of his own skin, I had to admit his face was as handsome as any man I'd ever met, blue or not. In fact, with his otherworldly colouring, he might as well have been an incubus—a deviant creature who invades dreams, lavishing others with his attention, with his touch, feeding off their lust. And yet, I sensed there was nothing like passion in him anymore—that his power lay within a hatred so cool it burned. It was there in the curve of his lips, in the sneer of contempt he wore, the way his eyes tracked everything and nothing.

"It won't budge," Mabel whined. She plowed her hands into the folds of Polyphemus' face, burrowing until even her forearms vanished with a wet, slurping sound. She gritted her teeth and strained, trying to draw out the massive eye which sat in the middle of the Cyclops' forehead. Only it wasn't an eye—not one like I'd ever seen, anyway. Metal gleamed where Ryan's light touched the gold cylinder, its surface crossed with unfamiliar glyphs.

"Come away, I'll do it." Ryan stepped forward. "Without it, we'll never be able to navigate this wretched realm."

"But the Doctor said you shouldn't touch—"

"Enough. That madman doesn't control me. Move."

Mabel yanked her arms free, accompanied by an audible pop that made me want to gag. The smell of pus and sharper, nastier odors followed her as she scrambled off Polyphemus, inadvertently gouging the Cyclops' ruined throat in the process. She fell to the far side, out of sight, with a muffled groan. Ryan turned his back to me completely, pinching his nose to block out the stench. He seemed to be studying the Cyclops, oblivious to anything but his prize. I flinched, realizing this might be my best chance.

I took one deep breath, then rushed into the opening with all the obscene speed I'd regained, swinging the blunt end of my spear towards the back of Ryan's head with every ounce of strength I had, praying it wouldn't cave his head in. He'd barely begun to turn when the wood caught him; his head whipped sideways as he fell to the ground, his body limp, navy blue blood trickling from his scalp. Ryan's light died, and Polyphemus' blood melted beneath my feet.

"Jack! Jack, where are you?" Mabel called, using Ryan's new title. I could hear her struggling to work her way around the head of the fallen giant in the dark. "Ryan?" she asked at last, fear and uncertainty mingling in her voice. "Ryan, are you there?"

I waited for the would-be assassin to come round, waited for her to notice me standing over Ryan's body. Not so long ago, she'd had me dead to rights in a jail cell, prepared to kill me out of jealousy and hate. Part of me wanted to lash out at her, to drive the end of my spear through her chest and pin her against the wall to rot. But I didn't. Instead, I jabbed with my spear the instant she stepped within range, planting the butt end in her gut with enough force to send her to her knees, wheezing.

"Hello, Mabel."

The Faeling looked up, squinting, her face a rictus of pain. The pointed ears which emerged from her lank blonde hair were scabbed, and her skin was sallow. She looked malnourished, somehow. Sick. Indeed, it reminded me of Tinkerbell and Tiger Lily, albeit far worse. Was this the fate of all the Faelings who dared sail the Eighth Sea? One glance at Ryan's immaculate face, however, made me think otherwise. Was it possible only the weaker, the less powerful, felt its effects? Or perhaps it was only a matter of time before he ended up like the others. But, then, what about me?

"Who is that? Who's there?" Mabel croaked.

"I'd say an old friend, but we weren't that close, were we Mabel?" I pressed the tip of the spear to the hollow of her throat, let her feel its iron against her flesh. "Not unless ye count that time ye tried to knife me in the jail cell."

"It's you! But—but how?"

"You'll need to be more specific with your answers than ye have been with your questions, I'm afraid." I nicked her, just enough to see her bleed, to watch her wince in pain as the iron tip sliced through her Faeling flesh. "What are you and Ryan doin' here? No lies, or I'll shove this spear through each and every appendage ye possess."

But what came out of Mabel's mouth was neither dismissive nor vague, as I'd expected. Instead, it was a plea. Pitiful and pathetic, she spoke like someone who'd been accosted by a savior, not an enemy; she crawled forward through the pool of blood, closing the distance between us before I could step back.

"Please! Please," she begged, "you have to take me with you. Get me away from this place. Away from him." Mabel snatched my spear and held it to her own throat. Her fingers had withered to little but bones covered by a thin coat of skin, the veins beneath floating to the surface like worms after a rainstorm. "Or, if you won't, then kill me. End it, please."

"End it?" I asked, disturbed by the Faeling's uncharacteristic behavior. "Are ye mad?"

Mabel shook her head so violently I had to yank my spear back to keep her from slicing open her own throat. She fell to the floor on all fours, panting like a dog. Indeed, there was something feral about her I hadn't noticed before—a manic gleam to her eyes that spoke of unimaginable suffering. The Faeling I'd hoped to pry information from began hyperventilating, drawing in ragged breaths.

"Please, please don't leave me with him...I'll do whatever you want, just...don't..." Mabel drifted off, then slumped to the floor, casting ripples in the crimson pool that lapped against Ryan's slack face. I stared down at the Faeling who'd tried to kill me, who'd sent me hurtling towards the Otherworld, and felt something I'd never expected to feel: a stab of pity. It wasn't just the plea, but the fact that there had been nothing left of Mabel in that pleading mess—nothing of the malevolent, plotting creature I'd known.

"What did ye do to her?" I whispered, staring down at Ryan. But he was in no state to answer, and I wanted to keep it that way. What I needed to do now, I decided, was to get him out of here. I needed to tie him up, to restrain his powers somehow. Only then would we be able to talk. I glanced back down at Mabel, then at the broken Polyphemus, a feeling of foreboding tugging at my gut at the thought of trying to negotiate with someone who was capable of doing what he'd done to the Cyclops and the Faeling who'd loved him.

Nonetheless, I snatched Ryan from the floor and threw him haphazardly over one shoulder. No longer forced to resort to stealth, I sprinted back the way I'd come, giving my eyes barely enough time to adjust to the burgeoning light ahead. Shadows moved outside the mouth of the cave, their silhouettes flitting across like insects. I slowed, realizing there were far too many, too oddly shaped, to belong to James and the Laestorgynians. It was only then, after the clatter of my own echoing footsteps died away, that I could make out the sounds of fighting.

I quickly took off again, bursting out onto the sand with my spear leveled, Ryan still perched over my shoulder. At first, I wasn't sure what I was looking at: naked giants—those Laestrygonians who'd crewed the Crow Boat as well as Obelius—appeared to be squaring off against smaller, far less nimble opponents. Covered head to toe in shades of blue trimmed in white, the assailants were tall and lithe, their skin so pale it seemed unpigmented, their eyes pink and larger than they should have been. Albinos, perhaps? Some other race indigenous to the Titan Realm? I had no idea. They lumbered among the giants, welding all manners of weapons, most of which were stained with rust and covered in barnacles. They did not howl as they fell, but collapsed in silence, their yellow blood staining the sands like piss. And yet, somehow, the Laestrygonians were losing; as I watched, one of the Vegiants fell shielding Obelius, sliced at the knees, his cry silenced by the descent of a blood-soaked hatchet.

The Queen's greatest warrior hurried to the side of his fallen comrade, wielding a sword in one hand and a javelin in the other. He chucked the javelin with a side-arm throw that took one attacker through the throat, then decapitated another with his sword. And yet, they kept coming, lurching inexorably forward.

"Quinn!" James shouted, slipping out from between the rocks to stumble to my side, his face ashen, a shallow gash seeping red across his chest.

"What's goin' on?" I asked, whirling. "Where did these bastards come from?"

"They came on that ship!" James pointed to a dark-hulled monstrosity that dwarfed our own, anchored far enough out to sea that I hadn't noticed after emerging from the cave. A Man-of-War, I believe they called such ships. The vessel had a vaguely Spanish look to it, though the flagpole was bare. And yet, I knew who it belonged to immediately; the sails were dyed blue and bore a single symbol.

A freaking snowflake.

I tossed Ryan to the sand, then drew him up by his hair, leveling the point of my spear so close to his throat that Mabel's blood stained his neck. But no one seemed to care; the attackers continued their awkward assault as though nothing else mattered. Not even the fate of their Captain—as I presumed Ryan to be.

"That's enough!" I screamed, pouring my frustration and anger into my voice. Power—raw and crackling—rode the air. Power I didn't even know I had. Green flames licked the edges of my spear, and my voice reverberated along the shore as though I'd used a megaphone. The pale-skinned bastards lowered their weapons immediately, followed in short order by the clearly exhausted Laestrygonians. All but Obelius, who hurried up to us with two blades in either hand.

"Where's Polyphemus?" he demanded.

"Dead," I replied, still eyeing the creatures who'd attacked the Crow Boat's crew. Ryan's men, I gathered, if men they could be called.

"Really? Tell me—"

"Not now. I'll explain later."

Obelius' face darkened. He reached for me, taking half my jacket in his hand, the leather whining beneath his fierce grip. "You'll explain now, mortal."

I glanced down at that hand, incensed that the moron was thinking only of himself and his vendetta in this moment, what with so many of his own people under seige. I looked up, meeting his eyes. I let him see in my face what I thought of his callous disregard, of his offensive touch.

"Get your hand off me."

Obelius jerked back with a yelp of pain, steam hissing from his fingertips. Green flames, again. Was this more of my mother's power? Or something else? I couldn't say and didn't have time to dwell on it. And so, rather than waste any more time arguing with the Laestrygonian, I turned my attention to the task at hand.

"I have your Captain," I said. "He is a prisoner, now. Mine. So, if ye don't want him dead, you'll throw down your weapons and get on your knees."

Ryan's men didn't so much as fidget. They simply stared at me with their sickly, bloodshot eyes. There was something wrong with them, I realized. Something beyond their unusual pallor and stiff, robotic movements. After a few heartbeats of silence, I realized what it was: they weren't breathing. Dead men. I was looking at dead men. The horror of it must have flitted across my face, because in that moment another voice cried out, this one from a small skiff moored not far from the scenes of the fight.

"Do you like them?"

The voice belonged to a frail, reedy man with a weak chin who sat on the lip of the skiff, cleaning his spectacles. He had wild, untamed hair and sported a thick, curling mustache that hid most of his face. "I made them myself, you see. I've done much better work in the past, naturally. But one does what one can with limited resources." The man donned his glasses and bowed his head, fingers steepled to support that wobbly chin. "Dr. Victor Frankenstein, at your service."

All I could do was gape. Doctor Victor Frankenstein—engineer of the horror which had nearly killed me beneath the earth outside Salem, the mad doctor who had created one of the world's most terrifying monsters—was sitting but a few dozen yards away. I shook my head, unwilling to believe it. I mean, I'd known he'd worked with Ryan in the past, of course, but I had no idea the doctor had joined him on this endeavor. What the hell was he after?

But it seemed there would be no time to get my answers; Ryan, who must have woken at some point during the doctor's speech, wrapped his hand around the shaft of my spear. Frost bled across its surface in an instant, and I jerked away to the sound of it shattering in two, leaving me with little more than a thin club in its place, the sharp end buried uselessly in the sand. After a word from Dr. Frankenstein, the dead men seemed equally revived; they raised their weapons as one to resume the fight. In seconds, chaos reigned as the recovered Laestrygonians roared, led by a charging Obelius. Ryan, mercifully, remained on the ground, clutching his wounded scalp.

"Quinn, we have to go!" James shouted, drawing me towards the shore. But my feet felt leaden, my mind muddled, my body exhausted. It was as if I'd run several miles in mere seconds, struck by a wave of fatigue unlike anything I'd ever experienced. Suddenly, I could hear Narcissus shouting, joining his voice to the Neverlander's. Flee, return to the ship, he was screaming. The others, even Obelius, heard and began to disengage. I struggled to free myself from James, shaking him off my arm. Ryan was so close, I thought. If I could only get to him, I could clout him over the head once more and get the hell off this island with my old friend in tow. I just needed to find him, hit him with something. As I fought to shrug off James, I stared down at the shattered hunk of wood in my hand, unable to recall how it had gotten there.

A stronger grip took over, dragging me backwards, my heels digging furrows in the sand. I turned to find Obelius and another crew member pulling me into the boat. They launched me at James and Narcissus and began pushing the boat into open waters, fending off the dead men as they went. I saw one of the Vegiants take a blow from behind and slip beneath the waves, his blood smearing the frothing surf as it rushed towards the shore.

I stumbled to my feet a few moments later, intending to see what had become of Ryan, but Obelius thrust me back down. "They want you! Don't give me an excuse to give you to them!"

"Me? Why?"

"That's what they were saying," James answered. "The blue one told them to get you. At any cost. Didn't you hear him?"

I hadn't. The blue one...was he talking about Ryan? I swiveled to study the shore, to find Ryan, but we were much further away than I thought we'd be; the mouth of the cave was dime-sized, the boulders on the shore little more than specks. Were we really moving that quickly? But how?

"What on Gaia's green earth is going on?" Obelius bellowed, his voice laced with so much anger I instantly regretted lashing out at him earlier. "What were those things?"

I opened my mouth to speak, but one of the crew members interrupted before I could explain. The Laestrygonian pointed, shouting to warn us that we were being chased. We turned as one to watch the massive warship take to the sea with incredible swiftness, to marvel as it angled towards us like some dark behemoth, propelled by a wind that sent shivers racing up my spine.

"It will catch us," Obelius said, his voice grim with certainty.

"Maybe. Then again, it might not."

The entire crew turned to look at Narcissus. The Greek shrugged artfully, looking less concerned with the thought of his imminent doom than I'd ever have expected; he stroked his chin as though he were pondering some great mystery, a smirk tugging at his lips.

"What's that supposed to mean?" I asked, adrenaline chasing away the last vestiges of the mental fugue I'd experienced on the island.

"It means we have one other option, if we're lucky. It all depends on how quickly this ship can move. And, of course, what you're willing to risk," he added, glancing sidelong at Obelius.

Obelius started.

"You can't mean—" he began.

"I've studied the maps, which means I know where the strait is." Narcissus pointed off to our starboard side where two landmasses loomed, their cliffs separated by a narrow, almost imperceptible gap. "Their ship is too big to survive the passage. This one, on the other hand..."

"You're insane."

"What are ye two talkin' about?" I demanded.

"He's talking about Charybdis! The whirlpool. It will break this ship into a dozen pieces, and we'll all drown." Obelius shook his head, but I noticed him tracking the other ship in his peripheral. "It's certain death, sailing that way."

"Well, sure, unless of course you steer towards the other side."

"And risk half my crew getting eaten by her?"

"Her?" James asked.

"Scylla," the Greek replied on Obelius' behalf, flashing his trademark smile. "The man-devouring monster who lives in the sea," he sang, merrily, working his arms back and forth like a child doing a dance. I flinched, recognizing the name of the six-headed monster who reputedly devoured any unwary sailors who happened to pass within striking distance—a fate made more likely by the existence of a nearby whirlpool that very few ships could successfully navigate.

"I won't—"

"Do it," I insisted, grabbing the Laestrygonian's forearm. He flinched at my touch, but didn't shy away. "I only barely remember the legends, but if they catch us, it will be worse than anythin' ye can imagine."

"Having seen Scylla once for myself, I doubt that. I doubt that very much." Obelius stared into my eyes, face stricken. In the end, however, he turned to his crew. "To the oars!"

The crew rushed to their places, taking up the heavy oars and moving as one. Soon, the Crow Boat was speeding along the waves, the warship gaining on us only incrementally. I turned to find Narcissus smiling, his arms folded across his chest. James, meanwhile, had his back turned, watching the enemy.

"What are ye so pleased about?" I asked the Greek, annoyed by his attitude.

"Oh, nothing. I've just always wanted to see Scylla in action." He flicked his eyes to me, then back to the strait. "She was like a horror story, even back then. One of the very first monsters. They say she was a nymph, before Circe turned her into a man-eater."

"Shouldn't you be scared?" James asked, looking back over one shoulder.

"She only has six mouths, and the giants make better targets." Narcissus shrugged. "What can I say? I like our odds."

$\mathcal{T}$he weather turned as we closed in on the strait, the sun blotted out by pregnant storm clouds. A resounding crack of thunder broke above our heads, drowning out the panting breaths of the Crow Boat's crew. They'd lost two Laestrygonians on the beach to the dead men, which meant there were no auxiliaries to spell the scullers as they fought to keep us out of the warship's reach. I'd offered to substitute in, but Obelius insisted I'd ruin their rhythm and draw us off course—something we really couldn't afford as we closed in on the whirlpool. The Vegiant had taken command at the prow, calling out a beat attuned to the fall of the oars while I could only sit back and watch, unable to do anything.

James joined me, leaving Narcissus to mope alone at the boat's aft end; I'd castigated him for his callousness, even going so far as to threaten to throw him to Scylla myself if we failed to skirt the gap. That, I learned, was the only chance we had: to survive intact, we had to sail between the monster and the whirlpool, threading the narrowest of needles. If we erred right, we'd be swept up by Charybdis, our boat destroyed, and likely drowned. If left, we had to fend off the six heads of a horrifying, seemingly immortal monster who'd spent millennia devouring hapless sailors like us. And now it seemed we also had to contend with choppy waters and a possible thunderstorm, to boot.

The only good news was that, should we survive, we would at least be able to return to the island of the Laestrygonians without being followed; the gap was far too narrow for a warship of that size, which meant Ryan and his crew would have to sail along the coast for hours before finding passage. By then, we'd be long gone. Of course, now that I'd had some time to really think, I had to acknowledge the bitter irony that Ryan was now the one chasing me.

The sad truth was that, until now, I'd only considered what would happen when I got Ryan alone, when we could finally talk. I hadn't factored the mad doctor into the equation any more than I had Mabel or his crew of undead mariners. Frankly, even if we were sailing the *Jolly Roger* right at this very moment, my crew of misfits at my side, I doubted we'd have stood a chance against that damned warship and her equally damned crew. I felt foolish. Reckless. Here I thought I'd been following the correct path all along, only to realize I was both figuratively outgunned and literally outmanned.

Sail to the Underworld. Find Atlantis. Secure the Treasure. Save Ryan. These had been my objectives, my benchmarks. They'd seemed so straightforward when I laid them out like that, one at a time—a grocery list complicated only by the fact that I had to go to different stores for each item. But what had I accomplished, really, since I left the Otherworld behind? Sure, I'd "saved" Neverland, but at what cost to Eve? What if that was the last time I ever saw the flying island? What if I never saw Cathal again? And now there were the Neverlanders themselves, potentially destined to fade and die before my very eyes, all because I'd insisted they join me. And for what? So I didn't have to do this alone? Because I thought they might prove useful? How selfish was that?

I groaned and angrily mussed my hair, disgusted with myself, wishing I'd never agreed to my mother's last request. Maybe then I'd be in Boston right now, enjoying a stiff drink at Christoff's bar, spinning tales of my time among the Curaitl, of my life as Ceara. It'd been cold when I retrieved Eve, probably only a few weeks out from Christmas, if memory served. Boston would be lit up, lights strung between the branches of skeletal trees, its inhabitants tucked away inside their warm houses. Cheer and merriment would be in large supply, highlighted by Sunday football and games at The Garden. There were other faces I longed to see, I realized. Christoff's children, Scathach, Robin, Othello, even Max—a man who'd kissed me what felt like a lifetime ago. All the people I'd abandoned to chase after someone who might very well be beyond redemption. A hard nudge brought me out of my own thoughts, and I found James leaning forward to study my face. The look was enough; he was worried about me. About me, of all people.

"I'm really sorry I got ye into any of this," I said. "It's all me fault."

James snorted a laugh, surprising me.

"What's so funny?"

"Just something my father, Peter, used to say, that's all."

"Go on, then."

"Well, I was always apologizing when I was growing up," James continued, shrugging. "I was never very good at the games he wanted to play. My eyes were weak, when I was young. They got better, but for a long time I couldn't see the things he threw or find the things he'd hidden. He got frustrated a lot. Said I wasn't trying."

I nodded, thinking that jived pretty well with the young Peter Pan I'd encountered in Neverland's reveries. Spoiled and easily upset. Not a great combination in any person, but especially not in a father figure.

"Until the day," James continued, "I stopped apologizing altogether. I realized I wasn't sorry, I was just mad. But Peter understood anger in a way he never could understand regret. We started playing different games. More violent, certainly, but these I could win. Anyway, after that, he used to say 'I'm so glad you lost your sorry.' Peter thought my misery was like his shadow, I think. Something you could simply misplace."

"But it is like a shadow," I said, morosely. I shook my head, my hair cascading over my knees in red waves as another thunderous boom shook the heavens. Rain began falling almost as if on cue, falling in a light mist that darkened everything it touched except my pale skin.

"What do you mean?"

"Misery is always there, isn't it? Followin' us, just waitin' to get noticed on an otherwise bright, sunny day. Least that's how it seems, lately."

"I thought so, too, once. And maybe you're right. But for Peter, I think it really was a choice. Happy, sad, angry...he taught me the value of letting each emotion fill you up one at a time. It made him seem childish, but it also let him live a more carefree life. See, right now, I'm scared. But I'm also eager to get back to my friends. I'm worried about what's happening to them without me there. And, deep down, I'm even more worried they'll realize that they don't owe me anything, and that they're better off without me."

"James! They aren't—"

"Those emotions are all inside me, churning," James interjected before I could finish. "Maybe more, even. But Peter? He'd take one look at that strait and swear by everything he was that we'd make it through. Then he'd be content, because he'd made his decision."

"He'd probably turn it into a game," I admitted, laughing a little despite myself.

James chuckled. "You're probably right."

"So, what you're sayin' is I should embrace the challenge? That I should keep pushin' forward, regardless of the cost?"

"I'm not saying anything. I was just trying to pass the time." James thrust his chin forward, urging me to look out towards our destination. Indeed, the strait was much closer now, the cliffs visible in far greater detail. Of course, when I turned the other way, I saw Ryan's warship closing the gap in minute increments, its vast array of sails trailing us like kites.

"Oy, James."

"Yeah?"

"I swear we'll make it to the other side," I said as I rose, holding out my hand. "You'll see Tiger Lily and Tinkerbell, again, I'll make sure of it. No matter what it takes."

He took it, stood, and squeezed.

"I'm glad you lost your sorry, Quinn."

I had to laugh.

Because honestly, so was I.

The rain began to fall in sheets so thick I could have raised my face to the heavens, opened my mouth, and drowned. And yet, we continued on, our course decided long before the storm hit in full; Obelius insisted he knew which direction we were going despite the impaired visibility. Frankly, without hard proof to the contrary, I had to take his word for it; the Vegiant might have been a lot of things, but I didn't think suicidal was one of them.

"Slow oars!" he cried.

And just like that, we moved at a crawl, jostled by the rise and fall of waves beneath the hull. A sucking sound—I wasn't sure how else to describe it—rose above the white noise of rain pouring down on us. Obelius motioned with one arm, and the Laestrygonians on the right stopped rowing altogether for a moment. We veered left to the beat of Obelius' fist on his chest, my own heart racing considerably faster as I considered what that sucking sound might be. I craned my neck to see, but the rainfall was too thick. If only I could see beyond the confines of our boat, I felt certain I'd be less afraid; given the material my imagination had to work with these days, not knowing what was out there was far more nerve wracking than being confronted by the reality.

Suddenly, as if honoring my wish, the rain died down. No, that wasn't it, I realized; I held out a hand and watched as a flurry of snowflakes descended, landing to puddle in the nooks and crannies of my palm. A glacial wind gusted at our backs a moment later, sending up cries of alarm from the Leastrogynians. I tried to shield myself from it, but my poor, ruined leather jacket was soaking wet and provided little comfort. Instead, I turned and watched as a colossal shadow moved through the gloom—Ryan's warship, hot on our heels. Was all this his doing?

"They're crazy," Narcissus said, eyes wide with shock, pointing to our starboard side "They'll never survive Charybdis."

I spun to look where Narcissus indicated and finally beheld what I'd been so desperate to see only moments before: Charybdis. A whirlpool as wide as a football field, its interior lined with serrated rocks that jutted out like ragged teeth. The sucking noise came from the whirlpool itself, caused by the swirling water as it spiraled to the bottom. We were perhaps a dozen yards away, saved from being sucked in only by Obelius' skilled navigation. On our left, visible as well now that the rain had given way to snow, loomed another set of cliffs—and these too close for comfort. To avoid Scylla, we'd have to sail around the whirlpool's edge, then race through the strait and pray she couldn't reach us.

Ryan's warship, on the other hand, was far too wide to pass between the cliffs without catching the frothing edges of the whirlpool—Scylla or no Scylla. Narcissus was right; chasing us through the strait was insane. Suicidal, even. Unless, of course, Ryan had a plan.

"We have to hurry," I muttered, mostly to myself. I faced Obelius and made a pick-up-the-pace motion. A flash of irritation flitted across his face, but he did just that—beating faster and harder against his chest, one arm thrown wide whenever we needed to readjust. Still, the warship gained on us with every passing second, until at last Ryan and his crew reached the whirlpool. The snowstorm died at that exact instant, revealing the warship in all her glory, even as she began to tip. The whirlpool had her, I thought. They were doomed.

Except she didn't get sucked in. Indeed, after watching for several seconds, it seemed the warship remained steadily on course despite the angle of her masts, sailing along the whirlpool's edges as opposed to skirting them. My companions on either side noticed it, too.

"How is that possible?" James asked. "Is their's a flying ship, as well?"

"No." I pointed to the far side of the warship, to the swirling water that should have been pulling the vessel in—only it wasn't water. Not in the strictest sense, at least. It was ice, forming along the hull like a bumper to keep the warship from turning with the tide. "It's Ryan. He's makin' sure they don't get pulled in."

"They'll clear the whirlpool," Narcissus said in a hushed, disbelieving whisper.

I was moments away from agreeing when I heard a shout from one of the Leastrogynians. I whirled around in time to see what had drawn his attention mere seconds before it hit us. An iceberg. Nothing massive, only perhaps the height of a man, and yet still it snapped three oars in two and sent the rest of us sprawling to the deck with the force of the impact. I groaned as I rose to all fours, only to find several more blocking our path—the misshapen blocks of ice bobbing like buoys between us and the other side of the strait. Shit. We couldn't afford to hit any more of those, or we'd risk sinking the boat.

Obelius seemed to come to the same conclusion; he roared a command even as he snatched up one of the shattered oars. His fellow Vegiants began rowing once more while Obelius used his makeshift pole to thrust the icebergs away whenever they threatened to close in. Once I realized what he was doing, I rushed to help; I took up another oar and monitored the starboard side while one of the crew took port. I didn't have his reach, but I was able to fend off a couple before they collided with the side of our boat. Unfortunately, there was no time to navigate. The best we could do was clear the strait, make for the island of the Laestrygonians, and pray.

Unfortunately, in our haste to survive the floating ice sheets, we drifted; it wasn't until the shadow of the cliff face fell over us that we realized our shortsighted mistake. It seemed that, while we'd survived the whirlpool and had thus far evaded Ryan, we'd also put ourselves in the clutches of the monster we'd all desperately hoped to avoid.

A stench hit me as I fended off the final iceberg. Reptilian musk mingled with the acrid bitterness of spoiled fish and the rankling scent of wet dog. Another gale of frigid wind pressed against our backs, chasing the odor away. I noticed hoarfrost climbing up the leather of my jacket. I quickly tossed down my oar and threw the jacket off, worried it would slow me down. I was midway through picking the oar back up when the smell returned. I saw something move beyond the crags. And it seemed I wasn't the only one.

"There!" A Laestrygonian cried.

To be honest, had I not first witnessed the horror that was Typhon and the Faeling monstrosity created by Dr. Frankenstein, I might well have said Scylla was the most hideous creature I'd ever seen. As it was, she definitely earned a place on the podium. Standing as tall as a tree on twelve writhing tentacles, Scylla was a study in contrasts: six sinuous necks emerged from her throat, spilling over like lilies from a vase, while the heads of six blind hounds snapped and snarled where the flesh of her waist met the limbs below. Her heads were somehow worse; four-eyed, lipless, and scaled like a fish, they were more teeth than anything, giving each the appearance of having a broad, maniacal smile. That is, until she unhinged those jaws to reveal forked, slithering tongues.

Unfortunately, Scylla seemed to take notice of us just as the Laestry-gonian spotted her; her six heads popped up at once, scenting the air even as the hounds began barking. The sea monster lumbered forward, the suckers on her tentacles so loud as they plopped that I might have mistaken the sound for gunshots.

"I take it back," I heard Narcissus mutter to himself, sounding utterly disgusted. "I could have lived forever without seeing that."

"Keep rowing!" Obelius roared. "Fast and steady!"

Scylla—perhaps sensing our intent—picked up her pace, rushing to the farthest edge of the stone outcropping she called home, spittle flying from her belt of ravenous hounds even as she gnashed her teeth. Each of her mouths were large enough to scarf a man whole, which meant even a Laestrygonian could be dragged off between her teeth. I tightened my grip on the oar, but knew deep down that there was nothing I could do, not against this creature. My improved reflexes, my increased strength, none of it would be enough. Hell, even with an arsenal of automatic rifles at my disposal, I'd have been hard pressed to do more than wound her. The only way to survive Scylla was to outrun her, and we simply weren't fast enough.

I dropped the oar and pressed my hand to the deck, ducking my head in defeat, my eyes pinched shut. Let it be me, I thought. I'd gotten us into the mess. Let the others survive, somehow. Take me if you must, I prayed, but let them escape.

An alien sensation hit me like a punch in the gut. It felt like...approval. And then, almost immediately afterwards, came a flood of warmth that practically boiled my blood, instantly fending off the chill Ryan had set upon us. I opened my eyes and found green flames licking the skin of my hand as well as the deck of our boat. I looked around, but Obelius and the others only had eyes for Scylla and were already preparing to defend themselves as best they could, seizing the few weapons we had onboard. Only James noticed me kneeling. The Neverlander's eyes were wide as dinner plates as he tracked the writhing flames to their source.

With a sudden jerk, the Crow Boat picked up speed, churning through the water as if propelled by an engine. More green flames flared up along the hull as another rush of power moved through me to the deck and beyond. Scylla, sensing her prey moving suddenly out of her reach, lunged for us, latching onto the boat with one tentacle, her heads rearing back like snakes about to strike. But the flames quickly swarmed to sear the flesh of her limb, and she fell away, screaming, her hounds whining like they'd been kicked. The boat rocked violently as she crashed into the sea, then took off once more.

"Quinn, is this you—" James yelled, excitement bubbling in his voice, only to be cut off as one of Scylla's tentacles wrapped around his torso. I watched in horror as it coiled, tightening as if in slow motion, unsure of its captive. In seconds, I knew, she'd draw back, returning to her spit of rock with her single, solitary victim. Would she gobble him up in one bite, or tear him into several pieces? In that instant, I pictured the Neverlander torn to shreds by those hungry mouths, the blood licked clean by those panting tongues. I couldn't let that happen.

I leapt for him, my hands haloed by green flames, and clawed at the tentacle like some demented harpy. Thick and rubbery, the limb resisted even as I gouged into its pink flesh, charring it black wherever the flames touched. James screamed as the arm tightened, reflexively drawing back from the source of pain. Suddenly, Obelius was there beside me, hacking away with his sword. The tentacle loosened and flailed, spurting scalding hot, black blood that rained like ink over us all. James fell to the deck, clutching his ribs. Obelius roared and thrust his sword into the air, reveling in his victory over at least one monster, today. Which is probably why he didn't see the second tentacle, thick as a tree trunk, flying at him. The others ducked, but I only had time to push the Leastrogynian out of the way. Which meant I caught the full force of the blow, myself.

The tentacle hit me around the middle and took me high into the air, so high I could see the entire Crow Boat from above, no bigger than a playing card; the eyes of the crows flashed emerald green and seemed to track me as

I was flung skyward. I hit the side of the cliff, hard, my head snapping backwards into the stone with a sickening crunch. Next, the sea. It met me like an abusive lover, crushing me in its embrace the instant I landed. I bobbed to the surface seconds later, dazed, guzzling salt water, and saw the Crow Boat speeding away into the distance. I could just make out Obelius being held back by his crew before another wave overtook me; he wanted to leap overboard and rescue me. Silly Vegiant. I wanted to laugh, but instead I slid beneath the water, too weak to fight its pull. That leaden sensation I'd experienced on the beach was back, though compounded by the head wound and my general exhaustion; I couldn't even fight my way to the surface. And so I sunk.

So, this was how it was going to end. I'd either drown, or be plucked out of the water by Scylla and devoured—the fact that it made so little difference to me told me how fatigued I truly was. I drifted, unable to do anything but stare down into the depths of the sea. My lungs burned from the lack of oxygen, and yet I refused to open my mouth. Something in the back of my mind told me that once I did that, it would all be over. And so I began to black out, my vision fading until all I could see was a shadow moving through the gloom...except the shape seemed to be moving towards me, emerging from the ocean floor like the spread of an ink stain.

My vision tunneled. And yet, for just a second, I could have sworn I saw a single eye open amidst all that darkness, flashing iridescent like a fish leaping in the sunlight. Then again, it was entirely possible it was just my mind playing tricks on me.

It wouldn't be the first time.

Though it might very well be the last.

～

Quinn returns in 2019... Subscribe to my NEWSLETTER to receive an email when it's live!

*Turn the page to read a sample of **OBSIDIAN SON** - Nate Temple Book 1 - or* **BUY ONLINE**. *Nate Temple is a billionaire wizard from St. Louis. He rides a bloodthirsty unicorn and drinks with the Four Horsemen. He even cow-tipped the Minotaur. Once...*

(Note: Nate's books 1-6 happen prior to UNCHAINED, but crossover from then on, the two series taking place in the same universe but also able to standalone if you prefer)

Full chronology of all books in the Temple Verse shown on the 'Books in the Temple Verse' page.

TRY: OBSIDIAN SON (NATE TEMPLE #1)

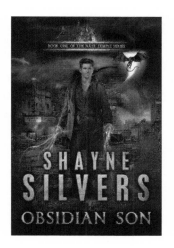

*T*here was no room for emotion in a hate crime. I had to be cold. Heartless. This was just another victim. Nothing more. No face, no name.

Frosted blades of grass crunched under my feet, sounding to my ears alone like the symbolic glass that one shattered under a napkin at a Jewish wedding. The noise would have threatened to give away my stealthy advance as I stalked through the moonlit field, but I was no novice and had planned accordingly. Being a wizard, I was able to muffle all sensory evidence with a fine cloud of magic—no sounds, and no smells. Nifty. But if I made the spell much stronger, the anomaly would be too obvious to my prey.

I knew the consequences for my dark deed tonight. If caught, jail time or possibly even a gruesome, painful death. But if I succeeded, the look of fear and surprise in my victim's eyes before his world collapsed around him, was well worth the risk. I simply couldn't help myself; I had to take him down.

I knew the cops had been keeping tabs on my car, but I was confident that they hadn't followed me. I hadn't seen a tail on my way here, but seeing as how they frowned on this kind of thing I had taken a circuitous route just in case. I was safe. I hoped.

Then my phone chirped at me as I received a text.

My body's fight-or-flight syndrome instantly kicked in, my heart threatening to explode in one final act of pulmonary paroxysm. "Motherf—" I hissed instinctively, practically jumping out of my skin. I had forgotten to silence it. *Stupid, stupid, stupid!* My body remained tense as I swept my gaze over the field, sure that I had been made. My breathing finally began to slow, my pulse returning to normal, as I noticed no changes in my surroundings. Hopefully, my magic had silenced the sound and my resulting outburst. I glanced down at the phone to scan the text and then typed back a quick and angry response before I switched the cursed phone to vibrate.

Now, where were we...

I continued on, the lining of my coat constricting my breathing. Or maybe it was because I was leaning forward in anticipation. *Breathe,* I chided myself. *He doesn't know you're here.* All this risk for a book. It had better be worth it.

I'm taller than most, and not abnormally handsome, but I knew how to play the genetic cards I had been dealt. I had shaggy, dirty blonde hair, and my frame was thick with well-earned muscle, yet still lean. I had once been told that my eyes were like twin emeralds pitted against the golden-brown tufts of my hair—a face like a jewelry box. Of course, that was two bottles of wine into a date, so I could have been a little foggy on her quote. Still, I liked to imagine that was how everyone saw me.

But tonight, all that was masked by magic.

I grinned broadly as the outline of the hairy hulk finally came into view. He was blessedly alone—no nearby sentries to give me away. That was always a risk when performing this ancient right-of-passage. I tried to keep the grin on my face from dissolving into a maniacal cackle.

My skin danced with energy, both natural and unnatural, as I manipulated the threads of magic floating all around me. My victim stood just ahead, oblivious of the world of hurt that I was about to unleash. Even with his millennia of experience, he didn't stand a chance. I had done this so many times that the routine of it was my only enemy. I lost count of how many times I had been told not to do it again; those who knew declared it *cruel, evil, and sadistic*. But what fun wasn't? Regardless, that wasn't enough to stop me from doing it again. And again. Call it an addiction if you will, but it was too much of a rush to ignore.

The pungent smell of manure filled the air, latching onto my nostril hairs. I took another step, trying to calm my racing pulse. A glint of gold reflected in the silver moonlight, but the victim remained motionless, hopefully unaware or all was lost. I wouldn't make it out alive if he knew I was here. Timing was everything.

I carefully took the last two steps, a lifetime between each, watching the legendary monster's ears, anxious and terrified that I would catch even so much as a twitch in my direction. Seeing nothing, a fierce grin split my unshaven cheeks. My spell had worked! I raised my palms an inch away from their target, firmly planted my feet, and squared my shoulders. I took one silent, calming breath, and then heaved forward with every ounce of physical strength I could muster. As well as a teensy-weensy boost of magic. Enough to goose him good.

"*MOOO!!!*" The sound tore through the cool October night like an unstoppable freight train. *Thud-splat!* The beast collapsed sideways into the frosty grass; straight into a steaming patty of cow shit, cow dung, or, if you really want to church it up, a Meadow Muffin. But to me, shit is, and always will be, shit.

Cow tipping. It doesn't get any better than that in Missouri.

Especially when you're tipping the *Minotaur*. Capital M.

Razor-blade hooves tore at the frozen earth as the beast struggled to stand, grunts of rage vibrating the air. I raised my arms triumphantly. "Booyah! Temple 1, Minotaur 0!" I crowed. Then I very bravely prepared to protect myself. Some people just couldn't take a joke. *Cruel, evil,* and *sadistic* cow tipping may be, but by hell, it was a *rush*. The legendary beast turned his gaze on me after gaining his feet, eyes ablaze as he unfolded to his full height on two tree-trunk-thick legs, hooves magically transforming into heavily-booted feet. The thick, gold ring dangling from his snotty snout quivered as the Minotaur panted, and his dense, corded muscle contracted over his human-like chest. As I stared up into those brown eyes, I actually felt sorry...for, well, myself.

"I have killed greater men than you for less offense," he growled.

I swear to God his voice sounded like an angry James Earl Jones. Like Mufasa talking to Scar.

"You have shit on your shoulder, Asterion." I ignited a roiling ball of fire in my palm in order to see his eyes more clearly. By no means was it a defensive gesture on my part. It was just dark. But under the weight of his glare, even I couldn't buy my reassuring lie. I hoped using a form of his ancient name would give me brownie points. Or maybe just not-worthy-of-killing points.

The beast grunted, eyes tightening, and I sensed the barest hesitation. "Nate Temple...your name would look splendid on my already long list of slain idiots." Asterion took a threatening step forward, and I thrust out my palm in warning, my roiling flame blue now.

"You lost fair and square, Asterion. Yield or perish." The beast's shoulders sagged slightly. Then he finally nodded to himself in resignation, appraising me with the scrutiny of a worthy adversary. "Your time comes, Temple, but I will grant you this. You've got a pair of stones on you to rival Hercules."

I pointedly risked a glance down towards the myth's own crown jewels. "Well, I sure won't need a wheelbarrow any time soon, but I'm sure I'll manage."

The Minotaur blinked once, and then bellowed out a deep, contagious, snorting laughter. Realizing I wasn't about to become a murder statistic, I couldn't help but join in. It felt good. It had been a while since I had allowed myself to experience genuine laughter.

In the harsh moonlight, his bulk was even more intimidating as he towered head and shoulders above me. This was the beast that had fed upon human sacrifices for countless years while imprisoned in Daedalus' Labyrinth in Greece. And all of that protein had not gone to waste, forming a heavily woven musculature over the beast's body that made even Mr. Olympia look puny.

From the neck up he was entirely bull, but the rest of his body more resembled a thickly-furred man. But, as shown moments ago, he could adapt his form to his environment, never appearing fully human, but able to make his entire form appear as a bull when necessary. For instance, how he had looked just before I tipped him. Maybe he had been scouting the field for heifers before I had so efficiently killed the mood.

His bull face was also covered in thick, coarse hair—even sporting a long, wavy beard of sorts, and his eyes were the deepest brown I had ever seen. Cow shit brown. His snout jutted out, emphasizing the gold ring dangling from his glistening nostrils, catching a glint in the luminous glow of the moon. The metal was at least an inch thick, and etched with runes of a language long forgotten. Thick, aged ivory horns sprouted from each temple, long enough to skewer a wizard with little effort. He was nude except for a beaded necklace and a pair of distressed leather boots that were big enough to stomp a size twenty-five imprint in my face if he felt so inclined.

I hoped our blossoming friendship wouldn't end that way. I really did.

～

Get your copy of OBSIDIAN SON online today!

～

If you enjoyed the **BLADE** _or_ **UNDERWORLD** _movies, turn the page to read a sample of_ **DEVIL'S DREAM**—_the first book in the new_ **SHADE OF DEVIL** _series by Shayne Silvers._
Or get the book ONLINE

Before the now-infamous Count Dracula ever tasted his first drop of blood, Sorin Ambrogio owned the night. Humanity fearfully called him the Devil...

TRY: DEVIL'S DREAM (SHADE OF DEVIL #1)

God damned me.

He—in his infinite, omnipotent wisdom—declared for all to hear...

Let there be pain...

In the exact center of this poor bastard's soul.

And that merciless smiting woke me from a dead sleep and thrust me into a body devoid of every sensation but blinding agony.

I tried to scream but my throat felt as dry as dust, only permitting me to emit a rasping, whistling hiss that brought on yet *more* pain. My skin burned and throbbed while my bones creaked and groaned with each full-body tremor. My claws sunk into a hard surface beneath me and I was distantly surprised they hadn't simply shattered upon contact.

My memory was an immolated ruin—each fragment of thought merely an elusive fleck of ash or ember that danced through my fog of despair as I struggled to catch one and hold onto it long enough to recall what had brought me to this bleak existence. How I had become this poor, wretched, shell of a man. I couldn't even remember my own *name*; it was all I could do to simply survive this profound horror.

After what seemed an eternity, the initial pain began to slowly ebb, but I quickly realized that it had only triggered a cascade of smaller, more numerous tortures—like ripples caused by a boulder thrown into a pond.

I couldn't find the strength to even attempt to open my crusted eyes, and my abdomen was a solid knot of gnawing hunger so overwhelming that I felt like I was being pulled down into the earth by a lead weight. My fingers tingled and burned so fiercely that I wondered if the skin had been peeled away while I slept. Since they were twitching involuntarily, at least I knew that the muscles and tendons were still attached.

I held onto that sliver of joy, that beacon of hope.

I stubbornly gritted my teeth, but even that slight movement made the skin over my face stretch tight enough to almost tear. I willed myself to relax as I tried to process *why* I was in so much pain, where I was, how I had gotten here, and...*who* I even was? A singular thought finally struck me like an echo of the faintest of whispers, giving me something to latch onto.

Hunger.

I let out a crackling gasp of relief at finally grasping an independent answer of some kind, but I was unable to draw enough moisture onto my tongue to properly swallow. Understanding that I was hungry had seemed to alleviate a fraction of my pain. The answer to at least one question distracted me long enough to allow me to think. And despite my hunger, I felt something tantalizingly delicious slowly coursing down my throat, desperately attempting to alleviate my starvation.

Even though my memory was still enshrouded in fog, I was entirely certain that it was incredibly dangerous for me to feel this hungry. This...*thirsty.* Dangerous for both myself and anyone nearby. I tried to remember why it was so dangerous but the reason eluded me. Instead, an answer to a different question emerged from my mind like a specter from the mist—and I felt myself begin to smile as a modicum of strength slowly took root deep within me.

"Sorin..." I croaked. My voice echoed, letting me know that I was in an enclosed space of some kind. "My name is Sorin Ambrogio. And I need..." I trailed off uncertainly, unable to finish my own thought.

"Blood," a man's deep voice answered from only a few paces away. "You need more blood."

I hissed instinctively, snapping my eyes open for the first time since waking. I had completely forgotten to check my surroundings, too consumed with my own pain to bother with my other senses. I had been asleep so long that even the air seemed to burn my eyes like smoke, forcing me to blink rapidly. No, the air *was* filled with pungent, aromatic smoke, but not like the smoke from the fires in my—

I shuddered involuntarily, blocking out the thought for some unknown reason.

Beneath the pungent smoke, the air was musty and damp. Through it all, I smelled the delicious, coppery scent of hot, powerful blood.

I had been resting atop a raised stone plinth—almost like a table—in a depthless, shadowy cavern. I appreciated the darkness because any light would have likely blinded me in my current state. I couldn't see the man who had spoken, but the area was filled with silhouettes of what appeared to be tables, crates, and other shapes that could easily conceal him. I focused on my hearing and almost instantly noticed a seductively familiar, *beating* sound.

A noise as delightful as a child's first belly-laugh...

A beautiful woman's sigh as she locked eyes with you for the first time.

The gentle crackling of a fireplace on a brisk, snowy night.

Thump-thump.

Thump-thump.

Thump-thump.

The sound became *everything* and my vision slowly began to sharpen, the room brightening into shades of gray. My pain didn't disappear, but it was swiftly muted as I tracked the sound.

I inhaled deeply, my eyes riveting on a far wall as my nostrils flared, pinpointing the source of the savory perfume and the seductive beating sound. I didn't recall sitting up, but I realized that I was suddenly leaning forward and that the room was continuing to brighten into paler shades of gray, burning away the last of the remaining shadows—despite the fact that there was no actual light. And it grew clearer as I focused on the seductive sound.

Until I finally spotted a man leaning against the far wall. *Thump-thump. Thump-thump. Thump-thump...* I licked my lips ravenously, setting my hands on the cool stone table as I prepared to set my feet on the ground.

Food...

The man calmly lifted his hand and a sharp *clicking* sound suddenly echoed from the walls. The room abruptly flooded with light so bright and unexpected that it felt like my eyes had exploded. Worse, what seemed like a trio of radiant stars was not more than a span from my face—so close that I could feel the direct heat from their flare. I recoiled with a snarl, momentarily forgetting all about food as I shielded my eyes with a hand and prepared to defend myself. I leaned away from the bright lights, wondering why I couldn't smell smoke from the flickering flames. I squinted, watching the man's feet for any indication of movement.

Half a minute went by as my vision slowly began to adjust, and the man didn't even shift his weight—almost as if he was granting me time enough to grow accustomed to the sudden light. Which...didn't make any sense. Hadn't it been an attack? I hesitantly lowered my hand from my face, reassessing the situation and my surroundings.

I stared in wonder as I realized that the orbs were not made of flame, but rather what seemed to be pure light affixed to polished metal stands. Looking directly at them hurt, so I studied them sidelong, making sure to also keep the man in my peripheral vision. He had to be a sorcerer of some kind. Who else could wield pure light without fire?

"Easy, Sorin," the man murmured in a calming baritone. "I can't see as well as you in the dark, but it looked like you were about to do something unnecessarily stupid. Let me turn them down a little."

He didn't wait for my reply, but the room slowly dimmed after another clicking sound.

I tried to get a better look at the stranger—wondering where he had come from, where he had taken me, and who he was. One thing was obvious—he knew magic. "Where did you learn this sorcery?" I rasped, gesturing at the orbs of light.

"Um. Hobby Lobby."

"I've never heard of him," I hissed, coughing as a result of my parched throat.

"I'm not even remotely surprised by that," he said dryly. He extended his other hand and I gasped to see an impossibility—a transparent bag as clear as new glass. And it was *flexible*, swinging back and forth like a bulging coin purse or a clear water-skin. My momentary wonder at the magical material evaporated as I recognized the crimson liquid *inside* the bag.

Blood.

He lobbed it at me underhanded without a word of warning. I hissed as I desperately—and with exceeding caution—caught it from the air lest it fall and break open. I gasped as the clear bag of blood settled into my palms and, before I consciously realized it, I tore off the corner with my fangs, pressed it to my lips, and squeezed the bag in one explosive, violent gesture. The ruby fluid gushed into my mouth and over my face, dousing my almost forgotten pain as swiftly as a bucket of water thrown on hot coals.

I felt my eyes roll back into my skull and my body shuddered as I lost my balance and fell from the stone table. I landed on my back but I was too overwhelmed to care as I stretched out my arms and legs. I groaned in rapture, licking at my lips like a wild animal. The ruby nectar was a living serpent of molten oil as it slithered down into my stomach, nurturing and healing me almost instantly. It was the most wonderful sensation I could imagine—almost enough to make me weep.

Like a desert rain, my parched tongue and throat absorbed the blood so quickly and completely that I couldn't even savor the heady flavor. This wasn't a joyful feast; this was survival, a necessity. My body guzzled it, instantly using the liquid to repair the damage, pain, and the cloud of fog that had enshrouded me.

I realized that I was laughing. The sound echoed into the vast stone space like rolling thunder.

Because I had remembered something else.

The world's First Vampire was *back*.

And he was still *very* hungry.

$\sim$

Get the full book ONLINE!

MAKE A DIFFERENCE

Reviews are the most powerful tools in our arsenal when it comes to getting attention for our books. Much as we'd like to, we don't have the financial muscle of a New York publisher.

But we do have something much more powerful and effective than that, and it's something that those publishers would kill to get their hands on.

A committed and loyal bunch of readers.

Honest reviews of our books help bring them to the attention of other readers.

If you've enjoyed this book, we would be very grateful if you could spend just five minutes leaving a review on our book's Amazon page.

Thank you very much in advance.

BOOKS IN THE TEMPLE VERSE

CHRONOLOGY: *All stories in the Temple Verse are shown in chronological order on the following page*

PHANTOM QUEEN DIARIES

(Also set in the Temple Universe)

COLLINS (Prequel novella #0 in the 'LAST CALL' anthology)

WHISKEY GINGER

COSMOPOLITAN

OLD FASHIONED

MOTHERLUCKER (Novella #3.5 in the 'LAST CALL' anthology)

DARK AND STORMY

MOSCOW MULE

WITCHES BREW

SALTY DOG

SEA BREEZE

NATE TEMPLE SERIES

(Origin of the Temple Verse)

FAIRY TALE - FREE prequel novella #0 for my subscribers

OBSIDIAN SON

BLOOD DEBTS

GRIMM

SILVER TONGUE

BEAST MASTER

BEERLYMPIAN (Novella #5.5 in the 'LAST CALL' anthology)

TINY GODS

DADDY DUTY (Novella #6.5)

WILD SIDE

WAR HAMMER

NINE SOULS

HORSEMAN

LEGEND

KNIGHTMARE

ASCENSION

FEATHERS AND FIRE SERIES

(Also set in the Temple Universe)

UNCHAINED

RAGE

WHISPERS

ANGEL'S ROAR

MOTHERLUCKER (Novella #4.5 in the 'LAST CALL' anthology)

SINNER

BLACK SHEEP

GODLESS

CHRONOLOGICAL ORDER: TEMPLE VERSE

FAIRY TALE (TEMPLE PREQUEL)

OBSIDIAN SON (TEMPLE 1)

BLOOD DEBTS (TEMPLE 2)

GRIMM (TEMPLE 3)

SILVER TONGUE (TEMPLE 4)

BEAST MASTER (TEMPLE 5)

BEERLYMPIAN (TEMPLE 5.5)

TINY GODS (TEMPLE 6)

DADDY DUTY (TEMPLE NOVELLA 6.5)

UNCHAINED (FEATHERS... 1)

RAGE (FEATHERS... 2)

WILD SIDE (TEMPLE 7)

WAR HAMMER (TEMPLE 8)

WHISPERS (FEATHERS... 3)

COLLINS (PHANTOM 0)

WHISKEY GINGER (PHANTOM... 1)

NINE SOULS (TEMPLE 9)

COSMOPOLITAN (PHANTOM... 2)

ANGEL'S ROAR (FEATHERS... 4)

MOTHERLUCKER (FEATHERS 4.5, PHANTOM 3.5)

OLD FASHIONED (PHANTOM...3)

HORSEMAN (TEMPLE 10)

DARK AND STORMY (PHANTOM... 4)

MOSCOW MULE (PHANTOM...5)

SINNER (FEATHERS...5)

WITCHES BREW (PHANTOM...6)

LEGEND (TEMPLE...11)

SALTY DOG (PHANTOM...7)

BLACK SHEEP (FEATHERS...6)

GODLESS (FEATHERS...7)

KNIGHTMARE (TEMPLE 12)

ASCENSION (TEMPLE 13)

SEA BREEZE (PHANTOM...8)

SHADE OF DEVIL SERIES

(Not part of the TempleVerse)

DEVIL'S DREAM

DEVIL'S CRY

DEVIL'S BLOOD

ACKNOWLEDGMENTS

From Cameron:

I'd like to thank Shayne, for paving the way in style. Kori, for an introduction that would change my life. My three wonderful sisters, for showing me what a strong, independent woman looks and sounds like. And, above all, my parents, for—literally—everything.

From Shayne (the self-proclaimed prettiest one):

Team Temple and the Den of Freaks on Facebook have become family to me. I couldn't do it without die-hard readers like them.

I would also like to thank you, the reader. I hope you enjoyed reading *SEA BREEZE* as much as we enjoyed writing it.

PLENTY more TempleVerse novels coming in 2020 0r sooner…

ABOUT SHAYNE SILVERS

Shayne is a man of mystery and power, whose power is exceeded only by his mystery...

He currently writes the Amazon Bestselling **Feathers and Fire** Series about a rookie spell-slinger named Callie Penrose who works for the Vatican in Kansas City. Her problem? Hell seems to know more about her past than she does.

He also writes the Amazon Bestselling **Nate Temple** Series, which features a foul-mouthed wizard from St. Louis. He rides a bloodthirsty unicorn, drinks with Achilles, and is pals with the Four Horsemen.

Shayne recently published the first book in the **Shade of Devil** series, which broke into the top 50 books on all of Amazon. Sorin Ambrogio, the world's first vampire, is awoken from a 500 year slumber by a shaman in present day New York City—only to learn that his old servant, Dracula, took credit for being the first vampire, erasing Sorin's name from the pages of history. If you enjoyed the BLADE or UNDERWORLD films, you'll love it.

Shayne holds two high-ranking black belts, and can be found writing in a coffee shop, cackling madly into his computer screen while pounding shots of espresso. **Follow him online for all sorts of groovy goodies, give-aways, and new release updates:**

Get Down with Shayne Online
www.shaynesilvers.com
info@shaynesilvers.com

facebook.com/shaynesilversfanpage

amazon.com/author/shaynesilvers

bookbub.com/profile/shayne-silvers

twitter.com/shaynesilvers

instagram.com/shaynesilversofficial

goodreads.com/Shaynesilvers

ABOUT CAMERON O'CONNELL

Cameron O'Connell is a Jack-of-All-Trades and Master of Some.

He writes The Phantom Queen Diaries, a series in The Temple Verse, about Quinn MacKenna, a mouthy black magic arms dealer trading favors in Boston. All she wants? A round-trip ticket to the Fae realm...and maybe a drink on the house.

A former member of the United States military, a professional model, and English teacher, Cameron finds time to write in the mornings after his first cup of coffee...and in the evenings after his thirty-seventh. Follow him, and the Temple Verse founder, Shayne Silvers, online for all sorts of insider tips, giveaways, and new release updates!

Get Down with Cameron Online

f facebook.com/Cameron-OConnell-788806397985289

a amazon.com/author/cameronoconnell

BB bookbub.com/authors/cameron-o-connell

🐦 twitter.com/thecamoconnell

📷 instagram.com/camoconnellauthor

g goodreads.com/cameronoconnell

Made in the USA
Middletown, DE
21 November 2019

79105169R10137